MIDNIGHT SHORES ON WHISLING ISLAND

A WHISLING ISLAND NOVEL

JULIA CLEMENS

PICKLED PLUM PUBLISHING

CHAPTER ONE

LILY GLANCED around her small but cozy home one more time, content that it was free of dust, grime, clutter, and anything that could mar Allen's return.

Allen was coming home. And everything had to be perfect. Especially after all Lily had done to make this day come to fruition.

She couldn't help the gigantic grin on her face. She'd fought and then fought harder for her husband, her marriage, and herself. Now she was finally reaping the reward.

Lily had sent her sweet little girl, Amelia, to hang out with her parents so that she could get some real cleaning and even baking done. The smell of Allen's favorite cinnamon rolls wafted to her nose.

Her parents would continue to watch Amelia while Lily drove down to the ferry dock to pick up Allen, and then they'd drop off Amelia a little while later. After Lily was able to give her husband a proper welcome home.

Lily hopped into her car and smiled as a few red leaves drifted down from the branches of the enormous maple trees in front of her house. They were gorgeous. This day was gorgeous.

The sun had even made an appearance, a rare treat during fall on Whisling Island. It was as if even the weather was on Lily's side. Which felt incredible after months of feeling like she was the only one fighting for her future.

That wasn't fair. As Lily drove, she remembered the way her family and friends had supported her. Her sister, Kate, had let Lily live with her, putting her own relationship on the back burner so that she could be the comforting shoulder Lily needed to cry on. Lily's parents had been saints and the best babysitters in the world, while Lily's friends, Gen, Bess, Olivia, and so many others on the island, had rallied around her, never letting her feel like she was alone. So she guessed this was a win for all of them.

Lily hadn't been sure she would ever convince Allen to move back to Whisling when he'd escaped to Alabama to live with his mom after a horrific car accident had left him paralyzed from the waist down. Especially because the accident had been Lily's fault. She had been the one rushing Allen to come home that fateful afternoon, on Valentine's Day of all days. But thankfully, she and Allen were growing past that. Allen seemed to have forgiven Lily for her part in the mess, and Lily was trying to forgive herself. That was the worst part in all of this for Lily. She was unwearyingly determined when it came to repairing her marriage, happy to try to heal Allen's broken soul. But when it came to forgiving herself, Lily couldn't do it. At least not yet. But she hadn't lost all hope.

As Lily pulled up to the ferry terminal—if one could call it that on Whisling—she saw the big boat just pulling up to the dock. Perfect timing.

Lily got out of her car and strained to see the passengers on the deck. Although Allen wasn't coming home with a car—for the duration of their marriage, he and Lily had always shared the one that Lily was driving—he had caught the ferry that was filled with them. Every three ferries that came into Whisling allowed cars to be transported. The other two were just passenger boats. Allen hadn't caught this specific ferry for the perk of being able to bring a car to the island—it was just the one that had worked best with his traveling schedule—and the many cars on deck made it hard for Lily to catch a glimpse of her husband. Man, did she miss him.

The ferry finally docked, and Lily knew this was it. The ferry would allow all of the passengers off before the cars for safety reasons. Allen would be one of the first off the boat.

Lily felt her throat close in anticipation. This was usually a bad sign for Lily, but she pushed the physical reaction from her mind. It wasn't a big deal that her anxiety was starting to manifest. Of course she was nervous about seeing her husband again. It had been months since their last physical meeting. Although the last couple of months had been filled with important conversations during everlasting phone calls and even a declaration of love or two, the months before that had been the worst of Lily's life. So it made sense that this big step was stirring up all kinds of emotions—good and bad.

Lily refused to dwell on any of the unpleasant ones. It was a great day. She wouldn't allow her emotions to mar this very great moment.

And then there he was. Allen navigated his wheelchair expertly down the gangplank as Lily stood by her car, squinting in the sunlight to get a good look at him. She wasn't going to miss a moment.

Her eyes drank in the sight of her husband who was finally so close to her. So close to home. And he was getting even closer. Of his own accord. He was choosing her. Lily's heart leapt at that. Come what may, that was enough for Lily to hold on to.

Lily fought the urge to run over to where Allen was pushing

himself across the gravel parking lot now that he'd left the gang-plank. The parking lot wasn't exactly wheelchair friendly, but Lily knew her husband would not appreciate being helped . . . even if he needed it. He'd told her as much over one of their calls. He had felt helpless for so many months after losing the use of his legs; he refused to be that man again. He'd worked hard to learn how to do practically everything on his own, and that was the way things had to be.

Lily hadn't missed the underlying threat of that declaration. She had to respect Allen's way . . . or else. Lily wasn't sure what the "else" was, but she wasn't willing to find out.

Allen arrived at her car, and Lily finally launched herself into his arms.

He laughed, sounding more than a little breathless after all the work it'd taken to get to her. But he was laughing. And Lily loved that sound.

"Did you have a good trip?" Lily asked, pausing at the sound of a female voice.

"Would you like these in the trunk of the car, Mr. Ander-sen?" a woman asked, and Lily hopped out of her husband's lap. She hadn't realized they would have an audience, but of course someone had helped Allen with his bags. He couldn't very well maneuver his suitcases along with his wheelchair.

"The trunk would be perfect," Lily said as she met the gaze of the beautiful woman who must work for the ferry.

The curvy blonde was the epitome of southern belle, although Lily wasn't quite sure why that thought popped into her head, considering they were way up north in Washington state. Maybe it was the slight drawl the woman had spoken with. She wore a cute, pastel green dress that perfectly matched her eyes and ... wait, didn't the ferry workers have a uniform? Lily guessed maybe the ferry owners weren't sticklers about the uniform when it came to young, beautiful blondes. But why was this woman pulling a cart full of bags? Allen had left with many of his belongings, but they hadn't filled more than two suitcases. The cart had at least five large suitcases, from what Lily could see. This had to be Allen's mother's doing. What had she sent him home with?

Lily pushed her questions away as she popped the trunk and helped the woman load up the items. Lily hoped they'd have enough room for all of this stuff in her sedan. She figured she'd have to use the backseat as well.

When the last of the bags were finally crammed behind the passenger's seat of Lily and Allen's car, Lily dug around her purse for a tip. But she hardly ever carried cash with her, and this was one of the many occasions she had none.

"I'm so sorry," Lily said as she came up empty from her purse. "We're so grateful for your help, but I'm fresh out of cash. I can come down tomorrow with your tip."

The pretty blonde seemed stunned by Lily's words, and Lily realized she might not believe that Lily would come back the next day.

"Unless my husband . . ." Lily turned to Allen, whose face seemed a bit red. How long had they been out in the sun? Lily needed to get her husband out of it.

"I can assure you, I'll be back," Lily said confidently before turning to go to the passenger door. As much as Allen didn't want her help, she knew he'd need some assistance getting into the car.

"Lily," Allen said, and she stopped, turning back to look at her husband whose eyes were on the ferry woman.

"I'm realizing I didn't say anything," Allen added, his face seeming redder than before. It was then that Lily realized the sun wasn't the culprit. Allen was embarrassed.

"Say anything about what?" Lily asked as she looked from Allen to the ferry worker, who Lily was beginning to suspect wasn't a ferry worker. But then why was she helping Allen with his bags?

"This is my in-home nurse, Belle," Allen said as Lily felt her heart drop.

A nurse? Allen had brought home a nurse? Who would live with them? They couldn't afford that. But as her thoughts raced, Lily quickly realized who would be footing the bill. This was Allen's mom's way of keeping her son in her sights, even while he was living across the country with his wife. Where he should be.

Of course Gretchen had hired a woman who was everything Lily was not. Blonde haired, blue eyed and voluptuous. Lily was a darker beauty—she wasn't going to sell herself short and not admit that she was beautiful as well—and she'd never developed the kinds of curves Belle boasted, even after bearing a child. She was sure Gretchen loved the fact that she could capitalize on this opportunity. Belle looked exactly like every woman Allen had dated before Lily.

Lily swallowed. What was done, was done. She would have a private conversation with Allen later about not saying anything about the nurse. But Belle was here. And apparently she would be living with them. Lily wasn't about to reflect on how she felt about another woman sharing their home.

"Belle. Lovely to meet you," Lily said as she extended her hand to the nurse. Lily might not've been raised in the south, but she knew a bit about charm.

"Likewise," Belle said, her drawl seeming even thicker than when she'd last spoken. "I've heard so much about you, Lily." Belle shook Lily's hand daintily.

Lily wished she could say the same about Belle, but to say Lily was blindsided was an understatement. She felt like she'd been knocked out, only to be brought back to consciousness in an alternate universe. So what now?

"I can help Allen into the car," Belle offered as she hurried forward and to the door that Lily had been just about to open.

"I can do that," Lily said after Belle had opened the door, waiting for Allen to make his way to her.

"We kind of have these things down to an art," Allen told his wife. And that was when it hit Lily. The "no helping Allen" speech hadn't been for the world at large. It had been just for her. He didn't want help from her.

"Oh, okay," Lily said as she walked around the car to her own door.

Lily felt a familiar sting in her eyes that she refused to give in to. So Allen's return wasn't going as planned, but she wasn't going to let this turn of events ruin things. Lily could live with a nurse. Heck, Belle would probably be helpful for them. Lily needed to look at Belle as a blessing. However, it would be so much easier to do so if Belle weren't so darn gorgeous. But Lily had never been the jealous type, and she wasn't about to start now.

Belle followed Lily to the driver's side of the car and met Lily's eyes as she began to open the car door. Lily suddenly realized just how stuffed the backseat was with bags and Amelia's car seat. Belle could fit, but it probably wouldn't be a pleasant ride home.

"It'll be quite the squeeze back there. Sorry about that," Lily said with a smile. She was determined to be polite and kind to the nurse who was evidently moving into her home. The only thing to do now was make some lemonade out of the situation.

"Oh, I'll be fine," Belle said, returning Lily's smile.

A returning smile. Okay. That was good.

Lily slipped behind the steering wheel. They could do this. She could do this.

LILY CLOSED her eyes for patience. She had realized on their way home that they had nowhere to house a nurse. They couldn't very well ask a health professional to share a room with their one-year-old daughter, but they only had two bedrooms. So unless they wanted nurse Belle to share their room with them, Amelia needed to have her crib moved into their room.

The space already felt smaller than it had ever been because of the adjustments Levi, Gen's husband, had made to make things easier for Allen. Levi had created an ingenious way for Allen to be able to park his wheelchair next to the bed and then use well-crafted bars to lift himself into bed. Allen wouldn't need Lily at all for that part of their nightly routine. But the new construction had taken quite a bit of the small amount of free space in the room. So where was Amelia's crib supposed to go? And her clothes? And toys?

Nope. Lily would not think of this as a burden. Belle was a blessing.

Lily smiled softly while she pushed Amelia's crib into her bedroom and up against the one free wall. Lily and Amelia would now be sleeping side by side, but that could be a good thing, right? And as Lily remembered the way Allen's eyes had lit up when he'd seen the ramp Levi had built next to the stairs that led up to their cottage, she was reminded that this was all worth it. The changes and adjustments, making their home accessible, were all worth it. Even if they did have to promise their landlord that everything would be undone before they moved out. Which would be a feat, but now wasn't the time to cross that bridge.

"I'm so sorry to make you move things around. After living with the Andersens, I never considered . . ." Belle said from the hallway and then stopped.

Lily knew just what Belle hadn't considered. That the son

of millionaires would live in such a tiny home. But he did. And if Belle wasn't happy with that, that was her problem.

Nope, that kind of pettiness wouldn't fly with Lily. She was going to be gracious. She had to live with Belle, after all. Why not make it as pleasant as possible for all of them?

"I didn't mean to imply that anything is wrong with your home. The bright white walls actually make it seem a whole lot larger," Belle said as she moved into the doorway of Lily and Allen's bedroom so that Lily could now see her. Lily shook her head.

"I totally understand. I'm sure our house is smaller than you expected. But I hope you'll still be comfortable," Lily said as she remade Amelia's crib with the blankets that had been rumpled during the move between rooms.

"I'm sure I will be. Thank you," Belle said. She turned to head back the few steps that would take her into their living space. Besides the small bedroom that would now be Belle's, this was pretty much the extent of their home. Fortunately, the cottage had two bathrooms. Lily wasn't quite sure what she would do if she had to share a bathroom with their new nurse. Judging by Belle's expert makeup, the woman liked her bathroom time.

"No!" Amelia screamed from the driveway, and that was Lily's cue.

She rushed through her living room where Belle sat on the edge of their tan sectional, which took up most of the room, speaking in hushed tones into Lily's husband's ear. Lily gave the scene a second glance before hurrying out the door to her daughter.

Why did Belle have to speak into Allen's ear? But as uncomfortable as the whispering made Lily, her upset little girl was the priority. It wasn't like Amelia to scream. The whispering was just one more thing to deal with later. Lily would add it to the list.

Lily hurried out her front door and crunched through leaves as she made her way to her mother's car, which was parked just behind Lily's.

"Stay Dammy!" Amelia shouted as she clung onto Marian, Lily's mother.

"Why do you want to stay with Grammy?" Lily asked as she extended her arms to Amelia. "I missed you."

"No," Amelia said adamantly as she wrapped her arms even tighter around her Grammy's neck.

Lily tried not to feel hurt by Amelia's rejection, especially after all that had transpired that day. Amelia always chose Lily over anyone else. Well, except maybe Allen before he'd gone to Alabama.

"What's going on?" Lily mouthed to her mom who just shrugged.

"No go home," Amelia said, showing just how precocious she was. Lily knew most eighteen-month-olds didn't have the language ability her daughter had, and Lily had always been so proud. But right now, Lily wished she had an eighteen-month-old who wanted to be in her mother's arms. Lily could use a good Amelia hug.

"But Daddy's here," Lily said happily, hoping her new tactic would work. They'd been talking about Daddy coming home for weeks. At first, Amelia hadn't seemed to understand, and Lily could sense her hesitancy. But earlier that morning, she'd seemed excited, or maybe *accepting* was the better word for what the little girl felt about her father's return. Lily wasn't sure Amelia really remembered Allen, even though the two had started video chatting during the last few months.

"No!" Amelia screamed again, and Lily realized that had been the wrong move.

"Is she worried about A-L-L-E-N?" Lily spelled so Amelia wouldn't understand.

Marian looked from the girl who clung to her to the cottage.

"Maybe?" she said. "Her a-t-t-i-t-u-d-e only started after I told her he'd be h-o-m-e."

Lily should've predicted this. Amelia felt things so much deeper than most kids. Her daughter was still practically a baby but rarely acted like it. The girl was beyond her years, not only in language skills but emotionally as well. Lily wondered if Amelia had picked up on much more about their dynamic than Lily had anticipated.

But what could Lily do now? Her daughter had to come home, and Allen was already here. They would just have to work things out. There was nothing else to do.

"Amelia, do you want to have a tea party?" Lily asked.

Amelia, who had had her head nuzzled into her Grammy's shoulder, looked up.

"Juice?" Amelia asked, and Lily knew she had her. Amelia loved a good tea party, especially one with real refreshment. Lily hardly ever allowed it because it usually meant a big mess to clean up. But now seemed like the perfect moment to use this elusive bribe on her daughter.

"Yup," Lily said.

Amelia immediately put up her arms, letting Lily know she wanted to be held by her.

Okay. One crisis averted. Lily wasn't quite sure how Amelia would respond to Allen, but at least she was willing to come home. One step at a time.

"Thanks, Mom," Lily said as she headed back toward her house. She wasn't going to take any chances on Amelia changing her mind by prolonging their time outside and talking to her mom. Although, Lily did wish that she could take a few minutes to unburden all of her thoughts about the nurse situation. But right now, it wasn't about what Lily needed.

"Anytime, Lil," Marian called out. "And let me know if you need anything else."

"Will do," Lily called back from her front door, quickly waving before entering her home.

Lily's eyes glanced around the space, catching sight of Belle sitting in the same spot with Allen's wheelchair quite near. He was laughing hard about something.

But his laughter stopped when Lily entered, holding their daughter.

"Amelia," she heard Allen whisper, causing Amelia to burrow her face in Lily's neck.

This wasn't a great sign.

"We were about to have a tea party. With real juice," Lily said, sounding way too cheery. But Amelia usually responded well to this voice.

"Oh, tea parties are my favorite," Allen said, right on cue, causing Amelia to look up. Lily hoped this would work.

Allen began to wheel his way across the living room toward the dining room table when Amelia howled.

"No!" she screamed, louder than she ever had.

Lily held on to her daughter a little tighter. The poor girl was shaking. And even though Lily had really wanted this day to go well, every motherly instinct demanded she forget about her wants and focus on Amelia.

"No tea party?" Lily asked as she lowered her head to Amelia's ear.

"No," Amelia said through her tears.

"Okay. No tea party," Lily said as she wrapped her arms around Amelia.

"Do you want juice?" Lily asked, hoping to help Amelia in some way.

"No." Amelia's tears weren't slowing.

"Hug mommy?" Lily asked, and she melted as Amelia nodded.

"I think I'm going to . . ." Belle's sentence trailed off as she headed for her new bedroom.

At least the woman knew how to leave during a family moment. Maybe they would survive living together after all. As long as she stopped whispering things into Allen's ear.

"What's going on?" Allen asked softly.

Lily just shook her head. The heck if she knew.

"Amelia?" Allen tried, and Amelia began screaming again at the sound of her father saying her name.

Allen met Lily's eyes, and Lily just shook her head again. She was at a complete loss. She thought she'd done all that she could to be ready for this day. She thought she'd been ready to see Allen, to rekindle what they had. She thought she'd prepared their daughter. Evidently, she had thought wrong.

CHAPTER TWO

ALEXIS GRINNED down at the card in her hands. The florist's delivery driver had just delivered a gigantic bouquet, the same one he'd brought every month since Alexis had started dating Dalton.

Happy five months. I love you! The card was simple and sweet. Everything she loved about Dalton.

She couldn't believe they'd been dating for five months. It felt like just yesterday they'd met at a bar for drinks, but it also felt like Dalton had been in her life forever. What a weird juxtaposition. Alexis grinned about it until she met the gaze of her mother, who was starting at the flowers in Alexis's hand.

Alexis stuffed the card into her jeans pocket as she met her mother's intense look. Even without the look, Alexis knew her mother disapproved of Dalton. She even disapproved of the flowers. The woman had been very vocal about her dislike for Alexis's boyfriend from day one. Which Alexis had never understood. Because when she'd asked her mom to explain, the older woman couldn't. At least not well. She told Alexis she didn't trust him, but if Alexis trusted him, what did it matter if her mother did or not?

So Alexis continued to date Dalton, driving a wedge between the typically close relationship she and her mother had. Talk about close, they even lived together.

When Alexis had moved back to Whisling after years away, she'd been happy to have her mom become her roommate after she'd bought a small, two-bedroom home a few blocks from Whisling's main street, Elliot Drive. It wasn't the prime beach location many sought, but it was home for Alexis. Some of Alexis's childhood memories on the island weren't great, but she held no resentment toward her mother for that because the woman had always shielded her the best she could.

Growing up the daughter of the girl who'd gotten knocked up in high school hadn't been easy. But Alexis had decided to give the island a second chance, and she was so glad that she had. Coming home as an adult, things had been different. People had been respectful, and Alexis's relationship with her mom had grown closer and closer . . . until Dalton. Well, the first part had stayed the same. It was just Alexis's relationship with her mother that had become strained.

Alexis hated that she couldn't delight in this flower delivery with her mother. Heck, she hated that none of her relationship with Dalton could be shared with the person who had always been her best friend and confidant. This was the greatest and most serious relationship Alexis had ever had. Sure, it was a bit late in life for a five-month relationship to be one of the most lasting in Alexis's dating career, considering she was now in her thirties. But she had avoided boys in high school like the plague. She'd been determined not to become her mother. And then when she'd moved off the island to bartend, the kinds of guys who'd hit on her hadn't been the kinds of guys Alexis had waited so long to date. She figured she deserved Prince Charming, and the guys she was meeting didn't fit the bill.

Except for Dalton. Alexis had met him during her early

bartending days. He was their club manager. But there was no way Alexis could've or would've dated him then, even though she'd known he was a treasure the first time they'd met. The club had a strict policy against employees dating, but that came secondary to the fact that Dalton had been married. So the two had become friends but never anything more. At least, not until recently, after Dalton's divorce.

Of course Alexis had dated over the years, but the result of the combination of her bad luck with guys and her fuller figure, which seemed to turn away half the male population of Seattle, was that she hadn't found Mr. Right. Not even a good imitation.

Then Dalton had come along again, and Alexis had been lost ever since. She would be completely and blissfully lost if it weren't for her mom.

"Sunflowers. Again," Margie, Alexis's mom, said as she stared at the flowers. On their four-month anniversary, when Dalton had sent a dozen fewer sunflowers, Margie had voiced her thoughts that the large bouquet was too over the top and hated that Dalton had chosen the flower because he thought they matched Alexis's disposition instead of buying her favorite flowers for her, red roses. But who could be mad at dozens of sunflowers? Margie.

"I think it's sweet," Alexis said, refusing to get into another argument with her mom. Arguing with her mom brought out a side of Alexis she didn't like. One that said cruel things, like *where did Margie get off trying to tell Alexis she'd chosen badly when Margie hadn't brought home a single winner in her life.* After Alexis had said that, Margie had left and hadn't come home for a week. When she had come back, she'd acted as if nothing was wrong. Alexis had tried to talk to her mother about it, to apologize, but it was like Margie couldn't hear her. So Alexis had let it go. Since apparently her mother had.

"Yeah, it is. But there are other ways to be sweet—ways that don't throw away a hundred bucks on flowers that you don't even like," Margie said from her spot on their blue loveseat.

"Mom, I like them. Actually I love them because they come from Dalton. And Dalton is just trying to show me how much he loves me," Alexis said. All that earned was a shrug from Margie before she turned back to her romance novel. Maybe that was Margie's downfall? She seemed to think love only came in one form. If it wasn't tumultuous and romance novel-worthy, it wasn't worthy at all. But Alexis had seen love in all shapes and forms, and one was never better than the other. All the variations were what allowed love to be right for everyone.

Alexis arranged the sunflowers in a vase she kept under her sink just for Dalton's flowers. She smiled as she moved them around, realizing that next month she might need a bigger vase for the sixth dozen. Alexis had never been happier with a man.

"So do all of those flowers come with some big date?" Margie asked.

Alexis nodded. Of course they did. Dalton loved to celebrate their love. At least that's what he told Alexis every time they had an occasion, big or small. He'd brought her Hershey's kisses on the one-month anniversary of their first kiss and an adorable stuffed puppy on the three-month anniversary of the time Alexis had made him his favorite meal, stuffed pork chops.

"So do you want me to do your nails?" Margie asked kindly, showing Alexis that even though she didn't approve of Dalton, she did approve of Alexis.

Nails had always been Margie's hobby, and she'd turned it into her career. She was the island's premiere nail technician. Even when people had still been judging her for being "a high school harlot," as many had called her, they'd come to her for their nails because there was no one better. Alexis actually counted Margie's job as one big reason why many Whisling residents could finally see past their own stupid judgments and recognize the woman Margie really was. The amazing, kind woman who'd single-handedly raised a headstrong daughter, worked long hours, and taught her baby girl how to cook. Alexis was a chef today thanks to Margie and her late night lessons in the kitchen.

Alexis smiled at her mother's offer. Margie being willing to do her nails for a date with Dalton was a big deal. Alexis felt she should return the favor.

"That would be great, Mom. And in fact, I was thinking. It might be fun for the three of us to do dinner together?" Alexis offered cautiously as she sat on the matching blue couch that was perpendicular to the blue loveseat on which Margie sat. Would her mom be willing?

"For this five-month anniversary thing?" Margie asked as she raised her eyebrows.

Alexis could see that wasn't something Margie wanted to join. "No. Maybe later this week?" Alexis asked hopefully.

Her mom met her eyes. Margie knew how important this was to Alexis.

"You could get to know Dalton . . .?" Alexis began, and she saw the way her mom's face pursed.

Margie felt she'd given Dalton more than enough chances. But the beginning of their relationship hadn't been the best time for Margie to get to know Dalton. He'd been so wrapped up in Alexis, and he'd wanted her to himself. He now knew that hadn't been the smartest move in winning over those whom Alexis loved. But most of them, including Alexis's boss, Bess, had given Dalton another chance. Only Margie hadn't. But she had to. Alexis could never fully bask in the delight of this incredible relationship until her mother was on board.

"Please, Mom," Alexis begged as she ground her bare toes into their gray carpet. Pleading was what it had come to. Alexis would do anything to help her mother's approval along.

Alexis could see that her mom was gritting her teeth, but Alexis wasn't going to give up.

"Fine," Margie said as she hit her book against her leg. "But you'd better be making my favorite."

Alexis beamed. She didn't care if she had to make fifteen bowls of ramen just for her mom or that Dalton wasn't a huge fan of Japanese food. Margie was giving Dalton another chance. Complete happiness now felt within Alexis's grasp. This dinner would work. It had to work. Besides, how could a man as charming as Dalton not win Margie over?

———

ALEXIS HAD BEEN SLAVING over a hot stove all day. Ramen broth was nothing to sneeze at in the culinary world. Alexis felt like she had a decent recipe, but even after years of trying to perfect it, she still felt her broth was mediocre compared to some of the places she'd been to in Japan. They somehow knew how to make a stock rich and light, all at the same time. It was probably a God-given gift, and Alexis was sure if Dalton could eat Japanese food in Japan, he'd fall just as in love with the cuisine as Alexis and her mom had.

She finally took a few moments to get ready and then drove down to meet the ferry. It didn't make sense for Dalton to bring his car to the island unless he had to, and if Alexis picked him up from the dock, he didn't have to. Besides, Alexis would be grateful for this time alone with her boyfriend. She hadn't seen him since their incredible five-month anniversary date, and she also felt the need to prep both of them for her mom.

Margie had been in a mood all day, and Alexis had been walking around on eggshells just hoping the atmosphere would improve by tonight. But Alexis knew better than to count on that. It would be wiser if she and Dalton were ready for what-ever Margie would throw at them.

Dalton ran down the gangplank as Alexis parked her car, and she was barely able to get out of it before she was wrapped in the arms of her man. It was the best place to be.

"You smell good," Dalton said as he sniffed Alexis's hair.

"It's my ramen broth," she said with a grin, knowing Dalton would hate that he'd complemented the cuisine he so often disparaged. He didn't exactly dislike Japanese food, but he felt it was overhyped. And as an owner of six French restaurants whose main competition were the Japanese restaurants in the area, Dalton felt he had to be true to the cuisine his chefs served. Well, except if Alexis cooked for him. And that was why Alexis was sure Dalton would love this ramen as well.

"What? *No*. Well, I guess if anyone could get me to like the stuff, it would be you," Dalton said.

Alexis grinned as she burrowed her face into Dalton's firm chest. How a man with a body like Dalton's could appreciate the fluff and curves that made up Alexis, she would never understand. But she sure would appreciate it.

"You look even better than you smell," Dalton complimented as his eyes roved over the tight jeans and fitted, red top Alexis wore. She would've never felt confident in this kind of outfit pre-Dalton, but now she couldn't help but feel like a million bucks. Dalton never let her feel like any less.

Dalton hungrily took Alexis's lips, and Alexis fell in to the kiss. It was familiar and thrilling all at once. He pulled her closer, and Alexis knew she had to stop him. They were about to go on a date with her mom. One of Margie's biggest complaints about Dalton was the fact that he was so physically attracted to Alexis. Alexis wasn't sure how that was a bad thing, but Margie had told her that men who look at women the way Dalton looked at Alexis couldn't be trusted. Alexis had written the advice off as crazy, but she also knew she and Dalton would have to tone back their intense attraction or mama bear would not be happy.

"So is Margie feeling any more pleasant?" Dalton asked.

Alexis shook her head. She'd warned Dalton over text that her mother had been on one earlier that day.

And when Alexis had left the house to go to the fery, her mom had still been every bit as ornery as she'd been that morning. Those worrisome thoughts caused Alexis to bite her lip as she thought about all that could go wrong that evening.

Dalton led her to her car door before kissing her lips softly. "No more of that. It will all be great."

"Promise?" Alexis asked, really hoping Dalton could bring to pass what he was saying.

"Promise," he said with a grin before pulling her in for another passionate kiss.

"Okay, last one. Until dinner with your mom is over," he said as he allowed her to step out of his grasp. "But after that, I'm making no promises."

Alexis grinned as she got into her car. It was a wonderful thing to be so wanted.

The drive went quickly as Alexis gave Dalton pointers about her mom. He'd arrived with the right gift. Margie might hate huge bouquets of sunflowers, but she was fine with exorbitant amounts of chocolate. So Dalton had brought the most delicious and biggest box he could get his hands on. Margie was going to be thrilled.

As Alexis parked on their street, since her home had no garage or driveway, she drew in a deep breath.

"Do you think she's watching us?" Dalton asked.

"I can guarantee it," Alexis said, glancing out her window and toward her cute home where she swore she saw the light blue curtains flutter.

"So no kiss?" Dalton asked, causing Alexis's stomach to flip flop.

"No kiss," she said as if she couldn't care less about having to keep physical distance from Dalton. But man if she didn't kind of wish their date was just the two of them.

"At least until later," Dalton said with a wink. "Get ready, Alexis."

Alexis drew in a fortifying breath—she would need it in order to keep her hands off of Dalton for a whole evening—and then got out of her car before she could change her mind.

Her mom had better appreciate her sacrifice.

"Mom?" Alexis called out as she and Dalton opened her front door.

"I didn't run, if that's why you're calling my name," Margie said, her tone halfway between serious and teasing. Dalton chuckled.

"She's funny," he said.

"She is," Alexis conceded, even though she wasn't sure she liked this most recent joke because she wasn't sure it was a joke.

From her bedroom, Margie joined Alexis and Dalton as they walked into the living room.

"It's a pleasure to see you, Margie," Dalton said politely as he extended his hand and then the box of chocolates to Margie.

Margie looked Dalton over, and Alexis wondered what her mom was seeing.

Alexis knew what she saw. Broad shoulders and ripped arms, covered by a brown polo. Wavy, dark hair that begged to have Alexis's fingers entwined in it and dark eyes that shone with laughter. Basically, a beautiful man.

Margie finally took Dalton's hand and the chocolates, although she didn't return his sentiment. But it was a start.

"I should check on dinner," Alexis said after a few seconds of the three of them just standing there.

When Dalton moved to follow her to the kitchen, Alexis subtly shook her head, letting her boyfriend know she wanted him to stay in the living room with her mother. Get to know her, hopefully charm her.

Dalton smiled, letting Alexis know he got her message loud and clear, before taking a seat on the comfy sofa in the living room. The thing was gigantic and had cost Alexis an arm and a leg, but the buttery, blue beauty and its loveseat counterpart were worth every penny. Alexis didn't know how many nights she'd fallen asleep right there instead of in her bed, and she always slept like the dead on it.

Her mother chose to sit on the far side of the loveseat—not a great sign—and although she wasn't smiling, at least she wasn't being outright hostile either. Alexis was going to take that as a win and hope things only got better once she took herself out of the equation, leaving the living room through the doorway that led to her kitchen.

Unlike many modern homes, Alexis's kitchen wasn't combined with the rest of her living space. There was a big, thick wall that divided the two rooms, and that wall was actually one of the reasons why Alexis had fallen in love with the home. She loved the separation of living room and kitchen, even though most others didn't. The kitchen had always been her escape, but if it was in the same area as the living space, what kind of escape would that be? And boy was Alexis's kitchen an escape. The dark gray, marbled countertops and stainless steel appliances of the kitchen were offset by yellow cabinets and matching yellow curtains, giving the space an overall homey feel. Alexis had painted her wooden table the same yellow in order to extend the cheeriness even further.

Alexis surveyed her kitchen and what she still needed to prepare for the meal as she listened to the rumble of Dalton's voice.

"How old was Alexis in that picture?" he asked, and Alexis wondered which photo he was pointing to.

Growing up, Alexis and her mom never had much, but Margie had always had a great camera. She bought them secondhand, but they were her prized possessions, and she took especially good care of them. Alexis was pretty sure her mother would've done something in photography if having a baby at sixteen hadn't necessitated that she find a paying job immediately. With Margie's ever-ready camera and incredible talent, much of her daughter's childhood was caught stunningly on film. The wall space in Alexis's home was covered with their favorite photos, some in color and many in black and white. That was Margie's specialty.

"Nine or ten," Margie said shortly, and Alexis tried to beg her mother telepathically to speak up more. Say anything.

Alexis checked on the broth and then began to drop the noodles she'd made earlier into a pot of boiling water. Since the noodles were fresh, they would only take about a minute to cook. Some of the traditional toppings of chashu, eggs, bamboo, scallions, and seaweed were ready on Alexis's cutting board. Then she just needed to plate the meal, or rather, bowl the meal, and dinner would be served. Hopefully her mom's favorite food would help to loosen Margie's tongue. In a good way.

"Was she a handful or an angel, like she is now?" Dalton asked.

The silence that answered Dalton's question unnerved Alexis. She needed to get dinner on so that the two of them would no longer be alone. Leaving them had been a very bad idea.

"She was Alexis," was all Margie said, and Alexis fought against an eye roll. How was that for a non-answer?

"Dinner's ready," Alexis called out, even though she had been planning to set the table nicely before allowing her mom and Dalton to come and join her. But helping the conversation along seemed much more important at this point.

"It smells delicious, love," Dalton said, causing Alexis to beam. She knew she was a good chef, but it still felt incredible for the man she cared about to praise her. She'd come to her calling later in life than many and hadn't gone to culinary school until her early thirties, so she still carried some insecurities in the back of her mind.

"Thank you," Alexis said as Margie grunted.

Her mother was about to get herself uninvited from this meal.

Alexis set bowls of piping hot broth and noodles in front of Dalton and Margie—she caught the tiniest of smiles on the latter's face when her mom beheld the beauty in the bowl Alexis had created—and then she served her own.

By the time Alexis was done serving, Dalton had found chopsticks, no thanks to Margie, and filled a water glass for each of them.

"This looks amazing," Dalton said as he sat in front of his bowl.

"You said that," Margie said bluntly.

"No, he didn't," Alexis said, knowing her voice sounded a bit whiny. But she was so done with her mother.

"Something like it," Margie said quieter this time, as if she might feel a bit of remorse.

"Let's just eat," Alexis said as she dug into her bowl. She didn't even look up to see if either of her guests did the same. Typically, Alexis liked to wait to see the reactions of others before tasting her food herself, but she'd lost all patience and had to hope some sustenance would help her endure the rest of the evening . . . since Margie was intent on making it a terrible one.

"You've converted me," Dalton, ever Alexis's ray of sunshine, said, causing Alexis to look up and see him struggle with his pair of chopsticks and the slippery noodles. She watched as he dug the two sticks back into his bowl, coming up with a sea of noodles but only managing to keep one ensnared long enough to get to his mouth.

She giggled.

"I'm glad my suffering doth please you, m'lady," Dalton said cheesily, only causing Alexis to laugh harder. How did he do this? Everything was falling apart, but it didn't matter. Because of Dalton.

"But I'm serious. This is some yummy grub," Dalton said, and Alexis couldn't help but beam again.

"It's called ramen," Margie interrupted.

Alexis turned to glare at her mom. Really? That was all she could say?

"Ramen. Right. Well, it's some yummy ramen," Dalton said with a wink toward Alexis.

"What was that?" Margie asked, turning her entire body toward Dalton, something she hadn't done all evening.

"I'm sorry, what?" Dalton asked, his eyes wide in shock.

And Alexis couldn't blame him. Mom had gone from icy to fiery in point two seconds. Why was she so upset?

"That wink. Were you mocking me?" Margie practically shouted.

"Mom, calm down," Alexis said.

Margie shook her head. "Calm down? Your boyfriend is mocking me, and you're taking his side. *His* side, the man you've known for a few months."

Margie crossed her arms across her chest, looking more like a petulant two-year-old than the fifty-something woman who'd borne Alexis.

"Mother," Alexis pleaded. This was so out of character for

her sweet mother. Sure, Alexis had gotten her mother upset over the years. But nothing like this anger.

"You are taking *his* side," Margie reiterated.

"Margie, I'm sorry. The wink was misunderstood. I just meant to tease Alexis a little. I do it often. I didn't even think about what it would look like to you. I'm so sorry," Dalton said.

Alexis looked from Dalton to her mother. She had to accept that, right?

But Margie's face turned stony, telling Alexis all she needed to know.

"I'm done here," Margie said, standing.

"Mom, please," Alexis begged. The meal couldn't end like this. These were the two most important people in her life. Her only family. She needed them to at least be able to coexist.

"I tried Alexis. This boy has shown me nothing but disrespect since he got here. You haven't done much better. You should see the simpering fool you become whenever Dalton walks into a room," Margie said, the cruel words nothing Alexis could've ever imagined her mother saying. Not to Alexis. Not in front of Dalton.

Alexis fought against the tears that threatened, and her mother at least had the decency to drop her head in shame.

"You can go, Margie." Alexis called her mother by her first name, something she'd never done in her life. But this woman wasn't the one who'd loved and raised her. Alexis had never felt this distance with her mother. She'd never worried that her mom might be the one to hurt her the deepest.

"Alexis," Margie said as she took a step toward Alexis's chair.

"This is what you wanted, right? Make your point. Leave. But don't think I'll be waiting with open arms when you come back," Alexis said, her piercing eyes locked dead on her mother's. Margie had to know Alexis was dead serious.

Alexis felt a rough, warm hand on her arm.

"It's okay, Alexis," Dalton whispered, but Alexis shook her head. It wasn't okay. Dalton had been nothing but kind and generous to Margie, and what had Margie done? Thrown all of the good behavior away and returned it with vitriol. Their relationship would never work if only two of them put in effort. And her mother had made it more than clear how much she was willing to sacrifice for Alexis and Dalton. Nothing.

"This is between myself and my daughter," Margie said at Dalton's whisper.

Alexis felt anger bubble up within. How dare she? Dalton was sticking up for Margie, and instead of gratitude, he was being told to butt out. Alexis knew she had to get out of the house immediately. Away from her mother.

"We're leaving, Margie. And when I come back, I want you gone." Alexis said the words she never thought she'd utter. Sure, it wasn't always a cake walk living with her mom, but Alexis adored Margie and vice versa. The positives had always outweighed the negatives.

However, this wasn't okay. This kind of disrespect wasn't healthy. And Alexis couldn't live with a person who felt it was okay to be so ugly to someone Alexis cared about. To Alexis herself.

"What?" Margie asked, sounding as shocked as Dalton looked. His round eyes and dropped jaw recovered before Margie did.

"Um, Alexis," Dalton said quietly.

"YOU STAY OUT OF THIS!" Margie screamed, only strengthening Alexis's resolve. It wasn't like Alexis was throwing her mother out on the street. But since Alexis had refused to take a cent of her mother's money while they'd lived together, she knew Margie had a bunch saved up. She could find a vacation rental on the island until something more permanent opened up.

With fury and the knowledge that her mother would be just fine on her own, Alexis stood and stepped away from the kitchen table.

Dalton followed her lead.

"I'll be back tomorrow. Please be gone," Alexis said calmly.

"You don't mean that—" Margie began.

"I meant every word I said. Just as I believe you meant every word you said," Alexis said, her head held high.

Alexis silently hoped that her mother would apologize for everything. If she would just say she was sorry, Alexis felt maybe they could work things out. But her mother had to offer the olive branch. She and Dalton had already offered so much, only to be turned away.

Alexis met Margie's eyes.

The emotions whirling in the blue depths of her mother's eyes were unlike any Alexis had seen before.

"You want me gone?" Margie asked.

Alexis nodded slowly, the action painful.

"You are choosing him over me?" Margie asked.

"That's not what I'm doing," Alexis defended.

"That's what it looks like from here," Margie rebutted, the hurt that had marred her face quickly replaced by wrath.

"I'm choosing me. You have disrespected me and the man I care deeply for. I hoped that you two would take this time to get over your differences. Dalton has only been courteous and gracious, but you've been nothing but mean." Alexis felt good being honest, no longer stuffing her feelings down because she worried what her mother might think or feel.

"You say tomato, I say tomahto," Margie said with a shake of her head.

How dare her mother say that what Margie had stated was the same thing Alexis had just revealed. She'd given her mother the most honest part of her, and this was the reaction she got?

Margie felt no remorse for what she'd said and done, and that didn't appear like it was going to change.

Alexis walked toward the door, knowing that if she didn't stop and give in to her mother, everything between them would change. But as much as Alexis loved her mom, she couldn't stop.

"Alexis," Margie warned, and Alexis knew exactly what her mother was saying. If Alexis walked out that door, Margie would leave. And things would never be the same.

But maybe that was what they needed? Maybe if Alexis stood on her own two feet, her mother would respect her and her decisions as a thirty-five-year-old woman.

For every step Alexis took, she heard Dalton with her. Right behind her. Telling her he was there, even as he gave her the opportunity to stop and make amends with her mother.

But Margie said nothing, so Alexis couldn't turn around. Her mother was in the wrong. Alexis couldn't give in. The only thing that would make Margie content would be if Alexis left Dalton, and that wasn't fair. If her mother loved her, shouldn't her only hope be for Alexis's every happiness? The exact hope she had for Dalton?

So Alexis walked out the door and cried the entire way down to the dock while Dalton drove her car. Alexis cried as Dalton parked and then took her into his arms.

"Do you want to go back?" Dalton asked softly.

Alexis shook her head. As much as this broke her, she couldn't.

"I'd offer my place for you tonight, but it's getting fumigated. I was going to crash at my brother's. I could always ask him—"

Alexis shook her head again. She couldn't put Dalton's family out like that. Not when this was all her doing.

"Rianne's couch is as good as your brother's. And that way I don't have to leave the island," Alexis said between shudders, referring to her best friend from high school. She'd cried so hard, her body was still recovering. "I need to be at work tomorrow."

It felt like Dalton nodded, but Alexis couldn't be certain since her head was still burrowed in his chest.

"It will be okay," Dalton said quietly.

Would it though? Her mother was her only true family. Sure, Dalton felt like he was now, but heaven forbid they broke up. What then?

"She's all I have," Alexis said honestly.

"You will always have me," Dalton said as he hugged Alexis even closer, and she hiccupped against him. "You might have even more. What about your dad?" Dalton asked hopefully.

Alexis knew this was Dalton's attempt at cheering her up, but if they were looking for more family for Alexis, her dad was a dead end. She shrugged. "What about him? Time old tale. Mom dated the wrong guy. Got knocked up. Had me. The end."

"Doesn't sound like the end to me. He's still your father."

"Mom calls him my DNA donor." And quite a few other names Alexis didn't want to utter aloud.

"Did he ever get a chance to man up?" Dalton asked. "Did you ever know him?"

Alexis didn't even have to think before shaking her head. "He had to know about me. The island is only so big. Mom did say something about his family moving away while she was pregnant, but I know that she told him about me. And he hasn't ever tried to contact me. Not once in over thirty years."

"Maybe he wasn't given the chance," Dalton said as he stroked Alexis's hair.

"What do you mean?" Alexis asked as she pulled away. She wanted to see Dalton's eyes during this conversation.

"I don't know Margie well . . ."

Alexis nodded. He didn't.

"But I do know the way she's treated me, the only person to

come close to you other than your . . . you know. Didn't you say she gave Rianne a hard time in high school as well?"

Margie had. She'd never thought Rianne would amount to much, but Rianne had been one of the only kids at school who'd never called Alexis names for the things her mother had done. Sure, Rianne didn't come from the best family—her mother was an alcoholic and her dad struggled to make ends meet—but she'd been loyal to Alexis. So Alexis had fought her mom for her one friend, and now, surprisingly, they all got along really well. Rianne often called Margie for advice, and Margie treated Rianne's kids as an extension of their family. Man was Alexis so grateful that she'd fought for Rianne way back then . . . or else where would she sleep tonight?

"She did. But that was in high school," Alexis admitted.

"Do you think your mom is trying to . . . I don't know," Dalton said.

But Alexis knew exactly what he was trying to say. "She wants to keep me to herself," Alexis said softly. She'd never even considered that. Margie loved her. Alexis thought that her mother was just a bit overprotective. But as someone who loved Alexis, of course Margie would want her to live a full and happy life. With plenty of people she loved in it. But Dalton wasn't wrong about Margie pushing Rianne away, although it had never been as bad as it was with Dalton. Had her mom kept her father away too? Alexis guessed it was a possibility.

"Do you want to meet him?" Dalton asked.

Alexis leaned against the head rest of her car. Did she? In all of her adult life, she'd never considered it an option. Because what woman wanted to meet the man who'd rejected her even before birth? But what if Dalton was right? What if her father hadn't rejected her? What if her mother had rejected him?

Alexis rubbed a hand over her face, not caring that she was smudging her makeup everywhere.

"I don't know," Alexis said honestly. Because she was still scared of rejection.

"Then you don't have to," Dalton said supportively.

Alexis nodded.

But she couldn't get the idea out of her mind now that Dalton had planted it. Did she want to find her dad?

Dalton leaned over the center console and suddenly began kissing Alexis a lot harder and stronger than she wanted that evening. She was still reeling from the confrontation with her mother. However, Alexis kissed him back for a few seconds because he'd been so good to her, but then she was done. She no longer had anything to give to anyone else. She pulled back and felt badly about the hurt look on Dalton's face.

"I just can't tonight," Alexis said, and Dalton nodded.

Of course he understood.

"Do *you* think I should look for my dad?" Alexis asked, her mind going right back to where Dalton had led it. Maybe she needed an opinion other than her own in order to move forward. She only trusted her mother more than Dalton, and heaven knew her mother wasn't one to go to for advice about this.

Dalton nodded slowly. "I do. I don't think it can hurt to start looking, can it?"

Alexis pondered his words as the ferry-riders began to disembark. That meant Dalton would have to get on the ferry soon.

Did it hurt to start looking? It didn't, right? Alexis could always change her mind.

"Okay. Yeah," Alexis said, feeling more hopeful than she had moments before. What did she have to lose? And didn't she have so much to possibly gain? A small part of her brain pressed that her mother might've kept her father away for a reason, but Alexis was too mad at her mom to give that part of her brain much credence. She wanted to move forward. She wanted to follow Dalton's advice. "I'm going to do it."

"*We're* going to do it," Dalton said as he took Alexis's hand. "I'm not letting you do this alone."

"Have I told you *I love you?*" Alexis asked as she pressed a soft kiss to Dalton's lips.

"Not today," Dalton said against Alexis's lips, and then he deepened the kiss.

And Alexis kissed him back.

CHAPTER THREE

"GOOD NIGHT, OLIVIA," Noah said just before hanging up the phone, causing Olivia to sigh at the sound of his deep voice and the immediate warmth it brought to her stomach. She dropped her cell phone on her comforter. Even the man's *good night* was sexy.

Olivia fell back in her pillows, listening to the calm rain falling on her roof. She was finally feeling good about the trajectory of her life. She hadn't felt this way in . . . well, she didn't know how long. Long before she'd divorced Bart, that was for sure. Maybe her discontent with much of life started just a couple years after getting married. When she was still so young. Sure, she'd found happiness, joy, and pleasure during moments and with specific people, like her daughters. But being so at ease with her whole life? Between her daughters, her job, her friends, and Noah, it felt like she had arrived. Or maybe close? Either way, she was quite pleased.

"Mom, I can't sleep," a very sleepy-looking Pearl said as she rubbed her eyes and wandered into Olivia's room, then climbed up into her bed.

"Oh yeah?" Olivia asked because it was quite obvious that Pearl had very much been asleep.

"Yeah. I keep thinking," Pearl said as she cuddled in next to Olivia, sure to get her fair share of the cream and white duvet.

"What do you keep thinking about?" Olivia asked. Olivia knew she shouldn't encourage this type of behavior. She should turn Pearl right around so that she could get a good night's rest in her own bed, but getting to cuddle with either of her girls was a treat Olivia knew wouldn't last forever. She decided listening to Pearl that evening was more important than sending her back to bed.

"Noah," Pearl said, and Olivia fought the urge to allow her mouth to drop open in shock. Noah was the last thing Olivia would've ever thought would be on Pearl's mind.

"What about Noah?" Olivia asked, now more than a little curious. Pearl liked Noah a lot, but she and her sister had been wary of Olivia's relationship in the beginning. However, Olivia felt like they were warming up to the idea of a man in Olivia's life, but maybe she was wrong?

"Is he going to live with us?" Pearl asked.

Olivia snuggled Pearl in closer as she wrapped an arm around her.

"Maybe one day. How would you feel about that?" Olivia asked candidly because she and Noah were getting quite serious. Of course Olivia had considered a future with Noah beyond just dating. But she hadn't been ready to delve into the specifics yet. However, it looked like her little girl was ready, so Olivia needed to be.

Pearl shrugged.

"Do you like Noah?" Olivia asked.

Pearl shrugged again.

"Will he be like Daddy?" Pearl asked, causing Olivia to look down and meet the sweet brown eyes imploring her.

"Will Noah be like Daddy?" Olivia clarified.

Pearl nodded.

Olivia wasn't sure how to answer that question. She felt the need for more information.

"Maybe in some ways. Do you want Noah to be like Daddy?" Olivia asked, wondering if Noah being like their father was a good thing or a bad thing for Pearl. Olivia knew for herself and her older daughter, Rachel, that Noah being anything like Olivia's ex, Bart, would be a nightmare. But Pearl didn't have the same harsh memories of her father and seemed to miss him more than the rest of them.

"No," Pearl answered quickly and easily.

Okay. Olivia only felt more confused.

"Daddy is Daddy," Pearl said, and Olivia guessed that made sense.

"What do you want Noah to be?" Olivia asked as she played gently with the ends of Pearl's hair. Where her and Rachel's hair were a vibrant auburn color with some natural wave, Pearl had her father's dark, thick hair. It was beautiful on her little girl.

"I don't know," Pearl said as she drew over the pattern of flowers on Olivia's bedspread.

"What do you *not* want Noah to be?" Olivia asked, thinking maybe that was the better question.

"I don't want him to live with us," Pearl said.

Olivia sat as still as she could, unwilling to show just how much Pearl's words had hurt her. Olivia wasn't on her way down the aisle or anything, but did she want Noah to eventually move into their home? Sure. And to know her youngest was against that idea . . .

Olivia drew in a deep breath.

"Why not? I thought you like it when Noah comes over," Olivia said. Her voice sounded strangled in her own ears, but thankfully Pearl seemed oblivious to Olivia's distress.

"I do. He brings us treats," Pearl said matter-of-factly. Olivia had worried that the girls' warming to Noah had been because of the candy and other gifts he showered on them, but she'd hoped it was more than that. Well, there went that hope.

"When Daddy would go on trips, he would leave us treats. But when he came home, he'd get mad," Pearl said, making it clear that she remembered a whole lot more about her father than Olivia gave her credit for.

"He sometimes did," Olivia agreed so her girl would know Olivia was on her side.

"If Noah lives with us, he might get mad. Like Daddy," Pearl said, causing Olivia to let out a small sigh of relief. This she could deal with and hopefully correct.

"Noah and your daddy are very different men," Olivia stated.

Pearl nodded. So far so good.

"Noah doesn't get angry like your daddy," Olivia continued.

"Did Daddy get mad before you married him?" Pearl asked.

Had Bart? Not really. Not in the way he had after they'd been bound together.

"No," Olivia answered.

"So if Noah lives with us, you guys will be married, and he'll get mad," Pearl said, her adorable attempt at logic completely flawed.

"It doesn't have to be like that, Sweetie. Lots of men are married and don't get mad the way your father did," Olivia reassured.

"Did Dean get mad at his wife?" Pearl asked, and Olivia felt like the girl had just spun a quick U-turn. Where were they going now?

"I don't know. But knowing Dean, I'm pretty sure he didn't," Olivia said honestly. She might not have ever dated Dean, but she knew in her heart of hearts that her landlord and friend couldn't hurt a fly, much less a woman he loved.

"Was Noah married?" Pearl asked.

No, Noah had never been married. He'd had a long term relationship for many years that had ended just the year before he and Olivia had started dating, but he'd never married the woman.

"No," Olivia said, still unclear on her daughter's train of thought.

"So we don't know if Noah will get mad when he's married. But we know Dean won't," Pearl said, as if she'd solved a problem.

But Olivia wasn't exactly sure of the problem, much less the solution.

Olivia's confusion must've showed on her face because Pearl continued. "You should marry Dean. He won't get mad."

Olivia wanted to fall back in her pillows. They were here again. The place where her daughters loved to imagine a future for their mother and Dean, even though there wasn't one. Olivia was with Noah, and Dean was dating every other woman under the sun. Olivia guessed that wasn't a completely fair depiction, but after his last long term girlfriend, Charlotte, Dean had begun serial dating and seemed to be very much enjoying himself. Olivia knew the single women of the island were loving it.

"Pearly. I can't marry Dean. And right now, I'm not marrying Noah either."

"You're not?" Pearl asked as her head began to feel heavy against Olivia's side. She was getting tired.

"I'm not."

"He's your boyfriend."

"He is."

"Boyfriends and girlfriends get married," Pearl said.

"Sometimes they do," Olivia said, not having the time, patience, nor soundness of mind to explain more than that to her nine-year-old.

"So you won't marry Noah?" Pearl asked.

"I'll tell you this, sweet girl. I will not marry Noah until you and your sister want me to," Olivia promised. It hurt her heart to think about leaving Noah, but given a choice between her girls and anyone or anything, her girls would always come first.

"Okay," Pearl said as Olivia looked down to see her eyes drooping closed. "I love you, Mama."

"I love you, my Pearl," Olivia said as she laid Pearl down on one of her pillows. She knew she should carry her ever-growing nine-year-old back to her room, but Olivia had a queen-sized bed. Why not share it?

Sleep didn't come as easily for Olivia. Her mind went in circles as she wondered what to do next. She knew she really liked Noah. She didn't want to lose him. But what if the girls never accepted him as part of their life? What if they never wanted her to marry him? Could Olivia ask Noah to wait around until they were ready for him? No, that wasn't fair. But could she really give him up?

If it came down to it, she guessed she would have to.

OLIVIA SAT in a dimly lit restaurant in downtown Seattle the very next evening. She'd hoped Noah would be able to make it to the island that night for an early dinner with her girls—she figured the more time they spent together, the better. But Noah had had to work late. So Olivia had left her girls with her mom and taken the ferry to meet up with him for a very late dinner. At least it was late for Olivia. She rarely ate dinner after six pm. And her growling stomach was telling her it wasn't pleased.

The rest of her wasn't too pleased either since Noah should've been there half an hour earlier. But Olivia told herself to be patient. She couldn't allow herself to become upset at such a little thing when the two of them had a big night ahead.

Since Olivia knew she'd be alone with Noah, she'd decided this would probably be the best time to discuss what Pearl had said. She felt it was the only fair thing. But she wasn't relishing telling Noah the girls still weren't his biggest fans. She felt confident that he thought, as had she, that the girls had overcome their initial trepidation.

"I'm so sorry I'm late," an out of breath Noah said as he slid into the seat across from Olivia. The waitress who'd been sending Olivia annoyed glances ever since she'd taken a table alone at one of the busiest restaurants in Seattle now came over to Noah with a gigantic smile on her face. Never let it be said that a handsome face and a fat wallet can't buy you friends. Noah had already made one tonight.

The waitress gave Noah the lowdown on their drinks menu, and Noah turned to Olivia. "Maybe a bottle of that—"

"I'm fine with just water tonight," Olivia said as Noah continued to peruse the wine menu. The waitress's scowl came back, but only for Olivia. When Noah looked up, the woman was all smiles.

"Are you sure? I hate that I made you wait. Let me make it up to you," Noah said.

Olivia shook her head. There was nothing to make up. He'd been a little late. Olivia had done as much quite a few times over their time dating. Besides, Olivia didn't want to drink when she still had to drive back to Whisling that evening.

"What if you didn't drive back?" Noah asked when Olivia gave him her reasoning.

Okay, this was really a conversation Olivia didn't want to have in front of a waitress who hated her. But the waitress wasn't moving until she got their drink order, and Noah wasn't giving up on that bottle of wine.

"I have to drive back, Noah. The girls."

Olivia didn't feel she had to say more. Of course the girls needed her, and Noah understood that. Besides, she was nowhere near ready for a sleepover. She knew men and women had them quite a bit sooner in relationships than where Olivia and Noah were at, but she wasn't most women and she was hoping Noah wasn't most men. He'd seemed understanding when she would put a stop to their kissing before it became too heated, but they'd never really talked it out. Olivia hadn't told him she wasn't ready to take things that far yet. She wasn't sure she'd ever be ready before marriage. She felt having sex too early had been a big part of the power Bart had held over Olivia. She had equated sex with love when Bart hadn't. And although she knew Noah was nothing like Bart and Olivia was much more mature than that seventeen-year-old girl, she still wasn't ready.

"I could always take you home," Noah said as he waved the waitress away. Finally.

"This isn't about the bottle of wine anymore, is it?" Olivia asked as she deciphered the implications behind Noah's offer.

Noah shook his head.

Olivia let out a breath. She wasn't sure she wanted to have this conversation in the middle of Pierre's with the smell of butter all around her, but then again, when did she want to have this conversation? Better to get it over with. And then go into what her girls were feeling. Might as well get it all out now.

"I don't think it's a good idea for me to bring a man home," Olivia said quietly, hoping they wouldn't draw any attention to their intimate conversation.

"I'm not a man, Olivia. I'm your boyfriend," Noah said.

Olivia nodded. He was right about that. "You are," she said. Then she decided she needed a bit more clarification before continuing. "Is this about sleeping over? Or about sex?" Olivia asked the question straight up.

"Both. I want to have sex with the woman I love, and then I want to hold you in my arms as we fall asleep," Noah said softly as he leaned his forearms on the table between them.

Olivia was hit with affection, sadness, and fear all at once. But mostly fear. And she didn't think it was a good thing that fear was the overwhelming emotion she felt at such a sweet sentiment.

"I'm not ready," Olivia said quietly, hating that she was disappointing Noah but needing to be true to herself.

"I respect that, Olivia. But then be honest. Don't tell me that you need to get home to your girls," Noah said as he looked down at the menu.

"*Do* you respect that?" Olivia asked because it seemed as if Noah was now upset.

"I do. I don't like it, but I respect it. I knew what I was getting into when we started dating."

"What you were getting into?" Olivia asked, trying not to sound as upset as she felt. But she hated that he was bringing up her baggage right now.

Even as she hated it, she understood what Noah was saying. Bart had done a number on her. She'd thought the same to herself plenty of times. But she didn't like that he was saying it at this point in their conversation, as if her baggage was the only reason behind her choices. Then again, maybe it was. Honestly, it made no sense because even while she saw Noah's point, she was annoyed. Maybe as annoyed as their waitress who had just brought back their waters.

"Would you like to—" the waitress asked.

"We need a minute," Noah cut her off curtly.

Well at least there went the waitress's smug smile.

Noah sighed.

"You know what I meant, Olivia. Bart left you with terrible scars. I didn't mean anything derogatory. I promise. I'm not sure how we got here. I respect you, Olivia. All of you. Including your decision to put off sex for as long as you want to. I knew when I started dating you that I would have to tread slowly and carefully in that respect. It didn't scare me off then, and it won't scare me off now. That's what I meant," Noah said.

Olivia nodded, feeling badly that she'd overreacted. "I'm sorry," Olivia said as she reached across their table to join her hand with Noah.

"Don't be. I shouldn't have pushed," Noah said.

"We need to have this conversation," Olivia said.

"Need?" he asked. Olivia realized he probably thought the conversation was done.

Olivia nodded and then drew in a deep breath. How would Noah react to the next part? Well, there was only one way to find out. "Noah . . . I might not be ready for sex until after marriage."

Noah rubbed his thumb against the back of Olivia's palm, calming her racing heart, and then met her eyes. "Well, it's a good thing I plan on marrying you soon then."

His sly smile made her heart flip until she remembered her conversation with Pearl. She wasn't sure how soon she could marry Noah. But she guessed they could probably use a bit of a break after their first near-argument. The next discussion could at least wait for their main course to be served since the waitress was coming back and they really needed to order their meal.

Olivia devoured her rocket salad appetizer while Noah explained the reason for his working late that evening, but she didn't even start to feel satiated until she was halfway done with her wild seabass. The fish, which had been cooked in lemon and ginger, was divine, but it wasn't enough food. Olivia would definitely be ordering dessert.

When her seabass was gone and the waitress nowhere in sight to take their dessert order, Olivia knew it was time to tell Noah the rest of what was on her mind.

"I had a conversation with Pearl last night," Olivia began.

Noah nodded. Olivia often told him about the chats she had with her girls.

"She doesn't want you to move in." Olivia said the words the same way she took off a band aid—in one fell swoop. But when she saw the press of Noah's lips and the scrunch of his nose, telling her how hurt he was, Olivia wondered if she'd taken the band aid off too fast.

"She doesn't?" Noah asked as he put down his fork next to his half-eaten filet mignon.

"I think she's scared of any new changes, and she's especially afraid of really letting a man into her life after Bart," Olivia tried to explain.

She expected Noah to nod and understand, but he didn't. Instead, he paused and looked down at the space between their plates. He drew in a deep breath and then said, "Any man other than Dean, right?"

Olivia bit her lip. Was that a fair assessment? She wanted to tell Noah it wasn't, but that might not be the truth. Had her girls let Dean fully into their lives? Olivia guessed they had. But only after months of patience and relationship building. Noah hadn't put in as much work or time as Dean had, so of course the girls trusted Dean more.

"I guess," Olivia admitted. As much as she wanted to make Noah feel better, the decision of who to let into their lives and hearts was up to her *and* her girls. She couldn't make them trust Noah any more than she could make them not love Dean. That wasn't Olivia's place.

"You know you promote that relationship," Noah accused.

Although Noah was upset, Olivia did not like where the

conversation was going. "I do. He's a man they love and trust. Who I trust with that love and trust. Why wouldn't I foster it?" Olivia asked, now feeling defensive of not only her own decision but of her girls.

"Because he's your *neighbor*." Noah emphasized the last word, also emphasizing the distance he felt Olivia's girls and the man next door should have in their relationship.

"He's a good friend to me, and he's been a salvation to the girls. When Bart wanted nothing to do with them, Dean was there. When Bart played with the girls' emotions, Dean was there. Dean has been a solid constant in their lives. I'm not sure what you're saying, but I am not willing to change that. Not even for a man I want a future with," Olivia said.

Noah's jaw tightened. "*A* man you want a future with. Not *the* man?"

Had she said that? Although Olivia wasn't sure she could tell the difference. Was *the* so much better than *a*?

Olivia stayed silent, unsure of what Noah wanted from her.

"Be honest with me, Olivia. Better yet, be honest with yourself. If the girls weren't around—"

"But they are," Olivia cut him off. She wasn't willing to imagine an alternative without her girls. Her girls were her life.

"Just hear me out," Noah said. By the strain on his face, it was apparent that his patience was wearing thin.

Olivia crossed her arms across her chest, all thoughts of dessert long forgotten.

"This isn't about your girls. You are once again hiding behind them. Do you want to know what this is about?" Noah asked.

Olivia raised her eyebrows, asking Noah to enlighten her.

"Even if your girls didn't love and adore Dean, it's obvious you do." Noah said each word firmly and then met Olivia's eyes with a look that asked her to defy him.

Alright. Noah was asking her to be honest with herself. So she reflected. Did she love Dean? Maybe she'd been in love with him at some point, and she knew she still had love for him. But how could she be in love with Dean if she cared so deeply for Noah? Did Noah doubt her adoration for him?

"I'm with *you*, Noah," Olivia said, matching the firmness Noah had had in his voice.

"I know. That's what makes this so hard. It's almost like living with a ghost in the middle of our relationship. Except he's not a ghost. He's a real man who lives next door to you and has a stellar relationship with your daughters." Noah sank back in his seat, looking defeated.

"I'm not sure what you want from me, Noah," Olivia said. She couldn't change things. She couldn't change that she had once cared for Dean as more than a friend and now cared for him as one of her best friends. She couldn't change that her girls loved the man and wanted him to be their father. She couldn't change her past, but she could choose her future. And she had chosen Noah. She thought he understood that. "I'm doing the best I can."

"But are you?" he asked as he leaned forward so that his elbows were on either side of his plate.

"Of course I am," Olivia said. How many hours, days, weeks, and months had she put her everything into this relationship? How dare Noah doubt that.

"There's always something between us. Your girls, your past, Dean. And if you look for a common denominator, I'm not the one putting those things between us, Olivia. That's all on you. *You* are the reason we can't make this work," Noah said.

Olivia felt her heart fall. That's what Noah saw? After all Olivia had done to try to make this work, he was accusing her of putting up walls? And he was bringing her girls into this?

Olivia put her palms against the table and raised herself out of her seat. Noah hadn't used his words to insult Olivia, but his accusation felt very much like an attack. She was brought back to a night, in a similar restaurant, where Bart had revealed in front of dozens of their friends and acquaintances that he was cheating on Olivia. That he had been for years. Olivia had promised herself after that night that she would never again go into a public bathroom and cry tears of pain. No man would send her to that place again.

So Olivia placed her purse on her shoulder and turned, walking right out of the restaurant.

"Olivia," Noah called out as he neared where she was waiting by the valet station for her car.

Olivia stood ramrod straight. She couldn't look at Noah. She was so done with having accusations thrown at her.

"Olivia, please. Don't leave like this. I'm sorry," Noah pleaded.

But the words sounded all too familiar to Olivia. Bart always did the same thing. Throw hurtful words her way and then give an apology that was as quick to come as it was to be forgotten. Because the next day the process would repeat again.

"What are you sorry for?" Olivia asked as the valet pulled her car in front of her.

"For what I said. I shouldn't have said it," Noah said. So far the words sounded okay. She knew Noah wasn't Bart and that she shouldn't hold Bart's sins against Noah. She also knew she and Noah had to fight. Every couple did. She just hadn't expected Noah to fight like this. Every time they'd disagreed in the past, they'd had rational conversations. Sometimes they became a bit heated, but Noah always treated Olivia with respect. This was the first time she'd felt disrespected and belittled. She didn't like it at all.

"I shouldn't have blamed this all on you. We're both in this, and the blame should be on both of us," Noah explained as the valet ran around the car and gave Olivia her keys.

"Thank you," she said quietly as she tipped the man and then walked toward her driver's seat.

"Olivia, let's talk this out. You can't leave like this," Noah pleaded.

Olivia stopped walking and then turned so that she could face Noah as she spoke to him. Noah took a few steps so that he stood just in front of Olivia.

"Your words hurt me, Noah," Olivia said, being as honest as she could because she didn't want to be accused of making another mistake. She ran down the list of things Noah had told her she'd done wrong that evening; it was a pretty extensive collection.

"I understand that. I'm sorry. I really am, Olivia. I don't want to hurt you."

Olivia believed him. And yet he had.

"We're going to have to have hard conversations. My baggage demands it." Olivia swallowed. She had thought Noah understood this. That Olivia came to the table with so much that could keep them apart. She wasn't putting those things there. They were with her forever. A part of her, whether she liked it or not. It felt like Noah could no longer accept that.

"I know. I'm sorry. I lost my head. I got jealous of Dean and wished the girls could accept me. I love your girls, Olivia," Noah promised.

Olivia nodded. "It's going to take time, Noah. All of this takes time," Olivia said, finally coming to a resolution that she didn't like but felt she had to follow through on.

"I get it, Olivia. I got impatient, and it wasn't fair." Noah said all the right words, and Olivia wanted them to make everything better. But they couldn't. It would take a whole lot of work for things to get better. And she wasn't sure Noah was ready for that.

"I think we need some time," Olivia stated.

Noah grabbed ahold of her hand. "Please, Olivia. Don't do this," he pleaded.

Olivia gripped Noah's hand just as tightly. She didn't want to take a step away from their relationship either. But it felt necessary. Not just for Noah but for herself and her girls. She and Noah had seen one another or talked on the phone every day since their first date. They all needed some time and space apart.

"It's what we need," Olivia said as she felt her eyes sting. Could she really do this?

"What I need is you," Noah said.

"This isn't the end, Noah. It's a step in our relationship. A step we all need."

"I don't need time apart from you. I don't need to take a step backwards," Noah said.

Olivia bit her lip as she tried to explain. "I need to concentrate on me and my girls. I know you may feel that what you said fell on deaf ears, but it didn't. I understand your concern, and I need time to reflect on myself. What I've done. What I'm doing. And what I want."

"And what if after this reflection you find you don't want me?" Noah asked as he tugged Olivia closer.

What could Olivia say? She knew she wanted Noah now, but who was to say what she would want after her reflection? She couldn't make any promises, and yet she knew she couldn't just go back to what they'd been doing.

"This is just a pause before breaking up. Don't do this to us, Olivia. Please," Noah begged.

Olivia was on the brink of giving in. Oh how easy it would be to tell Noah that she didn't need time, after all. That she only needed him. If Olivia didn't have her girls and her past, maybe she could've. But Olivia felt in her soul that without this time apart, nothing would change. They would just be brushing their issues under a rug, and Olivia couldn't do that. Not after having done it with Bart for so many years.

She had to ponder on what Noah had said. Find if there was truth to it, and then find where she should go from there. And she couldn't do that with Noah, at least not yet. In the future, she hoped she could recalibrate with Noah. But this time it was something she had to do alone. Especially after what Noah had said about Dean. She needed to make sure there was absolutely no truth to that.

Olivia dropped Noah's hand. "I wish I could."

"You can."

"I can't. Not if I want us to work," Olivia said.

Noah finally nodded.

"I'm doing this for us, Noah."

"I know that's what you think."

"It's what I know."

"If it's for us, why are you pulling away? Shouldn't anything that helps us be bringing us together?"

He had a point. But Olivia had one too.

"When you have a plant in a pot that's too small, the plant can't grow or reach its potential. It will either die or have its growth stunted. I'm trying to give our relationship a bigger pot."

"So let me move to the bigger pot with you. Why do you have to do it alone?" Noah asked.

"I just do," Olivia said, unable to explain herself further.

Noah met Olivia's eyes, and she knew he could feel her determination.

"Okay," Noah said, finally giving in. Then he gave Olivia one last piercing gaze. "But I'll miss you."

"I'll miss you too." Olivia spoke the truth. She was already aching with the knowledge that tomorrow would be without Noah. But she had to do this.

Noah looked like he was about to walk away when he turned and gathered Olivia into his arms. His mouth crushed down on hers in a desperate manner. Their lips had never met in this way, and Olivia could feel Noah's pain even as she felt their connection.

"I love you, Olivia Penn," Noah said. And then he was gone.

With shaky hands, Olivia got into her car and drove away, even as a big part of her heart screamed at her to stay. But she knew this was what she had to do. Had she used her baggage as a wall? Or worse, as a shield against Noah? Could she keep her past from getting in between them? Would her girls ever be comfortable with Noah in their lives? Was she keeping barriers between them on purpose? Olivia knew these questions and more had to be answered before she could go back to Noah. She liked him too much to give him anything less than all of her.

CHAPTER FOUR

JANA CAME out of the fitting room of the cute bridal boutique where she'd found her wedding dress with a gigantic smile on her face. She'd looked high and low for months before finally landing on the dress she'd deemed perfect. But because it had taken Jana so long to find "the one," many of her loved ones, including Bess, were just seeing the dress for the first time, even though the wedding was just a few months away. Bess had gone on the first few dress-searching trips with her future daughter-in-law, but Jana had stopped inviting all but her maid of honor after so many failed attempts. Today was the chance for the important women in Jana's life to see her in all her splendor.

As she walked toward her group, she was met with *oohs* and *ahs*, many coming from Bess herself. Stephen was going to be blown away.

Jana's dress was perfection. From its high neck to its gigantic train, the dress might've seemed a bit stifling if it weren't for the fact that the over layer of lace had lots of spaces between the pattern that were sheer. The bottom layer of the dress was a simple, long, silk slip dress with a low v in both the front and the back. Jana was stunning.

"I didn't think I was going to cry," Lindsey, Bess's daughter, said as she pressed her fingers under her eyes and then waved her hands in front of them. "I have to go back to work after this, and I can't do it with big raccoon eyes."

Bess chuckled and Jana grinned as she met the gaze of her future mother-in-law. Mother-in-law. The words hit Bess hard. Her baby boy was getting married. Suddenly tears threatened Bess as well.

"I know that look. You can't start crying, Mom. Then I'll never stop," Lindsey said, and Jana giggled.

"You are stunning," Bess said to Jana, who beamed with pleasure.

"Thanks, Mom," Jana said, sounding a little unsure before she actually allowed the second word out. Bess had asked Jana to call her mom just a few weeks before. It had felt like the right thing considering they'd be family soon.

"You're welcome," Bess said as she stood to give Jana a hug and then quickly stepped aside so that Jana's mother and her bridesmaids could have a turn to hug the bride.

"Soon she's gonna be stuck with Stephen forever. Poor girl," Lindsey lamented as Bess jabbed an elbow into her daughter's side. Bess knew her children loved each other, but man did they like to hide that love behind bickering and shallow digs.

"I mean, woo hoo. Lucky Jana," Lindsey said sarcastically as she jumped out of the way before Bess could jab her again.

After the women had had sufficient time to praise the beauty of both the dress and the bride, Jana went back into the dressing room where a woman from the store took her final measurements to use in the last alterations before the big day.

Bess chose that as her cue to leave. Although most of the women would be going to lunch with Jana, Bess and Lindsey both had to get back to work.

Bess's chef and friend, Alexis, had taken over Bess's

morning shift so that she could go to Seattle and see the dress, but she didn't feel right making Alexis work extra hours just so that she could join the girls for a nice lunch. It would've been fun, but work called. Thankfully Bess adored her job and her food truck.

The ferry ride back to the island went by quickly, and soon Bess was driving up the shoreline to the place where her food truck was almost always parked.

She reveled in the gorgeous view of the ocean right before pulling to park behind her truck. What a lucky life she led that not only did she get to ride a ferry across the gorgeous Pacific, she also got to work right beside it.

But there was no more time to look at the view, considering their line wound around the truck and back into the trees that sat around the clearing where Bess had set up a few tables for her patrons. It was going to take both her and Alexis some time to whittle away at that line.

"Hey, Bess," some of her regulars called out as Bess made her way toward the door of her truck.

She waved at all and then got to work.

"What do you need?" Bess asked Alexis as she washed her hands and put on her apron.

"Cassie just got a new order. Do you want to start that one?" Alexis asked without even looking up from the shrimp she was frying.

"Got it," Bess said as she squeezed past Alexis and went to the front of the truck where their cashier, Cassie, stood taking orders.

"Oh thank goodness," Cassie said as she noticed Bess. "That line just seems to keep growing."

Cassie handed Bess a ticket, and Bess got to work on the order of lasagna and fettucine alfredo. Even just looking at the words Cassie had written made Bess's stomach growl, but considering the line, Bess wasn't sure she'd get the time to take a lunch. Maybe dinner. Hopefully dinner.

The three women worked side by side for hours before Bess sent Alexis home. She'd already been working for over eight hours, and eight hours on a food truck were much more strenuous than eight hours in any other type work Bess had ever done. Alexis had argued that they still needed her to cook with them, and although they probably did, Bess wouldn't allow her chef to overtax herself. Fortunately, Cassie would be fine because she was the type of person to thrive with hoards of people, whereas Alexis was more like Bess, and the big lines only served to further drain her.

"Are you sure?" Alexis asked for the third time while she stood by the door Bess was kicking her out of.

"Positive," Bess called out as Cassie echoed the claim.

"Fine," Alexis conceded before exiting the truck.

The remaining two women continued to work as hard, if not harder, until the line finally died down around seven-thirty pm.

"I'm starving," Cassie said as she dug into one of the plates of shrimp scampi Bess had just prepared for the two of them.

"I'm so sorry about your lack of a break today," Bess said.

Cassie shrugged. "No biggie," the adorable blonde replied. "Some days I get bored during my break anyway. And besides, even if you never gave me a break, this would still be the best gig in town. I would work for free as long as you kept me fed."

Bess knew Cassie had exaggerated but returned the smile anyway. The girl really was a godsend.

"You can take that plate to go. You more than deserve to get off half an hour early after the day we've had," Bess said as she also dug into her pasta. She was partially tempted to close her truck for the day but knew her customers counted on her being open until eight. Even though she felt like she was practically sleepwalking at that point, it was important for her business to be consistent and a constant on the island.

"And leave you to your own devices? I think not," Cassie said with a sassy grin.

Bess decided then and there that her employees deserved an amazing bonus soon.

"How did wedding dress admiring go?" Cassie asked Bess between bites.

Bess cleared her mouth of the noodles she'd just shoved in and then said, "Wonderfully. I'm so glad they're finally getting married."

Cassie nodded. She knew the tough road Stephen and Jana had had on their way to matrimony, thanks to Bess's divorce. Stephen had taken the news of Jon's affair, Stephen's father and Bess's ex, harder than anyone had expected and had pushed his poor fiancé right out of his life. Things had improved substantially since then, but Bess would breathe a big sigh of relief when they finally made it down the aisle. Both of her children, because she now considered Jana as one of her own, deserved their happy ending. She told Cassie as much.

"What about your happy ending?" Cassie asked Bess with a pump of her eyebrows.

Nope, Bess was not going to go there. She knew exactly what, or rather who, Cassie wanted to talk about. Bess hoped she could divert Cassie's attention to another subject.

"Didn't you just start dating a new guy?" Bess asked, and Cassie giggled in response. That giggle told Bess she wasn't nearly as sly as she'd hoped.

"Caught me a week too late, dear Bess. I dated and dumped Walt. I'm now back in the singles scene with nothing to share. So where does that leave us?" Cassie tapped her chin in an exaggerated manner. "Oh right. What about your happy ending,

Bess? I know a certain eligible bachelor who would be thrilled to join you in that venture."

Cassie took another bite of her meal but kept her eyes on Bess, telling the older woman there was no way she was getting out of the truck that evening without revealing something juicy.

Bess placed her fork in her noodles so it wouldn't slide off her plate as she spoke. "I don't know."

Bess really didn't. She often thought about Dax, the man she was in love with. There was no getting around that now, not that she'd ever said the words aloud. But Bess knew she had fallen head over heels for the man. He was handsome, charming, smart, funny, for some reason attracted to Bess, and although he was many years her junior, he had a maturity that sometimes even Bess didn't possess. Basically he was her dream man.

However, Bess had spent most of her time and energy the past year trying to work things out with her ex. They'd called it quits *for real* a few months prior, and Bess didn't want to rush into anything new. Especially anything as real as what she had with Dax. She wanted to make sure she was wholly ready to love Dax and let Dax love her before she committed to him fully. She didn't want to mess this up.

"Why won't you just date him? It's easy to see he loves you, Bess. He practically worships the ground you walk on," Cassie said as she continued to eat.

Bess wasn't as fortunate as Cassie in that regard. Now that thoughts of Dax filled her mind, she found her stomach was too full of butterflies to eat. See, this was why she had to make things work with Dax. Being a grown woman who got butterflies at the mere thought of a man meant that this was a once-in-a-lifetime type of love. Bess wanted to keep that love forever, so she had to tread carefully.

"Are you scared?" Cassie asked when Bess didn't respond.

That was one word for it. Terrified, petrified, fearful were also adequate verbs.

"I just don't want to mess things up. It's the real thing. I think. I mean, we haven't even really dated, and I'm . . ." Bess let her words trail off.

"You're in love with him," Cassie said matter-of-factly. "That's easy to see too."

Bess guessed it was. She was usually better at hiding her emotions, but her complete adoration of Dax was hard to hide.

"But what if . . . now I'm just spitballing, so give me a chance before you deny all I'm saying," Cassie said, and Bess nodded. Cassie, although only twenty-six, was known on the island for giving good advice. Bess wasn't about to look a gift horse in the mouth.

"What if you waiting is hurting things instead of helping? What if all you're doing by waiting is just wasting time you could be spending with Dax?"

Bess set her plate on the counter so she wouldn't drop it. She had kind of hoped Cassie's advice would be so off the wall that she could completely disregard it, but she should've known it was going to be insightful. And what she'd said . . . well, it could be right on the money. What if Cassie was right?

"You know, I've been told that fear is the opposite of faith. When you allow fear in, you leave no room for faith."

Bess had heard that as well.

"What if you removed that fear or pushed it out with some faith in you and Dax?"

Bess knew the possibility of failing would be there, no matter how much faith she had. But she had to agree with Cassie that if she did have faith instead of fear, she and Dax might have a chance at making things work. And wasn't taking that chance better than just waiting around for who knew how long for who knew what to happen?

Bess's thoughts paused as she heard shuffling just outside of their truck's ordering window.

"Hey, Larry. Let me guess. Two caprese salads?" Cassie asked as one of their favorite regulars came up to her window.

Bess began to fill Larry's order, knowing Cassie had been spot-on even before hearing Larry's response.

"Exactly," Larry answered cheerfully. Fortunately, since the ingredients for the salad were already prepped, it was a quick and easy meal to make. Soon the salads were in their takeout containers, ready to go.

"How's it going, Larry?" Bess called out as she handed the salads off to Cassie.

Larry was an island lifer, born and raised on Whisling. And since he was nearing eighty, he was also one of the island's most knowledgeable residents.

"Not bad now," Larry said as he took the salads from Cassie. "I've been waiting for this meal all day."

"It's a bit late for dinner for you folks, isn't it?" Bess asked as she joined Cassie at the window.

"The Mrs. had us painting her precious sewing room all day. My Clara can be a taskmaster when she wants to be."

Bess and Cassie chuckled. They both knew and loved Larry's sweet wife. But when Mrs. Clara decided something was going to get done, whether it was a church social or, evidently, painting her sewing room, it was going to get done.

"We just finished up, and she promised me this salad as a reward. So I decided to be a good husband and order her one as well."

"Are you sure you don't want more than a salad?" Bess asked, thinking about the back-breaking work painting all day must've been.

"You want to know a secret?" Larry leaned forward to talk even though no one else was around.

"Of course," Cassie said with a flirtatious wink. The girl couldn't help but flirt with any man, and Bess loved her despite it. Or maybe because of it. Most times, not only was her jovial way adorable, it was also great for business.

"I get the salad so Clara thinks I'm being healthy, but I'm really in it for the garlic bread," Larry said about the side Bess served with each of her salads.

Bess grinned at Larry's admission and immediately turned around to wrap up the rest of the loaf she had prepared for the evening. She doubted she'd be selling any more garlic bread tonight anyway.

"Well, it's a shame then that a whole loaf of it made its way into your bag," Bess said as she handed Larry the bread.

"I couldn't," Larry said as he looked longingly at the bread.

"Yes, you could. On the house, Larry," Bess said with a grin.

"I shouldn't," Larry added before taking the bread. "But I'm going to."

Cassie laughed at the man's response and the quick way he left the food truck as if he worried they would take back the bread.

"I love this island," Cassie said as Bess looked at the clock. It was finally eight.

"I do too," Bess agreed as she began to clean the truck and Cassie closed up her register.

Bess wondered if Cassie would go back to talking about Dax, but since the conversation never strayed in that direction again, Bess guessed Cassie could understand Bess had said all she was willing to share.

In fact, Bess had told Cassie even more than she was typically willing to think about. As she drove home later that evening, Bess fought as her thoughts tried to wander back to Dax. At one point, she gave in, just long enough to wonder again if Cassie had been right. Should Bess really give herself and Dax a shot?

Her thoughts started going 'round and 'round, but Bess stopped herself quickly. The next afternoon she had an appointment with her therapist, Dr. Bella. She could pause her thoughts for a night and get a second opinion on what Cassie had said. Bess's continual worrying was helping no one.

It was only after that resolution that Bess was finally able to relax. She would let Dr. Bella determine her future.

BESS SHOULD'VE KNOWN it wouldn't be that easy.

"I can't tell you what to do about Dax," Dr. Bella said after Bess had explained what Cassie had told her.

But Bess was so very lost and confused about the situation that she was willing to push more than she typically would.

"Well, in your professional opinion, do you think that it's smarter to take the bull by its horns and begin a relationship right away? Or does it make more sense to cultivate the friendship longer, and then when I know I'm ready, start dating? Am I wasting time? Am I being unfair to Dax?"

There were at least a dozen more questions plaguing Bess, but she stopped there. Even if Dr. Bella was incredible at what she did, she was still human. And as far as Bess knew, humans still had to answer one question at a time.

"Are you not ready to date?" Dr. Bella asked.

Bess paused. She'd been hoping for an answer, not another question. But since Dr. Bella had yet to steer her wrong, Bess thought about what her doctor had asked.

Was Bess ready to date again? Sure, she guessed she was. But the real question was, was she ready to date Dax? That she wasn't sure of. Because if she ruined things with any other guy, she could forgive herself. But if she messed up with Dax . . . that just couldn't happen.

"I am," Bess answered truthfully.

"But you aren't ready to date Dax?" Dr. Bella asked.

"I don't know. That's why I asked you," Bess said as she met the doctor's eyes.

"I know. But I really can't answer that, Bess. I kind of wish that I could because I want only the best for you. But it's because I want what's best for you that I can't answer you."

Bess sighed. "I get it. It's just . . . I feel like if I make one decision, it could be the wrong thing, but if I make another decision, it could be a worse thing."

Dr. Bella nodded. "So which is the wrong thing and which is the worse?"

"That changes from day to day," Bess said as she leaned back on the couch.

"Let's go to worst case scenario," Dr. Bella said, causing Bess to fight a groan. She hated worst case scenario, but it was a good exercise. It had helped Bess to see that sometimes her fears were graver than the worst that could happen.

So even though she'd join the exercise begrudgingly, she would join it.

"If you waited to date Dax, what would be the worst case scenario?" Dr. Bella asked.

"He could move on and find another woman without so much holding her back," Bess said softly. Her heart literally ached just thinking about the possibility.

"He could," Dr. Bella agreed. "But in my professional opinion? There aren't many women around who don't have something holding them back."

"So you're saying if Dax found someone else for himself, it wouldn't be because she was better suited. It would be because she was more willing to get over her fears?" Bess asked.

"I didn't say that. You did," Dr. Bella said with a grin.

"You're right. I did," Bess laughed, but her laughter died down quickly as another thought came to her mind.

"But I think that's just worst case scenario one. I kind of wonder if Dax will wait around for me and then realize I wasn't worth the wait. Or resent me for putting us through so much. Man, there are lots of terrible scenarios with this one," Bess lamented.

Dr. Bella nodded. "Anything else?" she asked.

Bess leaned forward to think. "No. At least not now."

"Okay. So worst case scenario for option two," Dr. Bella said.

"If I get over my fears that I'll ruin things with Dax and start dating him now?" Bess asked.

Dr. Bella nodded.

Bess pursed her lips. What would be the worst case scenario? She imagined Dax coming home to see her more often. She imagined the deeper conversations she was holding back on because she was too scared to let Dax all the way in. She imagined really kissing him.

Option two had lots of positives.

But one huge glaring negative and the absolute worst case scenario finally came to mind.

"We could hurt one another the way Jon and I did." Bess's voice was barely above a whisper.

"You could," Dr. Bella agreed when Bess had been hoping she wouldn't.

"But what if you didn't?" Dr. Bella asked, causing Bess to shift so that she was once again looking the doctor in the eye.

"Every relationship has the potential for exponential hurt. But on the flip side, every relationship has the potential for inexplicable joy. There's no way to guarantee one or the other."

"But to pass on a potential good relationship is saying

goodbye to both possibilities," Bess finished, and the doctor nodded.

What did Bess want? Could she keep passing on Dax, knowing she could lose him? Was the possibility of joy worth the possibility of pain? Could Bess endure Dax becoming another Jon for her?

"You could keep waiting," Dr. Bella said. "But I don't know that that would change anything. If Dax is worth the risk in six months, why isn't he worth the risk now?"

Dr. Bella was right. As always. And she had kind of given Bess an answer as to what to do. That made Bess feel a little triumphant.

"So I should date him," Bess said.

"You should do what you feel is right."

"Can't you just say it?" Bess asked.

Dr. Bella grinned as she shook her head.

"Fine. But I think you pretty much told me what to do anyway," Bess crowed, and Dr. Bella laughed.

"I really am so scared," Bess admitted after she was finished joking.

Dr. Bella nodded. "I know. But do you trust Dax?"

"Completely," Bess said without hesitation.

"Then I think it's time you had a little faith in yourself, Bess."

CHAPTER FIVE

AS ALEXIS SHUT up the food truck for the evening, she thought about what awaited her at home. Nothing. No one. Her mom had been moved out for a few weeks now, and the island tongues were really waggin'. Most people were kind in their inquiries about her mom, but some, like Mrs. Camelli at the food truck that night, had just been downright rude.

The woman had asked Cassie to call Alexis to the front window, even while there had still been a line to serve. But both Alexis and Cassie knew better than to ignore Mrs. Camelli's requests. The woman, as wife of the island's mayor, felt it was her place to be in any and everyone's business. And if she wasn't placated, she made it her vendetta to knock the person down a few pegs.

When it came down to it, Alexis didn't care much about what Mrs. Camelli could do to her. But if Bess's food truck were hurt by association, Alexis would never forgive herself. So she'd gone to the window while Cassie had moved back to try to fill the orders she could.

"And why is your dear, sweet Mama living with Eleanor Bateman?" Mrs. Camelli asked Alexis immediately. Mrs.

Camelli had some nerve pretending to care about Alexis's mother's well-being when she was one of the very women who'd made her mother's life a living hell for many years on the island. But now that Mrs. Camelli got her nails done by Margie, evidently it was the mayor's wife's duty to fight her mother's battles.

Alexis pasted a big, fat smile on her face before replying, "Mrs. Bateman is Mom's best friend. They enjoy time together."

"Don't give me that kind of attitude, Alexis," was the immediate response.

Alexis had been unaware of any kind of attitude she was having, but still she opened her mouth to apologize when Mrs. Camelli continued. "I know for a fact that your mother isn't there by choice. I heard that you kicked her out. What kind of daughter does that, Alexis? And all for a man you've known for a few months? Who has been there for you your entire life? Not this man, I can tell you that."

Alexis clenched her teeth and wondered if actual steam was escaping her ears as she seethed, but there was nothing to do but stand there and be berated in front of a line of their patrons. That is, if she didn't want Mrs. Camelli doing anything worse.

So she stood tall and waited, not saying a word because she assumed Mrs. Camelli's questions were rhetorical. And when Mrs. Camelli said no more, Alexis decided it was time for the woman to move on.

"Can I take your order, Mrs. Camelli?" Alexis asked as politely as she could, considering she was about to blow a gasket.

"Is that all that you have to say for yourself?" Mrs. Camelli asked.

Alexis swore the entire line was judging her, and she wanted to convey at least a small portion of her side of the story. But she couldn't do that without yelling or crying, so she kept her mouth shut on the subject.

"I can suggest the scampi. Or the calamari special is pretty incredible," Alexis said, trying to keep her voice level.

With that, Mrs. Camelli huffed and then left the truck.

And only now, hours later, did Alexis have the time and brain power to dissect what had happened. The only way Mrs. Camelli could've known the kinds of details she'd told Alexis were if Margie had told the snooping busybody about their fight. Alexis knew her mother only put up with the woman as a client because she tipped well, they weren't actually friends, so did that mean Margie was sharing with the entire island things that had happened in the privacy of their own home? Things Alexis hadn't even revealed to her closest friends?

These thoughts accompanied Alexis her entire drive home, and at the last minute she took the turn that would take her to Rianne's house instead of her own. Alexis needed a distraction from her situation and, more importantly, her thoughts. She knew Rianne's rowdy four kids and husband would be just the ticket.

"You better get your butt back upstairs and finish your homework before you get started on video games," Alexis heard Rianne yell before Alexis had even gotten to their front door.

Alexis smiled. Yup, this would be perfect.

Alexis knocked and waited as she heard Rianne's oldest, Bridger, yell back at his mom that he had finished his homework. She continued to wait at the door while Rianne yelled to her husband that he needed to take care of his son. Then Rianne's only daughter, Allie, screamed that her twin little brothers had invaded her mascara collection and had proceeded to draw mustaches on all of her friends on the photos she had on her walls.

It was only after all of that, which happened in less than two minutes, that Rianne came to the door, ushered Alexis in, and then proceeded to yell at all of her kids to go to bed.

No one responded in any way. No whining that they weren't tired, no crying that it was too early, nothing. Alexis met Rianne's wary gaze. They both knew that wasn't normal, and not normal at Rianne's meant something was about to go very badly. And it did.

Jimmy, one of the twins, squealed as Allie's high pitched scream just about took down the rafters.

"What now?" Rianne groaned as she walked up the stairs.

"Make yourself comfortable," Rianne called down to Alexis. "And then pour us each a huge glass of something good."

Alexis chuckled to herself as she passed Bridger, who sat on the massive couch in the living room playing video games with his dad. Alexis was pretty sure this wasn't the way Rianne had been hoping Benny would take care of things, but she figured Rianne would have to deal with that after whatever had made Allie scream.

Alexis, a regular at Rianne's, dug around the fridge to find a big jug of milk. *Something good* in many households after a day like the one Rianne was having might've called for wine or something even stronger, but after Rianne's childhood with her alcoholic mother, she'd never touched the stuff, much less let anyone bring it into her home.

So Alexis poured the milk and dug into the cookie jar that had exactly two gigantic chocolate chip cookies left. Alexis might be the pro around a stove, but Rianne was the baker of their duo. She could outbake Alexis any day.

Alexis put the cookies on plates and then placed everything at their kitchen table. It was only after setting the stuff down that Alexis realized the table was still sticky from dinner. Deciding to make herself useful as she waited for Rianne, Alexis wiped the table and then moved on to all the counters. Alexis was going to guess one of the kids had cleaned the kitchen because, although the sink was empty, a pot sat on the back burner of the stove and a line of cups stood on the counter beside the sink. So Alexis continued to work.

"Seriously, Benny?" Rianne asked as she must've encountered the video game players.

"He said he finished his homework," Benny offered, but it was easy to hear that he was more interested in his game than in what his wife was saying.

"Did you check?" Rianne asked.

"No," Benny said, and a little of the fear he should've felt immediately could finally be heard in his voice.

"You do realize your son's progress report has shown missing assignments every day for the past week. And we just told Bridger two days ago that we would now be checking his homework, like he's a little child instead of a semi-responsible teen, because of that, right?" Rianne asked.

"You did," came the cautious reply. "We did," came more firmly. "Bridger, get your homework."

"But Dad, we'll die if—"

"Bridger." Benny finally sounded in command of the situation, and Rianne entered the kitchen just as Alexis put the pot on the counter to dry.

"Please tell me you weren't in here cleaning my kitchen," Rianne said as she noted the spotless place and that her friend was standing with wet hands by the sink.

"I wasn't cleaning your kitchen," Alexis lied, and Rianne laughed as she sat in front of a cookie and then waved Alexis over to do the same.

"I'll kill Allie for leaving it a mess. But I'll do it tomorrow," Rianne said as she leaned back in her seat and took a big swig of ice cold milk.

"She didn't leave it a mess. She may have forgotten a few steps, but the sink was empty." Alexis tried to stand up for the fourteen-year-old.

"Let me guess. Big pot left on the stove, cups on the counters, and every surface was a disgusting mess?"

"You are good," Alexis said as she raised her glass in a toast to her friend.

Rianne clinked her glass against Alexis's and then took a few gigantic gulps.

"I've had years and years of practice, especially with that oldest one," Rianne groaned as she set her glass down and then set her sights on her cookie.

"Bridger isn't all that bad. He's just fifteen," Alexis defended, remembering her own fifteenth year. It wasn't a pretty one.

"Oh, I know. I was talking about Benny," Rianne said as she took a big bite of her cookie, and Alexis burst into laughter.

"That's something they don't tell you," Rianne said around her mouthful of cookie. "You marry your biggest child."

Alexis's laughter died down, but she kept a smile on her face as she thought about the two very different paths her and Rianne's lives had taken. Alexis had dealt with her childhood by getting the hell out of dodge while Rianne had done the exact opposite. She was able to escape her home by marrying her high school sweetheart at age nineteen and then having Bridger at twenty. While Rianne had been establishing her home, Alexis had been living in a roach trap in Seattle, trying to make a living by waitressing and bartending. It had been rough, but Alexis had loved it.

Now, looking at Rianne with her four kids and settled life versus Alexis who was only just having her first really serious relationship, Alexis wondered if she'd missed out. If she was still missing out. However, her decisions had been made, and she always had Rianne's life to live through vicariously.

"What happened upstairs?" Alexis asked.

"Oh, besides the fact that those two eight-year-olds

happened to ruin two hundred dollars of makeup in less than ten minutes?"

"Noooo!" Alexis breathed. Rianne's house was usually quite the circus, but this was worse than normal.

Makeup was all Allie had asked for for both her birthday and Christmas last year. She had decided that after high school she wanted to get her cosmetology license, and although Rianne had cried every night for two whole weeks that her daughter didn't want to attend college, by day Rianne saved up and got Allie all that she needed in order to start on her dream path.

"It's not completely ruined but enough to make Allie sob. I don't blame her. So now the twins are in the landscaping business, earning money to pay their sister for what they ruined. Heaven help anyone willing to hire them," Rianne said as she bit the last of her cookie.

"I'll hire them. My grass could always use a good mowing."

"And this is why you should be nominated for sainthood, dear friend," Rianne said as she stood to go to the cookie jar.

"Sorry. These were the last two. You can have half of mine." Alexis offered her plate.

Rianne laughed. "Oh my sweet, naive friend. I will teach you my ways," Rianne said as she brought a chair to the refrigerator and opened the cabinet above it. She pulled down a ton of lightbulbs, a stack of books, and an entire toolbox. Finally, she emerged with a gallon-sized bag full of cookies.

"Always have your own stash for the really bad nights," Rianne taught.

Alexis looked down at her empty plate and then at her friend. "Why am I only learning about this trick now?" She had been at Rianne's on plenty of days when they could've used more cookies.

"These are for *true* emergencies," Rianne instructed, and Alexis nodded. Lesson learned.

"So I'm guessing you didn't come over for the fighting?" Rianne asked as she dug into the bag and set an extra two cookies on her own plate. "Do you want more?" she offered Alexis.

Alexis shook her head, so Rianne put the bag back in its hiding spot.

"Actually, I kind of did. Well, for that and the cookies," Alexis said, waving over the half a cookie left on her plate.

"Sounds like your day could've been even worse than mine," Rianne said as she bit into a cookie.

"Does Mrs. Camelli screaming at me at the top of her lungs in front of an entire line of customers at the food truck count as worse?" Alexis asked, sounding a lot more cheerful than she felt.

"She didn't." Rianne dropped her cookie.

"Oh she did. And then she proceeded to tell me how terrible a daughter I am. How I hurt my dear mama's poor feelings."

"This coming from the woman who actually shunned your mom for a full twelve years?" Rianne asked with a roll of her eyes. "That is just rich."

Alexis nodded. "Anyway, I'm over it."

"You aren't, but we can pretend that you are," Rianne replied.

This was why Alexis loved Rianne. She didn't let Alexis get away with any kind of baloney, but she also knew when to give Alexis a break.

"How are things with Dalton?" Rianne asked, knowing he was Alexis's favorite subject.

"Incredible," Alexis sighed.

Rianne laughed. "Did I ever feel that way about Benny?" she asked herself out loud as she bit into her last cookie.

"Of course you did. I fulfilled every one of your dreams and daydreams, baby," Benny said as he entered the kitchen to grab himself a soda.

"I should've dreamed bigger," Rianne muttered as Benny came up from behind her, pulled her into his arms and then smacked a loud kiss on her lips.

"You know you love me," Benny said, his lips still touching Rianne's.

"Unfortunately, I do," Rianne said, slipping back down onto her seat.

Alexis grinned up at her friends. Although Rianne was her best friend, she'd known Benny for almost as long. She loved the love that they had and had hoped for years to find it for herself. Now that she had it, she realized she should've coveted it even more. It was literally the best thing on earth.

Benny laughed as he left the kitchen, probably joining Bridger for more video games, considering the sounds coming from the TV.

"Back to you and Dalton," Rianne said, setting down her cookie to go back to her glass of milk.

"Nothing much to report. He makes my life worth living, and I count the seconds until I get to see him," Alexis replied, causing Rianne to scowl.

"I'm just kidding," Alexis said immediately because she knew that was Rianne's greatest fear when it came to Alexis finding love. She said Alexis lost herself too easily when it came to others. Alexis needed a man who would help her take care of herself, not just him.

"Not a funny joke," Rianne replied.

Alexis nodded silently, telling Rianne she'd heard her loud and clear. Dalton was everything Rianne wanted for Alexis and more. Alexis hoped Rianne knew that. When Rianne responded to Alexis's nod with a small smile, Alexis figured she did.

"Dalton is still talking about finding my dad." Alexis told her friend the only other real news she had about her boyfriend.

Alexis and Dalton were great, but that was nothing new. After the first couple of blissful months, there was really nothing to share about her relationship. Even though it was just as beautiful of a place to be in, it was still the same place.

"And how do you feel about starting the search?" Rianne asked.

"Honestly? I think that maybe I should. I told him I would after the fight with my mom."

Rianne nodded. She knew that.

"But I chickened out after the anger at my mom died down. I just couldn't do that to her."

Rianne nodded again. She knew that too.

"But now?" Rianne asked.

"Now, I think I might have to do this for me. At first it was for Dalton. And then I stopped because of my mom. But I really want to know who he is, Rianne. I mean, I'm scared to death. But I want to know. Even if it means being rejected."

"And talking to your mom about it is out of the question?" Rianne asked, causing Alexis to snort.

"Um, yes. Absolutely. She would kill me if she knew I was even considering this."

"But it's worth that?" Rianne asked. She knew Alexis acted like she didn't care what her mom said or did, but in the end, Margie was the only family Alexis had. Even if she was still upset with her mother, and now even more so because of the Mrs. Camelli situation, she would never do anything to completely sever ties with her mom. Margie was Alexis's whole world.

"I have to hope that my mom will have a change of heart. Because I realized, I need this."

"Then do it, Lex. I'm behind you ten thousand percent." Rianne said the silly phrase they started using in elementary school.

"I think I will."

———

"AND NOTHING ON TWITTER," Alexis said into her phone as she shut her computer, feeling frustrated. She and Dalton had been on the internet for hours scouring for any signs of Alexis's father.

Alexis had texted Dalton a few days before, telling him she'd decided that she wanted to start the search. He'd been thrilled for her but then had had to work crazy hours at his restaurant in the days since. So they hadn't been able to talk about the search until that evening, and even now, it was over the phone. Dalton had gotten off of work too late to come over to Whisling, and he didn't like Alexis traveling all the way to Seattle after her work day ended at nine pm. So that just left the phone.

When their call first started, Dalton had gotten them straight to work by checking all social media platforms for a Zachary Winters, aged fifty-three. They'd started with Facebook and ended with Twitter. But all their efforts were for naught because all they knew was that there were many many Zachary Winters in the world, and none of them seemed to be the man they were looking for.

"I'm sorry," Dalton said, his voice even lower than normal.

He tended to whisper the later it got at night, and Alexis had to admit she loved it. It made even their phone calls feel incredibly intimate.

"But we'll find him," Dalton said confidently. Dalton was still so sure of this process. That they would make it work.

"Promise?" Alexis asked.

"Promise."

Alexis smiled. She sure did love this man with every fiber of her being.

"Man, I miss you," Dalton added.

"I miss you." Alexis matched his whisper with one of her own.

"If I were with you . . ." Dalton said seductively, and Alexis wished he was there. If even just to hold her after their fruitless search.

"Are you going to be able to get away any time soon?" Alexis asked hopefully. She knew Dalton was busy not only running his restaurants but starting up a new one. His hours were insane, but somehow he still made time for her.

"We'll see. Hopefully next week," he said.

Alexis fought the urge to pout. Since it was just Thursday, that meant another weekend spent without her boyfriend.

"What if I came by the restaurant Saturday or Sunday? I'm sure Bess would be willing to switch shifts with me. I could come by between the rushes and maybe teach your chefs a thing or two," Alexis joked.

Dalton laughed. "I'm sure you could. But Sweetie, I don't even know where I'll be during that time. I'm running around between all three restaurants, and sometimes I'm just in a car somewhere in between, working over the phone with our restaurants in Cali. I don't want our moments together to be a stolen few. The next time I see you, I want to really see you," Dalton said.

Alexis nodded, even though he couldn't see her. She understood. Even if it did stink. Was it too much to ask to see her boyfriend once a week? But she knew it was. At least with Dalton during this phase of his life. And the last thing she was going to do was complain about it. Dalton had told Alexis early on that his ex's clinginess was the one thing he couldn't deal with. Alexis had told herself then and there that it was a good thing she was such an independent woman. Because she would never be clingy. And so far, she'd kept that promise. As she would continue to do forever.

"Okay. But I miss you," Alexis said.

"You *know* I miss you. And you also know I'll see you as soon as I can, but in the meantime, I'll make the wait a little more bearable. I know you're disappointed about not being able to find your dad tonight. However, I was actually kind of prepared for this to happen. So I've been asking around, and my friend knows a top-rated private investigator. What if we turn the search over to him?" Dalton asked.

Alexis's heart leapt. A private investigator. Of course. She or he could do what Alexis and Dalton couldn't. She'd thought they were stuck in their quest, but now . . . Dalton had just given her so much hope.

But she couldn't let Dalton pay for that. Weren't private investigators really expensive?

"I can't let you do that," Alexis said quietly. Maybe she could pay for one. She had some money saved up.

"Is this about the cost, Alexis? I really hope it isn't. I thought we discussed this," Dalton said, and Alexis smiled.

They had. Many times. Alexis knew her boyfriend was extremely successful, and with that kind of success came money. Lots of it. But she didn't want him to spend it on her. That didn't feel right.

"We did," Alexis replied.

"It's my money, Alexis. And I love spending my money on the people I love. Please let me do this for the woman of my dreams. The woman I love," Dalton practically begged.

Who could say no to that? Alexis grinned.

"You win. As always."

"I do love winning."

Alexis could easily imagine Dalton's smirk. He was so handsome.

"You're the best, Dalton." Alexis tried to express some of the overwhelming emotion she felt for this man.

"Remember that the next time you see me," Dalton said, his voice low and gravelly.

"I will," Alexis said.

Dalton groaned. "I'd better get off now."

Alexis laughed, loving how attracted Dalton was to her because she felt the same way about him.

"I love you," Alexis said.

"Oh, I really love you," Dalton replied, leaving Alexis with sweet dreams and no worries.

CHAPTER SIX

"NO! NOT IN THERE," Lily called to Maddie for the upteenth time.

If Lily had imagined it would be difficult to house a nurse in their home, she found it nearly impossible to do her job of watching three kids under the age of four in that same home now that the master bedroom was always occupied by Allen and the fun bedroom they'd always played in was off limits, thanks to said nurse.

When Belle wasn't working with Allen, she spent all her spare time in her bedroom, so poor Maddie, who was used to being able to play mostly anywhere in their home, was now confined to the tiny living space. Lily made a note to maybe talk to Gen about it. To ask if Lily and the girls could use Gen's home. She knew all three girls would be happier in the bigger space. But she also hated the idea of leaving Allen alone with Belle. There was something Lily just didn't trust about the woman.

Maddie turned on her heel, obeying Lily. But then she started running towards the master bedroom where Allen had gone to escape the noise of the girls.

"Not there either!" Lily called, causing Maddie to pause midstep and look up at Lily, her face full of confusion.

She wanted to agree aloud with Maddie's face, tell Maddie she didn't understand why Allen needed to escape the girls either. He had always been the type of man who loved playing with children, specifically Maddie and their own dear, sweet Amelia. But he'd asked for space that afternoon, and Lily had to give it to him. Even if she didn't understand it. She was working hard to keep peace in their home, and so far, what she was doing was working. She wasn't about to mess that up now, even if Maddie looked hurt.

"Why don't we go to the park?" Lily suggested. It was their third trip to the park that day, but they had to get out. Even if Gen would probably be by in the next half hour, she and the girls needed more space or they would go crazy.

Maddie nodded as if she, too, understood the need for them to be somewhere other than Lily's home. But she also didn't seem too pleased at the prospect of another trip to the park. It was starting to get cooler on the island, and the park just wasn't quite as fun when you were bundled in a coat and didn't have the sun shining down on your head. Thankfully, the drizzle that had made them leave the park the second time was no longer sprinkling down.

Lily got everyone in their coats and into the car about half an hour later, and then she drove down the street just in time for Gen to call and say she was on her way. Lily explained what had happened to a very patient Maddie and somewhat patient Amelia as she turned around and drove them right back home. Was this what her life had become?

Gen pulled up in the driveway just as Lily finished singing a third round of Old MacDonald. She breathed a sigh of relief that they didn't need to wait in the car any longer.

"You guys were on your way to the park again," Gen assessed. Then she added, "Didn't you already go today?"

Lily nodded.

"We went two times," Maddie supplied as Gen unlatched Cami's car seat.

"Two times?" Gen asked with a raised eyebrow, but Lily didn't get to respond because Gen moved to put Cami's seat in her own minivan.

Both women had upgraded or downgraded, depending on how you looked at it, their cars to minivans after Cami was born. Lily because of need—she couldn't get three car seats to fit in the back of her old car and she needed all three—and Gen because she felt it was the right step in her mom life. But while Gen's new car sported all the bells and whistles, Lily was lucky hers ran as well as it did for the price she got it second-hand. Gen had practically begged Lily to let her buy her a van as well, but Lily had to draw the line somewhere. Gen really would've been willing to buy her daughters' babysitter the moon if it would've helped Lily's job in any way.

"So this would've been a third?" Gen asked as she came back to Lily's van and undid Maddie's seatbelt.

Lily nodded, unsure of how to explain her home situation to Gen or even *if* she should. Gen knew that things weren't as rosy as Lily had hoped they would be with Allen coming home. She also knew about the nurse situation since Lily had come to Gen with questions of how to know if she could trust her husband. But even knowing all of that, Gen still wasn't aware of how distant Allen had become and how little he wanted to be a part of time with the girls.

Maddie slid out of her car seat and then jumped out of Lily's van to join her sister. She began to play a game of peek-a-boo with Cami, and Gen grinned as she turned her attention to Lily. Peek-a-boo was a favorite of the girls, and both women knew the sisters could play it for at least five minutes—which in baby terms was hours.

"Why the frequent trips to the park, Lily?" Gen asked as Lily went to take Amelia out of her seat. She'd become fussy because she was the last child left in the van. Lily propped Amelia on her hip as she turned to answer Gen.

"Our house is just . . ." How did Lily say these words without making Allen look bad? He was trying. She was trying. They were all trying. But so far, no matter how hard they all tried, things weren't working.

"You need more space with all three girls," Gen said.

Lily nodded, grateful that Gen had said it in such a matter-of-fact way instead of laying the blame at anyone's feet.

"Why don't you come to my place instead? We have all that space just sitting open all day. I think the girls would enjoy it, and it would give you and Allen a bit of a break," Gen suggested. It was the very thing Lily had hoped for, and yet she still felt the need to consider her options.

She really just wanted to say yes. Jump at the chance to be in a place where she didn't have to tell Maddie and Amelia every ten seconds that the space they wanted to go into was off limits. But that would leave Allen alone with Belle for hours on end, three days a week. Lily just wasn't sure. . .

"You have to trust him, Lily." Gen reiterated the words she'd said the first time Lily had come to her with the worries she had about Allen's nurse. The woman was just too friendly with him, and something rubbed Lily the wrong way. But Gen was right. And even though Lily was wary of Allen's nurse, Allen had never been anything but an upstanding husband, at least in terms of fidelity.

"I know," Lily said quietly. But she'd lost her husband in so many ways and felt like she was just getting him back. She didn't know if she could survive Allen stepping out on their marriage. But she couldn't base her life's decisions on *what ifs*, and she and the girls really needed a better situation.

"Thanks, Gen. More space is just what we need," Lily said.

Gen nodded her approval. "You are one strong woman," she said as she patted Lily on the shoulder and then headed for her car and a squawking Cami. Peek-a-boo's magic only worked for so long.

As Gen backed out of the driveway, Lily found herself replaying Gen's last words. She wanted to agree with Gen, but Lily just wasn't sure anymore. It felt like every small thing brought her to her knees these days.

Including thinking about preparing dinner. Lily stared at the small home, which served as lodging for three adults and one child. There was one too many adults in the home, if you asked Lily, but all four of them would need to be fed soon. And since they were living solely on Lily's income as a childcare provider, dinners could never be elaborate and eating out was a luxury they could rarely afford.

But she'd already made tacos and a slow cooker roast that week, none of which Belle had appreciated. So that made Lily gun-shy about her other go-to recipes. Lily didn't think Belle would be thrilled with fajitas or grilled pork chops either.

Nope, this second-guessing herself thing wouldn't work. Lily squared her shoulders as she walked toward her front door. She made good food that nourished her family. If Belle didn't like Lily's food, she could eat elsewhere. Nowhere in their contract did it say Lily would provide meals for their nurse . . . because they didn't have a contract. Lily assumed Belle had one with Allen's mom, but Lily wasn't responsible for anything Greta had promised. So if Belle didn't like grilled pork chops, too bad for her. Allen loved them, and Lily liked them. That was good enough for Lily.

As Lily entered her quiet home, she looked back toward

their bedroom where she knew Allen was probably sitting in his chair reading a book. She thought about taking Amelia back to him and asking him to watch her while she got dinner ready, but Lily wasn't sure how Allen would react to the request. Before the accident, Allen wouldn't have even waited for Lily to ask for help. He would've been out in their living space, playing with Amelia long before Lily needed to even start thinking about getting dinner on. But times had changed. Lily and Allen had changed. And Lily would have to get used to their new normal.

"Do you want an apple?" Lily offered Amelia, hoping the fruit would distract her daughter long enough for Lily to get a start on dinner.

Lily put Amelia in her high chair and then gave her daughter the whole fruit. She hoped that would entertain Amelia for a bit, and then Lily could cut it up for Amelia to eat. It was all about stretching any kind of entertainment these days.

Sure enough, Amelia seemed intrigued by the orb of fruit, and Lily got to work. She began with the apple slaw she typically served on the side of her pork chops and then got to work on the potatoes because they took longer to cook than the pork. Once the potatoes were simmering away, Lily threw the pork chops on the grill pan, and only then did Amelia complain that she was bored. Lily quickly cut up the apple and then gave it back to her daughter who grinned when she saw the fruit in the form she recognized. Amelia immediately devoured her snack as Lily flipped the pork chops, drained the potatoes and then began to set the table.

Somehow everything came together just as Amelia was finishing her pieces of apple, and Lily called the other two adults in her home to the table.

"Grilled chicken?" Belle asked excitedly as she came to the table.

Lily looked down at the plate that was easily recognizable as pork and then back at the nurse.

"Pork," Lily said, causing Belle's smile to slip off her face.

Lily made a note to make more chicken, even though she and Allen weren't huge fans of the protein.

Belle waited until Allen wheeled himself to the table before taking her seat. Well, at least their nurse was good at her job. She was always aware of Allen, and Lily told herself that was a good thing. That was what a nurse should be doing. Lily just wished their nurse was about thirty years older and didn't look at Allen like he was that piece of chicken she craved.

"Looks good," Allen said.

Lily grinned. Maybe she wouldn't be making chicken. Allen's compliments didn't flow as freely as they once had, so Lily savored every one of them.

"Thanks," Lily said as she noticed that Allen hadn't once acknowledged their daughter. Pre-accident Allen would've pulled her out of her seat to snuggle her or at least made some kind of comment about their cute girl that would make Lily laugh, but nothing.

Lily shook those thoughts from her head. It wasn't fair to compare Allen to anyone, especially the man he used to be.

Lily had been so deep in her thoughts that she hadn't noticed the others had already begun filling their plates with food. Lily noticed the huge portion of mashed potatoes and slaw Belle put on her plate, but she didn't even go near the pork. Oh well, at least their nurse was making do.

Lily took the smallest of the plates and began to cut up some pork for Amelia. She then placed a bit of slaw and a small mound of potatoes on the plate before depositing the food on Amelia's tray. Lily knew her daughter wouldn't be too hungry, thanks to the apple she just ate, but Lily saw no way around that. She'd had to amuse Amelia somehow. If her dinner was spoiled, it couldn't be helped.

Allen had also served his plate. His portions were smaller than Lily would've liked, but she'd learned better than to comment on Allen's eating. He'd given her a death glare the last time she'd mentioned she was worried he wasn't eating enough. He'd then told her that thanks to his now-sedentary lifestyle, he didn't need much food. That had effectively shut Lily up.

Although Lily didn't really believe that Allen led a sedentary lifestyle. She knew he worked his butt off at physical therapy three days a week, and he went on walks where he wheeled himself the other four days of the week. Lily appreciated the toned arms that were the result of said walks and workouts. Allen's shoulders were broadening, and if Lily was honest, she found her husband more attractive than she ever had. But she wasn't sure that was something she could say anymore. Honestly, she wasn't sure she was allowed to say anything anymore.

Lily served herself a modest portion as well—she didn't want to make Allen feel like he was the only one eating a small amount—and then dug into her meal. The pork was a bit overdone, but Lily often did that because she was scared about serving them underdone. She'd never perfected the art of grilled pork chops, but she continued to make them because they were a favorite of Allen's and pork was often cheap.

"A little overdone, right?" Lily said as Allen tried to cut through a piece.

"Not bad," Allen said, shooting Lily a smile.

Lily returned the smile and then sighed contentedly. Things were good. It was a good evening. Sure there was an extra person at their table, and sure things weren't as simple as they had been before, but that didn't keep them from having good times.

"Thanks for dinner," Belle said as she stood and left the table, leaving her dishes and the rest of them behind.

And so it would go again. Lily worked all day, made the meals, and then cleaned up after them as well. But Lily wouldn't complain. Because Allen was home. That was all she'd ever wanted, and now she had him. She could endure a bit of extra work. Anything was better than losing her husband for good.

Allen finished his meal, and Lily waited for him to do the same thing Belle had done and leave the table.

"It was delicious, Lily," Allen complimented, and Lily beamed. The meal hadn't been that good, but Lily would take it.

"I'm glad you liked it. Pork chops always remind me of the days right after we got married," she said as she stood to clean Amelia up. The girl was covered in mashed potatoes.

"And you burned them every time?" Allen asked, causing Lily to laugh.

"You said you liked them," Lily accused through her laughter.

"With enough mustard, anything is edible," Allen said, and Lily laughed harder. "And I would've eaten anything you prepared, Lily."

Lily's laughter stuttered to a stop. That was the sweetest thing Allen had said to her in a long time. Lily was beginning to see glimpses of the man he used to be. Not that he had to go back to that man in order for Lily to be happy, but Lily had to admit she missed that Allen.

Lily took Amelia out of her seat, and the girl ran right to her toys as soon as she was set on the ground. Lily turned, fully expecting to see Allen wheeling himself toward the bedroom. But he was still there. Watching Lily.

"How about you rinse and I'll load?" Allen offered as he looked at the kitchen full of dishes.

Lily thought about telling Allen there was no need, that just the offer was enough, but she realized that might hurt his feelings. He was offering the help that Lily wanted. Why not take it?

"That sounds great," Lily said as she brought the dishes from the table to the kitchen sink and then began to rinse them.

"How was PT today?" Lily asked about the only part of the day Allen had spent outside of their home.

"Rough. I'll be hurting tomorrow, but I think I'm improving," Allen said as he took a plate from Lily and placed it in the dishwasher.

"That's incredible," Lily said, but she didn't ask anything else. One of the first things Allen had accused her of was only wanting him if he was going to get better one day. Lily had understood Allen was paralyzed but had heard so many stories of people regaining their mobility and had wanted to share that hope with her husband. But it had been taken the wrong way, and now Lily did her best to hide that hope. Besides, she didn't care if her husband never walked again, at least for her sake. All she cared about was having her husband.

"Yeah, I guess," Allen said as he loaded a cup. "How were the girls?" he added.

"Rowdy, crazy, and perfect," Lily said about her charges. She truly loved all three of them so much.

"Sounds about right. It got quiet out here a few times during the day. Did you all go somewhere?" Allen asked.

Lily looked from Allen to the pot she was cleaning. "Yeah. The park. The house can sometimes feel a bit small."

"Oh yeah?" Allen asked as if he hadn't noticed how little their living space was.

"Yeah. Especially now with the bedrooms off limits." Lily tried to broach the subject in a tactful way, but she wondered if Allen would take offense. She really hoped he wouldn't.

"Off limits?" Allen asked as he took the pot from Lily and loaded it on the bottom rack.

"Yeah. I don't want to bother Belle or . . ." Lily paused. Should she say this? Was she being stupid? But Allen had asked, and Lily wanted to be honest. "You."

"Belle I get, but me? I love the girls," Allen said, and Lily wondered if she'd misread him. And if she'd misread him on this, where else had she made the same mistake?

"I just assumed that when you went into the room, it was your way of saying you needed space. Didn't you say you needed time alone this afternoon?" Lily asked quietly as she turned off the water. It was amazing how fast dishes went when two people were doing the job together.

"Yeah, right after PT I needed a break. But not the whole afternoon. I guess I could see why you would think that though. And if I'm being completely honest, I do sometimes stay in the room to escape the crazy out here. But I didn't mean to make things hard on you or on the girls," Allen said.

Lily smiled softly at her husband who was trying oh so hard. "It wasn't too bad. And actually, Gen offered a solution. She said we could come over there. That way you'd have more space around the house during the day and we'd have more space to play," Lily said.

Although Allen was smiling, Lily saw the way it didn't quite reach his eyes. She'd upset him. But how?

"That sounds like the perfect solution," Allen said before spinning around and wheeling back toward the master bedroom. He maneuvered expertly around Amelia and was almost out of reach. Lily had to say something. They'd come so far tonight. She didn't want to take any steps backwards.

"And on the days you feel like it, I'd love for you to join us at Gen's," Lily said, causing Allen to pause.

Had that been the right thing? Lily hadn't even analyzed the words the way she always did these days before speaking. But Allen had been about to leave, and she didn't want to lose her one shot. So she'd taken it. But had she missed?

"The girls would love it too," Lily added when Allen still didn't speak.

Allen turned back to Lily, even though his chair still faced the bedrooms.

"Do you think so?" Allen asked. "I just wondered . . ." Allen's voice trailed off as he turned forward again.

Lily took a step forward but paused. She didn't feel that now was the right time to press.

"Are the girls afraid of this?" Allen asked as he thumped his hands against the wheels of his chair.

"Your wheelchair?" Lily clarified because that didn't make sense to her at all. The girls had tried to use Allen as a jungle gym a number of times. Where would he get the idea that they were afraid?

"Yeah. Amelia's first response to my being home again wasn't great, and then Maddie asked me to stand up the other day," Allen said quietly.

Lily had no idea he'd been holding all of that inside.

"I'm sure they both miss the times where you used to play games with them, but I think once they realize how cool this new Dad is, they won't miss the standing at all," Lily said confidently. The girls would adapt.

"What about you, Lily?" Allen asked, his back still to her.

"What about me?"

"Do you miss me being able to stand?"

Lily felt tears well up in her eyes as her husband allowed a vulnerability to surface that Lily hadn't seen in a long time. She needed to tread with caution but also be honest. It was only fair.

"Probably less than you miss it," Lily said lightly. Then she added with more seriousness, "Allen, I have all of you that I need."

Allen turned his seat so that he was facing Lily.

"Are you sure?" he asked as he met Lily's eyes, his own searching hers intently.

"I am completely positive. I love you, Allen Anderson. Not despite this accident and the changes it has caused. I just love you. There are no *ifs*, *ands*, or *buts*."

Allen nodded. "I just love you too, Lily Anderson."

He then turned and wheeled back into his room.

Lily fought the urge to jump up and cheer in triumph; she didn't think Allen would appreciate it. And although she knew this one conversation wouldn't make everything better—tomorrow wouldn't be all cupcakes and roses because of it—it was a step in the right direction. And for that, Lily would quietly cheer.

—————————

CHAPTER SEVEN

HOW DID BESS GET HERE? She was on a plane at least thirty thousand feet up in the air on the way to Los Angeles. What the heck was she doing?

Bess breathed in a calming breath. This was a physical manifestation of her having faith in what she and Dax could have. This was Bess having faith in herself. She was going to go after who she wanted. And she wanted Dax. She wanted to give them a chance. A real chance. Something she couldn't say on the phone.

So she was on an airplane that was descending into LAX.

Ahhh!

But Bess pressed forward, walking herself off the plane, then walking through the airport and right to the car she'd ordered to take her to Dax.

She'd checked Find My Friends and saw that Dax was at a restaurant in Brentwood. Her first plan had been to call him and ask him where he wanted to meet up, but now that Bess was doing daring things like flying across two states to tell Dax she wanted to make things work between them, she was going all out on the daring front and had decided to surprise him.

Was it a good idea? She wasn't sure. But she was doing it.

The rideshare service dropped her off in front of the vine-covered restaurant that screamed, "I'm in LA!" and Bess made her way to the hostess before she could change her mind.

She needed to talk to Dax. Dax was here. It wasn't a big deal. Right?

Just as Bess was about to approach the hostess, another woman cut in front of her. So Bess waited in line. She wasn't the type to raise a stink—even when someone cut in line—on a normal day, and today wasn't normal. Bess's nerves were everywhere, and her mind was racing about so many things that a woman not waiting her turn didn't even reach Bess's top ten things to think about in that moment. She'd let the woman have her moment with the hostess, and then Bess would step up and ask about Dax.

As Bess waited, she scanned the restaurant and her eyes landed on the back of the head of the handsome man who'd somehow completely taken her heart. Some of the maneuvering had been slick—Bess hadn't even realized her heart was being stolen—but some of the moments had been so sweet and sincere, they were etched not only in Bess's heart but in her mind as well. And in the end, it didn't matter how Dax had stolen her heart. Just that he had.

His auburn hair glistened in the sunlight that the restaurant was full of. His broad shoulders filled out his blue suit in a way that made Bess want to sigh, and although she only saw the back of him, she could imagine the charming smile he was bestowing on his fellow diners. Yeah, they wouldn't stand a chance.

Dax turned his head to the woman on his left, and Bess noticed that although she was probably only a few years Bess's junior, her toned and tanned shoulders that peeked out from the white tank top she wore were nothing like the shoulders Bess's blue blouse covered. The woman also wore a pair of white, wide leg pants and had a pair of enormous, designer sunglasses in her glossy, blonde hair. Well, if that didn't tell Bess they were no longer on Whisling. Bess knew of no one in real life that dressed like this woman. Granted, the often puddle-filled streets of Whisling wouldn't be kind to an all-white outfit, but it wasn't just the weather that wouldn't have gotten along with such a look. Whisling was more laid back and LA was just . . . well, LA.

Bess noticed that not only did Dax have the attention of the gorgeous woman beside him, but every person at the table seemed to defer to him. The longer Bess watched, the more she saw that Dax was the center of everything happening at that table. They all needed him.

And suddenly it hit Bess hard. The one factor she'd been ignoring ever since she'd decided to follow through on this half-cocked, crazy plan. Dax's life was here. And Bess's was on Whisling. Not only did she have her business, but her kids were near there and her friends were there. Bess's entire life revolved around the island, whereas it looked as if LA revolved around Dax. How in the heck could they make this work?

Bess continued to stare at the table as the conversation ensued. People would speak, and then they would turn to Dax, apparently waiting for his opinion.

What was she doing? She had been so intent on having faith in them, on making things work, that she'd pushed all the doubts and reasons they couldn't be together aside. Including this very valid reason. Dax's life was in LA. She couldn't ask him to leave that behind. His entire business, his friends, the life he'd spent the last few decades creating, it was all here or in Nashville. Definitely not on Whisling.

Bess took a step back. She'd never felt so foolish in her life. She wasn't one for grand gestures, and now she knew why. She stunk at them. She'd pushed herself so far out of her comfort zone that she'd stopped thinking. And look where that had gotten her. In the middle of LA, waiting behind a woman who seemed really upset about something, and staring at the man she loved but was realizing she would probably never have. She was an idiot. Big time.

Suddenly, the woman who had cut in front of Bess to speak to the hostess screeched, making a sound that should've come from a bird instead of a human woman. Bess took a couple more steps away.

But all thoughts of the woman making crazy noises fled when Bess realized that noise had been loud. Loud enough to call the attention of the restaurants patrons. Loud enough to . . .

"Bess?"

Crap.

Bess thought about turning and running out the door. And then when Dax called her later that day wondering if she'd been in LA, she'd tell him he was nuts. Why would she be in LA? Then they'd laugh together about her doppelganger who stood in lines behind crazy, bird-calling women at upscale LA restaurants. But no such luck. Bess had remained frozen in thought for too long, and Dax's long legs had made quick work of the space between them.

"Bess?" he said again before gathering her into his arms. "You're here," he breathed into her hair as if Bess spying on him in the middle of his town wasn't completely insane and in need of an in-depth explanation.

Now that she was trying to come up with an explanation to give Dax, the craziness of her plan *really* came into focus. Had she truly thought she could just join Dax and his colleagues at their lunch? That was her plan? Well, technically she didn't have one. At least not a complete one. Obviously.

So she did the only thing she could do. She hugged Dax back.

"Surprise," she said into his woodsy smelling suit. Man, the guy smelled as incredible as he looked. And that was quite the feat.

"Yeah. It is." Dax held Bess even tighter. "Maybe the best of my life."

And this was why she had put her life on hold and travelled to LA to tell Dax she had to be with him. Not only was she in love with him, he said things that made her feel like the center of his entire world. How could she not be foolishly in love with him?

"Let me just tell them I've got better plans," Dax said, nodding in the direction of his colleagues and then grudgingly letting Bess out of his arms.

Dax began to move toward his table when he paused mid-step. "Wait, come with me. Let me introduce you," Dax said as he linked hands with Bess and pulled her in close again.

Bess glanced over to the table to see the way white tank top woman was glaring at her. The rest of Dax's colleagues didn't seem any more impressed, if their frowns could be trusted. Um, yeah, introductions didn't seem like the best idea.

"It's okay. I can meet them some other time," Bess said as she tugged her hand away.

"Really? I'm sure they'd love to meet you," Dax said.

"Yeah, but they're eating, and I don't want to interrupt them," Bess said as she bit her lip.

"I get it. I won't make you meet them. But I will be announcing that I'm leaving them for the most incredible woman in the world," Dax said with a grin.

"Dax," Bess admonished, feeling her cheeks getting red.

"What? You know I'm a stickler for the truth." Dax turned and jogged toward his colleagues, said something while glancing back toward where Bess stood, and then left them looking a bit shocked. White tank top woman's mouth even gaped open.

"Was that meeting important?" Bess asked as Dax joined her, took her hand, and then led her out of the restaurant. Bess's question was probably something she should've asked earlier. Like hours before when she was still back on Whisling.

"Nothing my senior agents can't handle. I've hired the best so that I can do things like this," Dax said as he handed the valet a ticket.

"Like abandon them because a crazy woman just shows up at your lunch?" Bess asked with a shake of her head. What had she been thinking?

"Like leave things to them so that I can concentrate on the things and people I really care about. You."

Bess's heart flip flopped. And Dax was only proving, yet again, that he had been worth this leap of faith and any other one Bess could possibly make.

The valet pulled up in a sleek, black car that matched Dax's LA persona. The young man waited at the driver's door for Dax to take his seat, but Dax walked to the passenger's side instead, opening the door for Bess. He waited for her to take her seat before closing her door and then getting in the door the valet held open for him.

Dax was charming, chivalrous, and the list went on. Why had Bess waited so long to start dating him? She looked at the palm tree lined roads ahead of them. Right. LA. And there had been many other reasons before, as well. But now that Bess was having faith, the distance was all that remained. Could they overcome this last hurdle? Bess didn't see how.

"Where are we going?" Bess asked as Dax pulled out of the restaurant's lot and into LA's afternoon traffic.

"Somewhere where you can tell me just why you're here," Dax said as he changed lanes abruptly.

"I'm here to see you," Bess said as she swallowed back her sudden fear. She had flown all this way, interrupted Dax's lunch, and it still made her anxious to think about telling Dax that she wanted to date him. What if he'd moved on? What if white tank top woman was more than a work colleague? Bess doubted it, considering every single one of Dax's actions. But she was still scared. Besides, hadn't she just realized they couldn't be together because of the distance? Would telling Dax that she wished things could be different just serve to make things harder on both of them?

"I know. But I also know you're here for more than that, Bess. I'll let you tell me when you're ready, though," Dax said as he merged onto the freeway.

Of course he knew why she was here. Bess was in so much trouble.

The noises of the surrounding cars were all that accompanied them as they drove along the I-10 and then moved onto the more peaceful Highway One.

"This is gorgeous," Bess said as they drove right along the ocean. "Is this the Pacific Coast Highway?"

Dax nodded.

"This reminds me of Whisling," Bess said as she took in the view right beside their car. "Well, if Whisling had about ten times the activity."

Dax chuckled. "This is often where I come when I'm missing home. When I'm missing you. This is my piece of home right here in California."

Dax missed her? Well, he had told her that dozens of times over texts and calls. But to hear it here in person, to know that his life in California wasn't enough to help him forget all about her was . . . well, kind of sad. She didn't want him to miss her. But then again, she did. Man, she was a confusing mess. Better not to dwell on that and move along with their conversation.

"Did you think this beautiful piece of road would help me

drop my inhibitions and tell you why I'm really here?" Bess joked.

Dax nodded. "Exactly."

Bess grinned. She guessed Dax's assumption that the scenic highway would get her to talk was partially right. Bess had admitted she was here for more of a reason than just to see him, and she guessed since she had been halfway honest, she might as well tell Dax the whole truth.

"I wanted to start dating you," Bess said slowly, and she watched as Dax's hands gripped the steering wheel tighter. That was the only indication he gave that he'd even heard what she'd said.

"I'm not sure I like the past tense in that sentence," Dax said as he pulled into a parking lot on the side of the road that housed some kind of restaurant. The outside of the building was painted in bright blues and oranges that Bess was sure had been used to distract people from the view of the ocean. With such a gorgeous sight as competition, the food establishment had to do something to get eyes on it. That was a big part of the reason why Bess had painted her own food truck red.

"This is the home of the best fish tacos on this side of the border," Dax said as he put his car into park. Then he pulled off his suit coat and began rolling up the long sleeves of his button up shirt. Bess watched as Dax revealed his toned forearms. Who knew such a mundane part of the body could be sexy? But Dax's forearms were.

"Care to try one?" Dax offered, and Bess nodded enthusiastically in response. If there was one thing Bess was always up for, it was trying a new food establishment.

Dax got out of the car and came around to open Bess's door as she remembered where they had just been.

"But aren't you full? You were just at lunch," Bess said as Dax opened her car door for her.

"It was a working lunch in LA. Basically code for lots of working and not much eating. Or in that particular meeting's case, no eating. Julia Price is notorious for choosing that exact restaurant because they serve her favorite soybean smoothie."

Bess blanched at the thought of soybeans in such a form.

"Yes, it's as gross as it sounds. But Julia has learned that she can't typically enjoy what she puts in her mouth. I guess this next role she's preparing for demands a certain look. Hollywood code for *she's got to lose a few pounds*. Which in any other business would be against the law, but Hollywood disguises their requests behind the need for characters to look a certain way. In the end, does it really matter if an assassin wears a size two or a size zero?" Dax said out loud some of the very same things Bess had been thinking as they found a small, circular table at the seaside restaurant.

The place had the laid back feel a California seaside restaurant should. There was no hostess, so everyone seated themselves. The rickety wooden tables each had a menu placed between the napkin holder and bottles of sauces. The only decor the restaurant had were photos of different beachfronts all around the world. This was Bess's kind of place.

As a server came to their table and Dax ordered for them, Bess thought more about what he had said. Julia Price had chosen the restaurant for his meeting. Wait, did that mean . . . white tank top woman was *the* Julia Price?

Bess felt her cheeks redden. How had she not recognized one of the most recognizable faces on the entire planet? Of course this would happen to her. Granted, Julia wasn't wearing the amount of makeup Bess typically saw her wearing since she'd only seen the woman on the big screen and magazine covers, but still. Oh my goodness. And she'd pulled Dax out of a meeting with his most important client? She was a full-fledged idiot.

"Please tell me you weren't meeting with Julia Price," Bess whispered after Dax finished their order and the server walked away.

"Okay. But then I'd be lying," Dax whispered back.

Bess's entire face flamed. What had she done? Dax worked with big names, but Julia's was the biggest.

"It's okay, Bess. I told you my senior agents can more than handle those kinds of meetings. It's what I've trained them to do," Dax said with a grin that was way too easygoing considering what Bess had just done.

"Yeah, but . . . but Julia Price," Bess stuttered, and she could tell Dax was biting back laughter.

"It isn't funny," Bess said as their server came back with their drinks.

Bess had been so preoccupied with her thoughts about Julia Price that she hadn't noticed what Dax had ordered them. Bess sniffed her drink and liked the fruity smell, so she took a huge gulp.

"Oh my gosh. This is fantastic," Bess said as soon as her mouth was free of liquid.

"The place is famous for them," Dax said, pointing to his own drink that looked just like Bess's. "Frozen fruit punch. Much better than a soybean smoothie," he said with a nod, and Bess giggled. Okay, maybe the situation was a little funny.

"Are you sure I didn't ruin things for you, Dax?" Bess asked.

"Bess, I'd like to make one thing crystal clear. You can't ever ruin *anything* in my life. Because you're my priority. As long as things are good between you and me, my life is good."

Bess's mouth dropped open with Dax's declaration. He often said that she meant a lot to him, but this was another level. Bess had to admit she liked how much she meant to Dax. Especially right at that moment when she was trying to dispel her fears surrounding getting into a relationship with the man. If he felt that way about her and she felt the same about him, how could they not work?

"So I assure you, all is well with my work. Now let's get back to the important conversation. Why did you say *wanted* in the past tense, Bess?" Dax asked as he put his elbows on the table and leaned forward toward his dining partner.

"I walked into that restaurant, and I was hit with a realization."

"And what was that?"

Bess leaned forward to match Dax's sitting position. "Your life is here and in Nashville."

"And your life is in Whisling," Dax finished.

Bess nodded.

"That's something that has occurred to me as well," Dax said with a smile, as if Bess hadn't found a fatal flaw in their plan to date one another. How could they make this work? Sure, if either of them had plans to one day move to where the other lived, maybe they could make long distance work for a short amount of time. But even if Bess could give up all that she'd made for herself on Whisling, she couldn't bring herself to leave her children, despite the fact that they were really adults already. And Dax's entire career counted on him being in either Nashville or LA. Where was the fix to this problem, and why was Dax smiling?

"You are so cute when you're annoyed," Dax said as he ran a finger along where Bess's forehead was puckered in consternation.

"And you're annoying when you say I'm cute," Bess responded, causing Dax to let out a rumble of laughter. "I just don't understand how you can be so nonchalant about this. I really want to date you, Dax."

"And I think I've proved I really want to date you too, Bess."

Bess nodded. He had. Not only with his words but with many of his deeds.

"But wanting something doesn't make it happen," Bess stated.

"It does if you want it enough," Dax said, and he leaned back.

His movement caused Bess to look around and see their server coming toward them with their order.

Was it all so easy? If Bess wanted it enough, could they make it work? Bess didn't think it was that simple. But then again, Dax had proved her wrong in the past.

"You have to try this," Dax said as he held out a taco.

Bess leaned forward to take a bite of his offering and immediately moaned as the flavors of savory fish exploded with the sweet and tangy slaw.

"Delicious," Bess said as soon as her mouth was free of food.

Dax set down the taco and took both of Bess's hands into his own.

"Bess, we can and will make this work," Dax said confidently.

Bess wanted to believe him, but the idea that they were leaving this one, huge variable unsolved scared her.

"Look at me, Bess."

Bess met Dax's beautiful eyes that nearly matched the color of the sea just next to them.

"I love you, Bess. I have never been so committed to anyone or anything in my life. I don't have every detail ironed out today, but I promise I will do everything in my power to make this work. Just give us a chance. Please, Bess?" Dax asked as his grip tightened around her hands, telling her he would never let her go.

"Okay," Bess squeaked. And then she yanked a hand away from Dax to cover her mouth. Had she really just said that?

"Okay?" Dax asked, and Bess nodded, even with her hand still over her mouth.

But she couldn't take it back. She wouldn't take it back. She trusted Dax. And if he was promising he would help her to make things work, she was in this.

Using his one hand that still held Bess's, Dax tugged her out of her seat as he stood and pulled her into his arms.

"Really?" Dax asked.

Bess smiled as she nodded.

"So . . ." Dax's voice went low and gruff, just the way Bess liked it. "You're my girlfriend."

Bess giggled. It felt like such a juvenile term for what she felt for Dax, what Dax was to her, but she guessed it was the only one they had.

"Yup."

With that *yup*, Dax dropped his lips to Bess's, pulling her tight against him. Bess felt him share a part of himself with her through that kiss, deepening it so it was very much not appropriate considering they were standing in the middle of a seafood restaurant.

Bess's stomach warmed as her heart pounded against her rib cage, and she tugged Dax even closer to her.

"Ahem," a male voice said right next to them, and Bess pushed away from Dax. She was sure her entire body had to be red from the embarrassment she felt at being caught during that kind of kiss.

Needless to say, Bess and Dax were offered their tacos to go. But Dax didn't seem to mind in the least, if the kisses they continued to share the rest of that afternoon were any indication.

By the time Dax dropped Bess off at the airport, she was feeling lighter than air with promises that he would see her soon and they'd definitely be continuing their kisses.

CHAPTER EIGHT

———————

OLIVIA FELT her hair getting bigger by the second as she sat next to the indoor pool where her daughters were in the middle of swimming lessons. The humidity and heat of the room were quite impressive, and Olivia might've enjoyed it compared to the quickly cooling evening outside if it weren't for the fact that her hair was well on its way to Dolly status.

"Mom, mom! Watch this!" Pearl called out just before she dove into the pool.

Olivia clapped loudly so that Pearl would be able to hear her when she came up from under the water moments later.

Pearl waved happily at her mom before continuing to swim across the pool.

With both of her girls busy enjoying their lessons, Olivia's thoughts wandered to the place it always went to when she wasn't busy with other things: Noah.

Olivia reread the text Noah had sent the night before, just as she was falling asleep. The one she was at a loss about how to answer.

How much longer are you going to need?

That was a good question. Even as she'd debated the merits

of dating Noah against what her daughters wanted, Olivia still wasn't any closer to a decision. All she knew was that it was now much easier to live her life. Not having to divide her time between Noah and her girls. Not needing to worry that she wasn't enough for either entity.

Olivia hadn't answered Noah because she wasn't sure how to. She really liked Noah. But her girls didn't. They'd expressed that plainly when Olivia had told them she was taking a break from dating the man. But to be fair, they'd also told Olivia that they didn't want her to date anyone. Well, anyone other than their precious Dean. Which wasn't a good wish for any of them considering the way Dean was acting like a dating machine. Okay, maybe that was a bit of a stretch. But Olivia was noticing that he came home late almost every evening, and she'd heard too many rumors concerning the trail of broken hearts being left behind her handsome neighbor. Not that Olivia was keeping tabs on the man.

Back to her girls and Noah. If her girls didn't want her to date, was it really okay for her to do so? But then again, should she give in to their every whim? But was this their every whim? If she was being completely honest with herself, there really wasn't much her girls had asked of her since her divorce. And if they were so uncomfortable with Olivia dating, wasn't her answer clear? Didn't she need to honor what they'd asked of her? Even if it meant being single for many more years. Maybe forever? On the other hand, was it fair for her girls to ask that of her?

Olivia realized that with them being only nine and eleven, it wasn't up to them to decide. It was Olivia's decision as their mother. So now that the choice was back in her hands, did she make it for selfish reasons because she liked Noah and didn't want to be alone forever or for more noble reasons like showing her girls that sometimes we sacrifice for those we love? Did

Olivia ask her girls to make that sacrifice or should she do it herself? Therein lay the circles she'd traveled for the past few weeks and why she had ignored Noah's text.

Right after that last date, Olivia and Noah hadn't contacted the other for a couple of days. Then Noah had called, apologizing for overreacting. Olivia had told him she didn't feel it was an overreaction. She could see why he'd behaved the way he had, and then they'd talked into the night about anything and everything. Even if her girls weren't fans of Noah, Noah was a big fan of her girls and wanted to know all about them. And that was part of the issue as well. Olivia knew if her girls would just let Noah in, he'd be fantastic for them.

The calls had become more frequent, for a week or so, when Olivia had had to pull the plug on them. She needed space to think about Noah, and she was getting none of that space talking to him every night. Because as much as she loved their conversations and looked forward to speaking to the man she'd begun to truly care about, this time had been set aside for her to figure out her future. And she couldn't do that if she was keeping every minute full of Noah.

So they'd reduced their contact to texting, and Olivia readily admitted that she missed the man. A lot.

But her girls, on the other hand, were thriving. They were both excelling in school and their swimming lessons, and Pearl had the record for the most goals made on her soccer team, which was coached by Dean.

They came home after school every day full of stories and were back to the bubbly selves they'd been in the months before Olivia had dated Noah. For some reason, when Noah had been a part of Olivia's life, it had been like a small, dark cloud over their little family's head. Maybe because Olivia had to divide her time? Or maybe it was because her being with Noah killed her girls' dreams of Dean one day becoming their step-father?

However, the first would be inevitable if Olivia ever dated again, and the second was a necessary truth her daughters needed to learn.

So again, Olivia was stuck. She wanted her vivacious girls to thrive in life with no dark cloud. But was the dark cloud of their own making? Something that they could dispel, that they needed to learn to dispel. Or was this something Olivia should shelter them from?

Where was the single mom manual when you needed one?

"Olivia!"

Olivia cringed at the sound of her name being called by that voice. This was the one bad thing about her daughters' swimming lessons. Marsha Tuttle's son and daughter had lessons at the same time.

Marsha had been a friend once upon a time. Her kids had gone to the same school as Olivia's girls when they'd lived with Bart, and she and Marsha had been on many committees together. But as Olivia's old life had dissolved, so had her ties to many of the people in her old circles. Not that they were bad people, but they weren't necessarily true friends either. Marsha had been overheard to say that Olivia just needed to suck it up and figure out how to make things work with Bart. All women endured *things* during their marriage. It was up to them to shut up and deal with it. Olivia couldn't even truly blame Marsha for this distorted view of reality considering it had once been Olivia's very same view, but she also didn't want to surround herself with people who thought that way. Olivia's old way of being and those kinds of thoughts had been toxic for her. People like Marsha were part of that problem. But Marsha was a decent, if not misguided, woman, and she still thought of Olivia as a friend. So Olivia tried to be cordial . . . because what was her alternative?

"Hello, Marsha," Olivia responded, cringing at how formal

her voice had become just speaking to Marsha. This was country club Olivia, and Olivia wasn't that woman anymore. So to make up for it, Olivia added informally, "How's it going?"

Marsha tilted her head as if she wasn't quite sure how to answer Olivia's question. Then she said, "I'm so glad that they keep these classes small. I wasn't sure about allowing Peter and Brittany to take lessons anywhere other than the club pool." Marsha mentioned the country club Olivia used to frequent pre-divorce.

"I can imagine," Olivia muttered. What else could she say?

"But I've heard amazing things about Elliot's methods, and since the club couldn't steal him away . . . the sacrifices we make for our children, right?" Marsha said with a laugh that Olivia joined in because that seemed easier than responding to the absurd notion that taking her kids to lessons at a place other than a country club was a motherly sacrifice.

Olivia turned toward the pool and noticed the kids were all taking turns racing across it. Olivia hoped that would be exciting enough to keep Marsha's attention so she would no longer have to hold a conversation with the woman.

"We haven't seen Noah around the island recently," Marsha said, and Olivia didn't have to ask who *we* were. Marsha and many from Olivia's old circle were part of a group of women who made it their top priority to know the goings-on of the entire island. They disguised themselves as a book club, but everyone on the island knew that a book had never been discussed at one of those meetings.

Olivia would put money on the fact that Marsha's "book club" knew about Bart's cheating long before it was revealed at Olivia's class reunion. Olivia was also pretty sure they greased a few palms to know the comings and goings of the people they deemed important on the island, and for some reason they'd deemed Noah important. Probably because he was a good-looking, high-powered attorney from Seattle. Just the kind of man the country club would try to recruit.

"Oh really?" Olivia said as if she didn't know any more about the Noah situation than Marsha and her croonies.

"You are a hoot, Olivia," Marsha said as she pretended to smack Olivia's arm, but her hand hit nothing but air.

Olivia gave a wide smile that felt fake, but she doubted Marsha would know the difference.

"Why hasn't Noah been around?" Marsha asked, and Olivia now understood why Marsha had come and joined her today.

Marsha had sat on the sidelines next to Olivia and watched her children for their first few lessons but hadn't been around since then. Olivia had noticed their nanny was the one to come to lessons after that. But Marsha's posse must have sent her in to do some digging. And now Olivia was caught. Because Marsha wouldn't leave without some good intel. Olivia swore if these women put their minds to it, they could solve more wrongdoings than every crime-fighting unit in the state.

"Noah's been busy. His job is pretty demanding." Olivia spoke in terms Marsha would understand. A demanding job was the only kind of job men in Marsha's world would ever want to have.

"I understand. But his job has always been demanding. Somehow he still made time to come see you. Or for you to go see him. Did you know you've only been off the island once in the last three weeks?"

Olivia would've been shocked that Marsha knew that about her if she hadn't already had her run-ins with this particular group in the past. They were scary. And honestly, Olivia was actually more surprised that Marsha hadn't mentioned the reason for Olivia's trip off island. She was pretty sure the women knew that as well.

"I do," Olivia said. She didn't add, *Because it's my life,* the way she wanted to; that would just be picking a fight with Marsha. And the last thing Olivia wanted was to be in a fight with Marsha. The only thing these women did better than fact-finding was drama. And a good fight would only serve to further thrill Marsha.

"So why not?" Marsha asked.

Olivia fought the urge to say, *Don't you know? Because you seem to know everything else.*

She wondered if the book club knew everything but just wanted to get the truth right from the horse's mouth. They knew so much, there were some days that Olivia wondered if she should just ask these women about her future. Maybe they could solve the Noah dilemma for her. Olivia's own thoughts were a jumbled, confusing mess. But she was pretty sure the book club would be happy to make the decision if Olivia would allow it.

"We're taking a bit of a break," Olivia said honestly because she had a feeling Marsha wouldn't leave until those words were said. And since swimming lessons would be coming to an end soon, she might as well get it all out there. The last thing Olivia wanted was to be pressed to say anything about Noah in front of her girls.

"I knew it!" Marsha exclaimed.

Olivia raised her eyebrows at Marsha's loud declaration.

"Oh, excuse my exuberance. It's just Penny Larkfield said Noah had broken it off with you, and I came to your defense. You know, you're much prettier and more capable than you give yourself credit for, Olivia. Bart was an idiot letting you go. Anyway, so I told Penny there was no way Noah broke up with you. He was head over heels. Am I right?" Marsha spoke so quickly, Olivia felt like her head was spinning. But from what she'd caught, she was pretty sure Marsha had stuck up for her. That was nice.

"It's just a break," Olivia said instead of directly addressing anything Marsha had said because she wasn't sure if she could.

"Which always leads to a breakup," Marsha said knowingly.

Wasn't that exactly what Noah had said? But Olivia wasn't about to tell Marsha that. "Maybe? Maybe not," Olivia said ambiguously. Evasive maneuvers were a must when dealing with Marsha Tuttle.

"I knew Penny was wrong. You just let me know when you break it off for good, Olivia. I was always on your side," Marsha said as she stood and went toward the door a good five minutes before lessons were over. Just as Marsha slipped out, her nanny came in, making Olivia feel as if she'd been part of some kind of covert operation.

The last five minutes of class were spent with Olivia trying to recover from her encounter with Marsha. It hadn't been bad, per se, but it hadn't been good either. And Olivia just needed a minute to breathe.

As soon as her girls got out of the pool, her moment to breathe was done as both girls excitedly told Olivia about the new skills they'd learned in the pool that afternoon.

"I'm the best diver in the class. That's what Mr. Elliot said," Rachel said gleefully.

Olivia was quite certain her older daughter had a bit of a crush on their swimming instructor. Olivia smiled as she remembered having a crush on her own swimming teacher when she was about the same age. Olivia guessed it wasn't that abnormal considering the men who taught their lessons were typically older teens or young men in their early twenties, and they spent most of class time in swim trunks, often without a shirt.

"He said *I* was the most improved," Pearl said proudly. "Improved means better than best, right, Mom?"

Oh dear.

"No, dummy. There's nothing better than best," Rachel snapped.

Olivia drew in a deep breath. Why did half of parenting feel like refereeing?

"Rachel, don't say dummy. And improved means you got even better than last time," Olivia responded, causing her older daughter to sulk as she got into the back of their car while her younger daughter sent her sister a triumphant smile.

With both girls settled in the car, Olivia got in on the driver's side and pulled them out of the pool's parking lot.

"See, I'm better than you," Pearl said smugly.

"No you aren't. I'm the *best*. You're so dumb!" Rachel screeched.

"Rachel! What did I say about that word? And Pearl, no more talk about who is better. Got it?" Olivia said as she stopped at a red light and then turned in her seat to discipline her girls.

"Got it," both girls muttered.

Whatever. Olivia would take muttering. She'd gotten a response from both of them. For right now, that was enough.

Silence reigned for about two seconds while both girls sulked. Then Olivia heard Rachel sigh, and she knew her older daughter had thoughts of her coach on her brain. The crush was mostly cute but maybe a bit disconcerting. Olivia wasn't ready for Rachel to like boys.

"Did you know Mr. Elliot is training for the Olympics?" Rachel said with admiration.

Olivia bit back a smile. So that was why Marsha had been willing to come down from Country Club Drive to allow her children to take lessons with the average people of the island. Olivia had heard Elliot was good, but Olympic training? That was pretty dang awesome.

"Do you know why he's on the island if he's training for the Olympics?" Olivia asked, knowing it was kind of sad that her gossip source was her eleven-year-old. But Olivia usually avoided the stuff, so no one ever told her anything. Including information she actually cared about, like why a young man who was training for the Olympics had come to Whisling.

"His coach moved here last summer because he was going to retire, but Mr. Elliot still wanted to be trained by him. So they made a compromise. The coach would come out of retirement to train Mr. Elliot, but Mr. Elliot had to move to the island. Mr. Elliot said he got the good end of the deal because the island is beautiful, and it has good swimming and the best students."

Olivia looked in her rearview mirror to see Rachel grinning proudly. Olivia was pretty sure her daughter had taken that last compliment to mean only her. With her slicked back, auburn hair and blue eyes that matched Olivia's, Olivia knew her daughter was growing into quite the beauty. Olivia worried Rachel's looks would hurt her and bring unwanted attention at too young of an age, the same way it had for Olivia. Olivia recognized that it was up to her to protect her daughter. To teach her that what was on the outside only went so far, and anyone who focused solely on that wasn't worth her time. Feeling good about her future game plan, Olivia's thoughts went back to the moment at hand and what her girls needed immediately.

"Who's hungry?" Olivia asked, wanting to direct the conversation away from a certain swim instructor.

"Me!" both girls called out.

What was it about swimming that left people ravenous?

"Good. I left slow cooker beef stew simmering all day. You both hop in the bath, and I'll have dinner ready when you come out," Olivia said as she pulled in the driveway.

Olivia looked into her rearview mirror in time to see her girls nod and then jubilant expressions cross both their faces. "Dean's home!" Pearl called out as Olivia glanced over at their shared yard and saw that, sure enough, there was her handsome neighbor. Sans shirt, even though the evening was quite nippy. Olivia was going to guess he'd just gotten back from his run.

Olivia knew Pearl's excitement was largely due to the fact that they hadn't seen the man around as often these days. Sure, he was at soccer practice every Tuesday and Thursday, but he and his dog, Buster, hadn't been just hanging around the back-yard the way they used to. Probably because of Dean's many dates.

"Dean!" Rachel called out as soon as she got out of the car, and she ran over to give their neighbor an enthusiastic high five.

"Hi, Dean!" Pearl said as she followed her sister's lead but gave the man a hug instead of a high five.

"Hi, girls! Olivia," Dean said, his signature grin covering his face.

Geez-louise, the man was attractive.

"Hey, Dean," Olivia said in a much more subdued manner than her girls had, even though she'd been missing Dean as well. He'd been such a fixture in their lives, but ever since she'd started dating Noah, he hadn't been around as much. And it had been hard on all of them, especially her girls.

"Can Dean come over for dinner?" Pearl asked her mom right in front of Dean.

Olivia looked down to give her nine-year-old *the look* because she knew better. "Do we invite friends over in front of them?" Olivia asked Pearl.

Pearl shook her head. "But Dean isn't *my* friend. He's *our* friend. Don't we all want him to come to dinner?" she asked sweetly because she knew she was in trouble.

Olivia didn't know whether to be impressed or to scold Pearl.

"We do," Olivia conceded. She decided now wasn't the time to discipline her youngest. But Olivia would continue to watch for more of that sneaky behavior from Pearl. If it went on, then she'd punish her.

"Dean, would you like to come for dinner?" Olivia asked, sure he was going to turn her down. He was certain to have a dinner date that evening, right?

"Can I shower first?" Dean asked Pearl, who giggled.

"You have to shower first," Pearl said.

"He doesn't *have* to," Rachel said, looking embarrassed for her little sister's faux pas.

"But you can," Olivia answered for all. "The girls are going to bathe as well. See you in ten to fifteen?"

Olivia wondered if it was weird that she knew how long it took her neighbor to shower, but considering they'd been friends for so long, she doubted it.

"Sounds good," Dean said as he and Buster jogged towards their door while Olivia and her girls went on to their bungalow.

Fifteen minutes later, Dean knocked on the door just as Pearl placed the last bowl of stew on the table. Olivia had had time to warm up a loaf of French bread she'd picked up from the grocery store as well as throw together a quick salad.

"Smells amazing," Dean said as he drew in a deep breath. "Beef stew?"

"How did you know?" Pearl asked, sounding astonished. But considering Dean had been over to their home for dinner a few dozen times and nearly half of those times had eaten beef stew, it wasn't really a stretch. But in Olivia's culinary defense, beef stew was easy, her girls ate it well, and it warmed them all right up.

"He's had it before," Rachel said with that attitude that Olivia wished she could bottle up and send far, far away.

"Rachel," Olivia warned. She didn't even need to say what the warning was about. Rachel had been reprimanded for her attitude often enough.

"Have a seat," Olivia offered Dean as they all sat down, her girls on either side of her and Dean across the table. It was quite the quaint domestic scene. Well, if Olivia weren't maybe dating another guy and Dean wasn't dating the entire single population of the Pacific Northwest.

The girls dug into their meals, content with the scene they sat in, as Olivia noticed she wasn't the only one sensing there was something wrong with what was happening in their little dining space.

Dean took slow bites of his stew, his eyes cautiously darting from each of the girls to Olivia. Even his chewing seemed less vigorous than normal. Did he feel guilty because he was finally dating just one woman again and this meal felt like it was a traitorous action against her?

Olivia didn't like that the idea of Dean in a relationship didn't sit well with her. She wanted to be happy for her friend. But she wasn't. She was jealous.

Olivia paused on that thought. She was jealous. Oh for the love of all that was holy. If Dean had a girlfriend, she was jealous. Now. When she'd been sure she no longer had any feelings for Dean. *What?* This revelation wasn't a pleasant one.

"Mom, I don't think Dean likes the stew," Rachel said as she set her spoon in her empty bowl. Olivia looked over to see Pearl's bowl was just as devoid of food. But Dean's was still nearly full. The same as Olivia's.

Olivia met Dean's eyes that said so much and yet nothing because Olivia had no idea how to read them. They'd been friends for long enough that she thought she knew all of Dean's expressions, but this was new.

"I like it. I like it a lot. And I think that might be the problem," Dean said as his eyes dropped down to look at his bowl. Was he talking about the stew? But why would that be a problem? Unless he was talking about Olivia. Could he be talking about Olivia? It was the only thing that made sense and yet . . . Olivia didn't dare get her hopes up. Besides, she was still dating Noah.

Oh crap. She was still dating Noah. Why had her thoughts strayed so far when she still had a boyfriend? She was a terrible, horrible person.

"It's a problem?" Rachel asked as she cocked her head to look at the man who sat next to her.

"Just while it was too hot," Dean said as he dug into his stew with vigor.

"It's not hot anymore, Dean," Pearl said.

Dean nodded. "Yeah, I know."

Olivia tried to concentrate on her own meal, but those words had been like a siren's call and she couldn't help but look up at Dean. Their eyes connected, and Olivia felt something inside of her click.

Whatever that something was scared her, so she ignored it and turned her attention to her daughters instead.

She watched as Rachel and Pearl both beamed up at their dinner guest, more pleased during a dinnertime than they'd been in months. Than they'd been ever since Olivia had started dating Noah. But was this fair to any of them—this pseudo family they'd created—if it couldn't last?

Olivia suddenly recognized that none of them had viewed this scenario as a family scene until Olivia had begun dating again. If Olivia had never started dating, her girls would've been fine with Dean just staying Dean, their friend and neighbor. But when her daughters had seen that Olivia wanted to fill that void in her life, of course they'd hoped Dean could fill it. He was their Dean. He was comfortable for them. Noah was a brand new entity. One that had uprooted all that had been.

The girls didn't dislike Noah because he was Noah. They disliked him because with him around, Dean couldn't be. At least not in the capacity he had been. That was all her girls had wanted, and Olivia had selfishly taken that from them. That hadn't been fair. To any of them. Because if Olivia was honest with herself, she'd missed this as well. She might've even missed this closeness more than she missed dating Noah.

So wasn't that her answer? She wasn't giving in to her girls' every whim by breaking up with Noah. She was helping them regain the solid ground they'd secured when they'd had Dean in their lives. She was promising them that they would come first, no matter the cost. And she was doing the same for herself. Because, as much as she hated to admit it, right now she needed Dean in her life as well. Maybe one day Olivia could date again, but she realized that day wasn't today.

And with that decision, Olivia wondered to herself how she could've been so selfish for so long. How had she put her relationship with a man above her girls? She had tried so hard not to do that by splitting up her free time fairly and by always putting her daughters' events above Noah's. But that hadn't been enough. She'd hoped that if the girls got to know Noah better or if they were all given some more time, it would all work out. But it wasn't in the cards for Olivia to find a partner at this juncture in her life. As much as she hated to give up on her relationship with Noah, as much as she hated to lose the one man who'd been willing to look past all of her baggage and see her, she had to break up with him. The thought landed in her heart with a heavy thud.

"Who wants to help me clear the table?" Dean called out, and both girls hopped to their feet and joined the race in taking over all their dishes.

"Are you finished eating?" Dean asked softly as he stopped at Olivia's side. They both looked down at her nearly full bowl, but Olivia nodded. She wouldn't be eating anything more that evening. Her stomach was too full of the knot of worry over what she had to do. Noah wouldn't be happy. Heck, she wouldn't be either. But her girls would be. And that was her first priority right now.

Dean took Olivia's bowl but then paused, looking at her.

"Anything I can help with?" he asked, obviously sensing her distress.

Olivia shook her head. Nope. No one could help her. This was something she would have to do all on her own.

Dean nodded, taking Olivia's bowl into the kitchen and then tackling the dishes with the girls as Olivia wiped down their table.

Olivia thought about telling Dean he didn't need to clean up, but she figured it would be wasted breath. She'd told him many times before that just because she invited him over didn't mean he had to clean up. But he'd ignored her each and every time, always doing the dishes and sometimes even more, and getting her girls to join him in the process.

"Can we watch a show?" Pearl asked as she, Rachel, and Dean finished loading up the last of the dishes into the dishwasher.

"Brush your teeth and get all ready for bed," Olivia replied.

"Then we can?" Rachel asked hopefully.

Olivia nodded, causing the girls to squeal and run for the bathroom, leaving Olivia alone with Dean.

"Rough day?" Dean asked as he leaned against Olivia's kitchen counter.

Olivia thought back on her day. The morning had been nice because she'd worked all of it. She adored her job keeping the books for Bess's food truck. But then swimming had happened, and she remembered Marsha and her last words of *let me know when you break up with him*. That conversation hadn't been terribly pleasant, but it hadn't been awful either. So no. Her day hadn't been too bad so far. But it was about to get a whole lot worse. So overall, yes, it would be a really rough day.

"I guess you could say that," Olivia finally responded.

Dean shot her a look she knew well. He knew she was holding back what she was really thinking.

Olivia bit her lip as she considered what she should do. Could she tell Dean she was going to break up with Noah before she told Noah? Granted, Dean was Noah's friend. And he had also been the one to go out on a limb to introduce the two. Now that Olivia was breaking that limb, shouldn't Dean get a heads up? Olivia's decision was made.

"I have to break up with Noah," Olivia said with a sigh as she crossed her arms over her chest and sat on the very edge of her table.

"Oh," Dean said as he looked down at the kitchen counter.

"Yeah," Olivia said, dropping her head as well. "I'm sorry it turned out this way. I know you and Noah are friends, and I really hope he won't blame you for this."

"Whoa, don't worry about me, Liv. My *oh* was for you. It sucks to break up with someone. Especially someone you like as much as Noah," Dean said as he rounded the kitchen bar that stood between himself and Olivia and paused a few steps away from her.

"Yeah, it does," Olivia said. Then she let out another long sigh. "But I have to do what's best for my girls, and I guess in the end, it's also what's best for me."

"Is it?" Dean asked.

Olivia shrugged. She hoped so. Because she was doing it.

"Wait, Noah didn't hurt the girls, did he?" Dean asked, his voice becoming gruff.

Olivia quickly shook her head. "He would never," she responded.

Dean nodded once. "Good. I thought I was going to have to kill a friend," he said.

Olivia cracked a smile. One thing that could never be denied? Dean loved her girls.

"So why is it best for Rachel and Pearl?" Dean asked as the girls came running into the living room.

"I get the remote," Pearl called out. "I asked Mom if we could watch!"

But Rachel got to the remote first, causing Pearl to scream.

"Hey! No screaming," Olivia reprimanded. "And you'd better share the remote or it's off to bed for both of you."

Both girls drooped their heads in disappointment but then glanced over at the other, realizing they had to get along.

"Yes, mom," Pearl muttered as Rachel murmured, "Fine."

"How about I get the remote, but you get to choose the show?" Rachel offered.

Pearl nodded, and Olivia sighed. She had diverted world war three. Again. It was honestly an hourly battle.

The theme song to Pearl's favorite YouTube family sounded on the TV, and Olivia looked back to find Dean waiting for her. Right. They'd been in the middle of a conversation.

"Do you want to go outside?" Olivia asked.

Dean nodded and he waited as Olivia grabbed a jacket. Then the two of them went out onto her front porch.

"I'll be right out here," Olivia called into her house before she closed the door, but it seemed like neither girl cared.

Dean sat on Olivia's porch swing and then patted the spot next to him. Olivia took the offered seat but then scooted to the far end of the swing, careful not to touch Dean. Physical contact with Dean tended to mess with Olivia's mind. That was the last thing she needed considering what the night still held for her.

"They've just never felt comfortable with Noah," Olivia said, answering Dean's earlier question.

"Why?" Dean asked.

Olivia thought back to the dinner when her girls had met Noah, then to some of their more recent interactions.

"I think he was doomed from the start," Olivia said, and then she wondered how honest she wanted to be with her friend. She figured she'd better say it all. Dean needed to know the truth.

"Really?" Dean asked. "Noah's good with kids, isn't he?"

Olivia shrugged. She really wouldn't know because her girls never gave him a shot.

"So the first time the girls met Noah was on my birthday," Olivia explained.

"Right, you had that dinner here."

Olivia nodded. "The girls wanted you to come."

"I did come." Dean remembered.

"Just for dessert. By then, I think the damage had already been done."

"Damage?"

"The girls had asked for you to join us earlier, but my mom had thought it would be best for the family to meet Noah without anyone else. . ." Olivia's voice trailed off because she wondered if that was rude.

"Understandable," Dean said, relieving Olivia of any worry.

So she went on. "But I think the girls took it as Noah keeping you away from them. In their minds, it pitted you against Noah or Noah against you from the start. So Noah was doomed to fail. It didn't matter how many times I tried to tell them Noah wasn't taking your place, I think our actions spoke louder. You came over less often, and Noah was here instead."

"Wow," Dean breathed as he kicked back on his heel so they swung slightly.

"Yeah."

"I don't know whether to feel flattered or terrible."

Olivia felt a whisper of a smile on her face. It really was

hard to stay all that sad when Dean was around. Even if she was going to be doing one of the hardest things she'd had to do in a long time later that night.

"Do you think if I talked to the girls—?" Dean started to ask.

Olivia shook her head. The time for words was over. Besides, this was about more than Dean and Noah now. It was about proving to her girls that she was on their side, whatever side they chose. And it was what Olivia wanted . . . she was pretty sure.

"Do the girls know you're breaking up with him?" Dean asked.

"I think they think I already did. We've been on a break for a few weeks—"

"Ugh. A break? Poor guy," Dean lamented.

Olivia nodded. But it seemed like the only option at the time. She hadn't been ready to let Noah go. And to be honest, she still wasn't. But it was time to pull the plug.

"He hasn't been around. And the girls have been getting along better, talking to me more, just all around happier. I think they were holding a grudge against me while I dated Noah. In reality, it might've all just been too soon for them. Even though I was ready to date, they might not have been ready for a new man in my life. So Noah and I might've been doomed from the start in that respect as well. I was so worried about my own dating readiness that I didn't even consider the girls. But in my defense, they seemed okay with it during the conversations we'd had before I started dating again. I guess talking is much different than reality."

Dean nodded and then stood.

"I really am sorry, Liv."

Olivia kicked back so the swing swung once again. "It's not your fault. Well, I guess if you could've been a little meaner to my girls . . ."

Dean laughed because they both knew Olivia would've sacrificed anything if it meant her daughters had more people to love them.

"Really, I am so grateful for you. If this teaches me anything, it's a testament to how much you've helped our entire healing process after Bart. We couldn't have done it without you."

"Yes, you could have. You are so much stronger than you know, Liv."

Olivia shrugged. She doubted that. "Well, thankfully I won't ever know. Because you *were* here. I'll forever be in your debt, Dean."

Dean shook his head. "It was nothing. I just tried to be a good neighbor."

"What you've been for all of us has been much more than that, and I think you know it," Olivia said as she cracked a smirk. She thought about standing up to give her friend a hug, but when she touched Dean, her thoughts went beyond friendly fast. So it was better for her to stay just where she was.

"Good luck, Liv. I'm here if you need me."

"Thanks, Dean," Olivia said.

Dean turned to walk off her porch and to his home. He stopped by his back door and turned to look at Olivia, who still sat on her swing. He shot her a smile that buoyed her, and she knew it was time.

She pulled her phone out of her pocket to call Noah.

CHAPTER NINE

ALEXIS SAT up at the pounding on her door. She had just finished her shift at the food truck, so it was late for visitors. At least nine-thirty in the evening.

"Alexis." She heard Dalton's voice from the other side of the door. Dalton? Was here?

Alexis hadn't seen her boyfriend in nearly a week, so she ran straight for the door, opened it, flung herself into Dalton's arms and then returned his kiss that would've been greeted by catcalls, had they any observers.

"You're here," Alexis said happily, relishing the fact that her boyfriend was with her before wondering why he was there. At nearly ten pm on a Thursday night.

"I'm here," he whispered into her hair, tugging her behind him as he led her to the couch.

They continued their kiss there for far too short, but Alexis's curiosity was getting the better of her. Dalton never just showed up. Their dates were often planned at least days, if not weeks, in advance.

Dalton had pulled Alexis on top of him during their kissing, so it was up to Alexis to sit up and bring Dalton with her.

"As you can tell, I'm happy to see you," Alexis said, and Dalton grinned cheekily. "But why are you here?"

"I've got news that I needed to tell you in person," Dalton said, causing Alexis to sit up straighter. News? As in something Dalton wanted to say to her? Could it possibly be a question? Alexis hoped for a moment that Dalton had a ring hidden in his pocket, but she knew it was way too soon. At least for him. Alexis already knew she wanted to spend the rest of her life with this man, but Dalton was a little gun-shy because of his first marriage. Alexis understood that, but it didn't keep her from hoping he'd one day pop that question.

It was only after her thoughts had strayed toward such a fantasy that Alexis remembered something else. Another reason why Dalton could be there. The private investigator.

"About my dad?" Alexis asked.

Dalton nodded. "He found him."

"He did?" Alexis felt her eyes go wide as her heart dropped. It had only been a couple of weeks. And her father, the man who had been elusive to her for so long, had been found.

Alexis swallowed.

"I know it's a lot," Dalton said as he tugged Alexis in by his side and held her close.

Alexis nodded. That it was.

"What are you thinking?" Dalton asked.

What was she thinking? The question was, what wasn't she thinking.

"What would you be thinking?" Alexis asked.

"If I got news about my father, a man I'd never met?" Dalton asked, and Alexis nodded, even though she knew Dalton would have to use his imagination to answer her question. Dalton's parents were the ones people dreamed of. His dad had been the type to be home from work at five so they could play ball in the yard until it was dark. Dalton had learned how to ride a bike, charge a car battery, fix a running toilet, all from his father. His mother kept their home immaculate and baked the best chocolate chip cookies. At least that's what Dalton had told Alexis. She had yet to meet Dalton's parents herself, but she knew she would one day soon. Dalton had just been so busy with work that even their dates were squeezed in whenever they could. Alexis held out hope that with the holiday season approaching, she would get to meet not only Dalton's parents but his three brothers and their families. However, Alexis refused to push Dalton to this next step before he was ready. She would not be the same person to Dalton that his ex had been.

"I think I'd want to meet him," Dalton said slowly.

Alexis gnawed on her lip.

"Don't do that unless you want me to kiss you," Dalton practically growled.

Typically, Alexis would be all for that, but she had a big decision to make. She let go of her lip.

"Smart girl," Dalton said, still giving Alexis a brief peck, as though he couldn't completely restrain himself.

Alexis grinned before she remembered what she'd been considering. What should she do? Her father. She could meet him if she wanted to. Didn't she want to? What was the point of looking for him if she didn't? Wouldn't it be a complete waste of the money Dalton had spent?

"I think I want to meet him too," Alexis said as Dalton pet her hair and twirled it around his fingers.

"But?" Dalton asked.

He knew her so well.

"I'm scared. What if he doesn't want to meet me? He *has* stayed away for over thirty years," Alexis reminded him.

"If it was his choice," Dalton said, reminding Alexis that he thought her mother might've kept her father away.

"Right." Alexis leaned her head against Dalton's chest.

"I could ask the PI to talk to him first. Test the waters. See how your dad would feel about meeting you. At least that way you wouldn't have to be the one to tell your father the news. The PI would do so, and if your dad is amenable, we could go from there," Dalton said.

Alexis threw her arms around him. "You would do that?" she asked.

"I think by now you know I would do absolutely anything in the world for you, Alexis," Dalton said, and all Alexis could think as she met Dalton's lips was that he was the perfect man and she was the luckiest woman alive.

———

"ALEXIS!"

The sound shot Alexis out of her dreams because it was a voice she knew all too well. But why was she here so early in the morning? Alexis wanted to relish the way she'd felt being held by Dalton until he'd had to leave on the last ferry the night before. She had hoped he might sleep over now that her mom no longer lived with her and judged her every action, but Dalton had told Alexis he loved her too much to take such a big step lightly. Just because he was there didn't mean he had to sleep over. He knew she wasn't well-versed in serious relationships and wanted to take each step with extreme caution. Another reason why Alexis adored the man: he treasured her.

But the pounding on Alexis's door reminded her Dalton was long gone and a possible problem stood on her doorstep. Alexis pondered if she had to open the door. She hadn't spoken to her mother since that fateful day when she'd asked her to move out. And Alexis had missed her, but she hadn't missed this angry version of her mother who came out anytime anything about Dalton came up. Alexis couldn't help but think her mother's reappearance had to do with Dalton, considering the fact that he'd been on the island just the night before. Did Alexis want to deal with it all?

"Alexis! I know you are in there. Open this door right now!"

Alexis guessed she had no choice. She pulled down the hem of the nightshirt she slept in so that when all of her neighbors, who were undoubtedly looking out their windows at the scene her mom was making, saw her, she would at least be half-dressed. Because she really doubted her mother would give her a chance to get fully dressed.

"Alex-is!" her mother called out again, this time going up an octave with the third syllable of Alexis's name. That was a nice touch.

"I'm coming," Alexis yelled back as she walked toward the door. Apparently, not fast enough for her mother since she shouted Alexis's name one more time.

Alexis opened the door to see a seething Margie on her front step. Alexis could imagine literal smoke pouring out of her ears, that's how mad she looked.

"Mother," Alexis said as she stood in front of her opened door, unsure if she wanted to let in steaming Margie.

But that choice was taken from her as Margie barged right past her, going straight to the couch. Alexis did a quick glance of her neighbors' windows before closing her front door, and sure enough, at least three sets of curtains fluttered shut as she turned their way. Well, there went her hope that this most recent display of anger by her mother wouldn't fuel the island gossip.

Alexis leaned against her closed front door, asking for strength before walking into the living room where her mom sat ramrod straight.

"Were you even going to tell me?" Margie asked.

Alexis bit back the snarky response on her lips that she had no clue if she was or not because she had no idea what her mother was talking about. But instead, Alexis waited for her mother to charge forward. She didn't have to wait long.

"Did you think I wouldn't find out? Do you know the percentage of women on the island who get their nails done at my salon?" Margie asked.

Nope. Alexis had no idea. She'd guess twenty, maybe thirty?

"Thirty-two percent."

Alexis's guess was close. And that was really weird that her mother knew such an exact number. But again, Alexis's conversation in her head was wildly different from the one happening in her living room.

"Are you going to say anything?"

Maybe Alexis would if she had the chance.

"Argh!" her mother screeched. "I know you're looking for your father, Alexis!" Margie accused.

Oh. That was why she was here. Now this was making sense.

"Behind my back. How could you?"

Alexis drew in a deep breath. If she could continue the entirety of the conversation without saying a word, she probably would. But her mother would not be content with Alexis saying absolutely nothing. So it was time for her to speak.

"So if I had told you my plans to find my dad, you wouldn't have tried to stop me?" Alexis asked sassily, knowing she was adding fuel to the fire. But at this point, she was beyond tiptoeing around her mother's feelings. Where had a lifetime of doing that gotten her? To a place where she felt she had to hide the fact that she wanted to meet her biological father and where she had to defend her boyfriend at every turn. No, Alexis was done tiptoeing. She was going to stand up for herself.

"Don't call him that," Margie seethed.

"What? Dad?"

"Yes! He has done literally nothing for you. If anything, call him father. But the most accurate term would be sperm donor," Margie spat.

Alexis reeled back. "Really? That's what you want me to think of half of my DNA? Just some chance donor?" Alexis realized her voice was beginning to match her mother's, but she was too furious to care.

"Yes! It's better than the alternative."

"And what's that, Mom?"

"Getting to know that poor excuse of a man. I made my biggest mistake getting involved with him. I won't let you make the same mistake."

"Except, Mom, you've forgotten one thing. I'm a product of that mistake."

"You aren't a mistake," Margie tried to backpedal.

"Let me finish!" Alexis yelled as she put her hand up, startling Margie into silence. "I am an adult," Alexis said when her mother was properly stunned. "I am making a choice. You have to respect that choice."

"Alexis, all I've done is try to protect you."

"That isn't your job anymore, Mom."

Margie stood, seeming to understand that Alexis wasn't going to back down. No amount of yelling, screaming, or guilting would dissuade her.

Margie shook her head. "That's where you're wrong, Alexis. It will always be my job to protect you."

Margie walked toward the door and then paused. "I know we haven't been seeing eye to eye. But make no mistake. I love you, my dear, sweet girl. I am always here for you."

With that, Margie opened the door and let herself out.

That last moment had shown Alexis a glimpse of the mother she'd always known. This was the woman who had loved and raised her. Alexis wanted to run after her mom and tell her that she did need her, but she paused. Giving in to Margie now would mean giving up the search for her father, and maybe giving up Dalton, because Margie always knew best. But Alexis couldn't give either up. So for now, even though she missed her mom with all of her heart, Alexis had to let her go.

CHAPTER TEN

BESS AWOKE with a huge smile on her face. The same smile that had been accompanying her every day now that she was Dax's girlfriend.

She blushed and then felt silly. What kind of grown woman blushed because of her boyfriend? The lucky kind, she could imagine Gen telling her.

Bess looked down at her phone, knowing what she'd see. Dax hadn't let a morning go by without texting, *Good day, Lovely*, which wasn't just a sweet sentiment but the title of Bess's very favorite country song. She loved all country music, which helped her and Dax find more common ground since Dax had lived in the country music world for most of his career as an agent to some of the biggest stars Nashville had to offer. But for some reason, the sentiments of that pretty ballad really hit Bess's heart. Dax especially loved that his client, Ellis Rider, had penned and sung Bess's very favorite lyrics. He often threatened that instead of a text with the words, one day he would have Ellis show up on Bess's front door step, singing the song. Bess had warned Dax with all the fiercest words she knew that he better the heck not. She knew what she looked like in the mornings, and no one should be subjected to that kind of horror while singing such a beautiful song.

Sure enough, her phone read, *Good day, Lovely.*

Bess grinned even wider as she whistled the tune of the ballad and got ready for the day. She had thought being Dax's best friend had its perks, but being his girlfriend was infinitely better. She was one blessed woman.

Bess got to the truck a few minutes later than she should've, thanks to the daydreaming she'd been caught up in, and was surprised to see Olivia waiting by the truck's back door.

"Olivia," Bess greeted with a smile before hugging her friend and employee. "Did I forget about a meeting we had scheduled?"

Olivia didn't often come to the food truck since her job was mostly on the business side of things, but she sometimes met with Bess while she prepped for the day so that Bess could get two things done at once. However, Bess was pretty sure this morning they didn't have anything to discuss. They'd just hammered out the details for Stephen and Jana's wedding menu, even though it wasn't for a couple of months and they only had to put the food order in a couple weeks before the big day. But the wedding would be their first catered event, so they were leaving nothing to chance. Details were getting sorted out early, and they were staying on top of every step of the process.

But since that had been done, Bess wasn't sure what more there was for her and Olivia to talk about. The food truck now ran like a well-oiled machine, each person knowing her job and getting it done well. Bess knew she was beyond blessed that things had worked out that way for her, but she prided herself on having found the very best of the best when it came to her employees.

"We don't have anything on the books," Olivia said slowly.

"Oh, so this is an off-the-books meeting?" Bess asked as she opened the door to the truck and let Olivia in.

"Something like that. I have a request from Mrs. Hennison." Olivia said the name of her mother's best friend, and Bess raised an eyebrow.

"She and Mr. Hennison will be celebrating their forty-year anniversary in February."

Bess knew what was coming next. She'd been asked to cater quite a few events since her truck had become a success but had said no to every one of them. She loved to feed people, but the truck's day-to-day work alone kept her and all of her employees swamped. She guessed she could cut back the hours of the truck's operations or she could hire more people, but she wasn't sure she wanted to do either.

"I was told I had to bring the request to you in person," Olivia said with an eye roll that told Bess she wasn't here of her own accord. Bess guessed Mrs. Hennison had gotten the backing of Olivia's mother, and poor Olivia had had no choice but to show up this morning.

Bess began to laugh.

"I told Mrs. Hennison an in-person request wouldn't assure her of anything, but she made me promise to try," Olivia added.

"Well, good on you for trying," Bess said as she patted her friend's shoulder and then got to work. There was much to do, and Bess was already about fifteen minutes behind.

"But we'll be saying no?" Olivia asked.

Should they say no? Probably. Bess really shouldn't be considering private events right now. Maybe after seeing how the wedding went?

"You want to see how the wedding goes before committing to anything else?" Olivia asked as she watched Bess work.

"Now, am I a fortunate woman or what? I hired an employee who can read my mind," Bess said with a chuckle as she began to sauté the meat mixture for the lasagna.

"You *are* a very fortunate woman," Olivia agreed. "Even

more so because I anticipated this very conversation and told Mrs. Hennison as much. She said she'd be happy to wait."

"Until after December? But what if it's too late for her to secure a caterer at that point?" Bess asked.

"She said she's willing to take that risk," Olivia said, raising both of her eyebrows. "People adore your food, Bess."

That they did. Yet another reason why Bess was a fortunate woman. It was almost like her past dreadful years with Jon had been the precursor to wonderful times. She just had to endure that phase before being blessed. And honestly, she wondered if without those trials she would've been as open to seeing her blessings today. Enduring the worst really did make the best of times that much more beautiful.

"So I guess we'll put a pin in that?" Bess asked, and Olivia nodded. "Anything else we need to discuss?"

"That pretty much covers it. I was going to text you today that I put our food order in for next week, and there is a shortage on pumpkins this season. I could get most of what we ordered for next week, but our supplier told me we might want a different special after that."

Bess nodded. Fresh pumpkin lasagna had been a hit, but she'd had it as a special for three weeks in a row, and she didn't think her clientele would mind the change too much.

"And now that's really it," Olivia said.

"Sounds good," Bess said as she heard Olivia's footsteps move toward the door. Bess realized they often discussed business, but she hadn't inquired after Olivia personally for a bit. She was pretty sure things were going well, what with her girls thriving at their sports and other activities and Olivia seeming very happy in her new relationship with Noah. But Bess realized it was probably a good thing to be sure.

"Before you go, Olivia. How are things going for you? Anything I can help with?" Bess offered.

Olivia's footsteps paused. "Well . . ." Olivia drawled. "I'm guessing the rumor mill will let you know soon enough, but I broke up with Noah a few nights ago."

"Oh," Bess said softly. "I'm so sorry."

She turned to Olivia who was batting her eyelids as if she were trying to stave off tears.

"It was for the best," Olivia said.

Bess turned off her burner and went to hug her friend. "But that doesn't make it any easier."

Olivia shook her head from within Bess's hug.

Bess held Olivia for a few moments longer, but then felt it was right to step away. Olivia was a private woman and probably didn't like that she'd already shed a few tears in public, even if Bess was the only person around to see them. So Bess was surprised when Olivia spoke again.

"Nothing I say will leave this truck, right?" Olivia asked.

"Never," Bess promised sincerely.

"The girls were having a hard time coping with my dating."

Bess nodded. She could only imagine. Getting back into the dating scene had been hard on Bess, and she'd only had adult children to appease. She couldn't imagine what it would have been like if her kids had still lived in her home.

"Noah, himself, wasn't the problem. More of what he represented. Pearl began asking what life would look like after Noah moved in with us, and even as I tried to assure her things would be different than they had been with Bart, she was scared that Noah would one day become the man her father was."

"Poor Pearl," Bess muttered.

Olivia nodded.

"I had hoped more time would help. I even tried taking a break from Noah to let the girls know I'd always put them first, but . . ."

"They've had a hard go of it."

"Don't I know it," Olivia said before sighing.

"But so have you."

Olivia shrugged. "But my choices got us to where we were, so I deserved it. My poor girls didn't."

"I'll agree with you on the second half of that, but the other? Olivia Penn, you know better than to think that loving a man was a crime worthy of all that you endured."

"Loving the wrong man," Olivia amended.

"Still not a crime."

"It sure does feel like it on some days."

"Olivia, I wish you could see how incredible you are," Bess said softly.

"Bess, you're a good friend. Thank you. But I'd better get going. I have a list that's longer than I am to get done today," Olivia said. But she stopped before leaving the truck. "I think you know this, Bess. But I want to tell you again how grateful I am for you and all that you've been for me. You gave me a job when I needed it and have been a listening ear and incredible guide."

"I'm just glad I got to snatch you up before someone else did. This truck's success is thanks to you, Cassie, and Alexis."

"That's where you're wrong, Bess. We were all support pillars, but you held this whole project up with your own two hands," Olivia said. Then she opened the door of the truck and was gone.

Bess felt her heart swell with gratitude but then got to work. Because now she was really behind.

An hour of whirlwind prep work later and Bess was almost caught up. She knew Cassie would be there any minute, and then the fun would really begin, especially because Bess would be working all day. Alexis had asked for the day off, a personal matter that Bess hadn't asked any details about, and Bess had been happy to give it to her. But working twelve hours would wipe Bess out, so she drew in a deep, fortifying breath that would hopefully get her through the day.

The door to the food truck opened, but Bess was so close to her finish line that she didn't even look up.

"Morning, Cassie," Bess said as she finished chopping the last of the tomatoes. Her truck used a whole lot of tomatoes.

"Good morning," a deep voice that was very much not Cassie's responded, causing Bess to drop her knife on her cutting board and look up.

"I guess it wasn't a good move to startle a woman with a knife," Dax said, but Bess was too thrilled to see him to care that she'd almost cut her finger off. She threw herself into his arms, and he happily hugged her tight.

"What are you doing here?" she asked as she nuzzled closer against Dax's chest. She might be questioning why he was there, but she wouldn't be letting go anytime soon.

"I came to surprise my woman," Dax said as he ran a hand up and down Bess's back. Bess felt her entire body tremor under Dax's touch. How did he do that to her?

Bess chuckled at Dax's use of the word *woman*. He knew it got under her skin, so it made him use it all the more. The man loved to tease Bess, and Bess had to admit, she loved to be teased . . . at least by Dax.

Bess suddenly realized Dax was there. Holding her. But she would be stuck in the truck all day. How unfair was that?

"I'm so glad you're here—" Bess began.

"But you're working all day," Dax finished.

Bess looked up at him with a raised eyebrow. How the heck did he know?

"I ran my plans by Cassie. She told me another day might be better, but this was the only day I could completely clear my calendar."

"So you're here just for today?"

Dax nodded. "And I plan to make the best of it. What do you say to having a sous chef?"

"You?" Bess clarified because, although Dax could cook, he wasn't exactly a skilled chef.

Dax laughed. "You don't have to look so appalled. Yes, me."

Dax really did know his way around a kitchen, and Bess could totally use his help. But she decided to keep up with her joke a little longer.

"I'm not appalled. Worried, fearful, a bit terrified, but not appalled." Bess grinned through her words. She loved to tease Dax just as much as he loved teasing her.

"Oh yeah?" Dax said as he pulled Bess in closer and then pressed his lips to hers.

Bess enjoyed every moment of that long kiss until the door to the food truck opened again.

"Sorry to ruin the party, but some of us have to work today," Cassie called out as she entered the truck.

Bess finished her kiss with her boyfriend before turning to the cute girl who ran her register and so much more.

"You don't look sorry," Bess said, seeing the grin on Cassie's face.

"That's 'cause I'm not really," Cassie said sassily. "If I don't have a handsome boyfriend to kiss, I'd rather not watch you get to kiss yours," she added with a laugh.

"Fair enough," Bess said.

"Hey, do I get a vote?" Dax asked.

"Nope," Bess and Cassie said in unison before the women got to work.

"Are you really going to hang out here all day?" Bess asked Dax as she finally finished the last of the tomatoes.

"The gig comes with free food, right?" Dax asked.

"When we actually have a moment to eat," Cassie answered.

"It gets that busy?" Dax asked.

"Oh boy. You are in for a ride," Cassie warned.

And that was how the rest of their day went. Bess lost track of the number of times Dax asked if it was always so eventful and Cassie responded that it was and sometimes even busier.

They whizzed through cooking, cleaning, and plating up food for hours on end. Dax had been happy about the fifteen-minute break to stuff some scampi down his throat before they all had to get back to work.

"This job is no joke," Dax said as the three of them finally closed the truck for the night.

"Your girlfriend works hard," Cassie said as they all left the truck and she set off toward her car. "See you tomorrow, Bess," she called back over her shoulder.

"Bye, Cassie. Thanks for your hard work," Bess called back.

"I didn't doubt that," Dax said, referring to Cassie's last remark, as he took Bess into his arms again the moment Cassie was out of view. "But I just didn't realize 'hard' meant working at a superhuman pace."

"It's only that tough the first day," Bess said as she relished the feel of Dax's embrace.

"Really?" Dax asked.

"Okay, maybe not *just* the first day. But the first day is the hardest."

"So you're saying I am dating not only the prettiest and smartest woman I know. But also the most hardworking and humblest?" Dax asked.

"Something like that," Bess said before Dax chuckled and leaned in for a kiss.

Bess sank into his kiss. She'd been waiting all day to do this.

"Don't hate me," Dax said as he came out of their kiss, causing Bess to groan. She could've kept on kissing him for a whole lot longer.

"But you have to get to the ferry?" Bess asked.

"I'm taking the last flight out of SeaTac to LA, but it's getting late."

Bess nodded. She'd assumed as much when Dax had said he only had today off.

"But I get to give you a ride to the ferry?" Bess asked when she looked around and didn't see a rental.

"If you don't mind," Dax said.

"More time with you? There is no part of me that would say no to that," Bess said, and Dax grinned as he opened her car door for her, then moved to his side of the car.

Bess thought about their long day. Dax had made it so much better just being by her side. It was definitely the most fun she'd ever had at work. But she wondered if it had been the same for Dax. She would've had to work anyway. But it couldn't have been the way Dax really wanted to spend his day, could it? Especially considering he rarely got days off.

"I'm sorry about how we had to spend today," Bess said, voicing her thoughts.

"Why? I'm not. I got to spend all day in a small, confined space with the woman I love," Dax said.

Bess felt her eyes widen. Dax had said things that he loved about her and even that he was falling in love with her, but the woman he loved? Was he saying . . .?

Bess pulled into a parking spot just in the nick of time because her thoughts were about to run wild and then she'd be in no shape to be behind the wheel.

"I love you, Bess," Dax said as he turned in his seat toward her. Then he gazed around the car and the ferry dock. "Not exactly the way I imagined telling you, but I can't keep it in any longer."

"I love you too, Dax," Bess returned without any hesitation. She'd felt it for a while now—probably too long, considering she'd loved Dax before she'd been willing to date him. But it felt good to let it out. Even if it did seem early. She and Dax had only been together for a few weeks.

"Don't be scared. I see it in your face," Dax said as he placed his warm hands on Bess's cold cheeks. The warmth felt so good. So comforting.

"I'm not scared."

Dax nodded, knowing Bess had more to say.

"It's just soon, right?" Bess asked.

"Maybe. For any other couple. But we were a long time coming, Bess. I'm not gonna lie. I loved you way before I should have. I'm pretty sure I fell in love with you when you tried to drop off those cookies to me and you stuttered through that conversation on my parent's porch."

"I did not stutter."

Dax cocked his head.

"Okay, I stuttered a bit. But you had to know your hand-someness was getting to me," Bess defended, and Dax laughed.

"I guess it was a long time coming," Bess admitted after Dax's laughter died down.

"It was. But it's also being said at just the right moment. Can you feel that, Bess?" Dax asked.

Bess was sure she felt something; her stomach was alive with butterflies and her heart was so full. But what exactly was Dax talking about?

"Maybe?" Bess said honestly.

Dax smiled and pulled Bess in close. "We're at the starting line of something extraordinarily beautiful," he said, and then he placed his lips gently on hers.

Bess realized she did feel it. And she had to agree.

CHAPTER ELEVEN

"DID you want your sandwich cut into triangles or rectangles?" Lily asked, and then she realized how silly it sounded to be asking a grown man that question. But she'd gotten so used to trying to make sure everything was just the way Allen wanted it that she was asking him about everything, even stupid things like sandwich shape.

"Either way is fine, Lily," Allen said in a tone that told Lily he knew what she was doing. But he was letting go of his annoyance at her babying him because that was what they were both doing: letting everything go in order to keep the peace.

"Do you mind if I take this into the bedroom to eat it?" Allen asked tentatively after Lily gave him the sandwich. Again, a question that might seem unnecessary, but Allen was asking just in case. Just in case his actions annoyed Lily. Just in case what he was doing could possibly, even one day down the road, cause a fight.

Because that had become their common cause: to not cause a fight.

When did we become this couple, Lily thought to herself as Allen wheeled away. They were partners in life, there was no denying that, but that was it. They were hiding from any kind of spark, good or bad. And because of that, they were robbing themselves of passion, fire, and excitement, as well as fights, cruel words, and maybe the end.

And that's what it came down to. Lily was afraid that one wrong word, the smallest action or inaction, would end them. And Lily wouldn't allow that to happen. She couldn't. If the last year had served to teach her anything, it was that Allen was her world. She didn't want to be without him, so she'd keep on keeping on. Anything to be sure that he would always be right there by her side.

Lily's phone rang, letting her know that Kate was calling. The timing couldn't have been more perfect since Amelia was down for a nap and it was a pretty, lazy Sunday afternoon. Belle was out shopping or something in Seattle, since Sunday was her only full day off each week, and for the first time in a long time, Lily thought she might be able to get a little privacy. Lily couldn't remember the last time she'd had an uninterrupted call with her favorite, albeit only, sister.

"Hey," Lily said happily as she took the call. She used her quiet voice to answer because, although their sound machine was running during Amelia's nap, she didn't want to risk waking her little girl. As Lily strained to look into their bedroom, she could see that Allen was sitting next to the far side of their bed with headphones in his ears, watching something on his phone. Lily couldn't see Amelia from that angle, but she was guessing her little angel was fast asleep in her crib.

Lily took that as her cue to be able to slip out her back door and into their small yard. It wasn't much, just a small patch of grass and then a fence that divided them from their neighbors, but it was enough.

"How are things going?" Kate asked, and Lily heard the clanking of pots and pans in the background.

"Are you trying to cook?" Lily asked instead of answering Kate's question.

"Of course not," Kevin's deep voice answered instead of Kate. "Neither of us have a death wish."

Lily laughed as she heard a noise that sounded suspiciously like Kate smacking Kevin. Then Kate said, "You've officially lost all phone privileges."

Lily heard the background noise go quiet, letting her know that she was no longer on speaker phone.

"Kevin is cooking," Kate said into the phone.

"That sounds nice," Lily said.

"It's the only way we both stay safe," Kevin called out loudly, and Lily could easily imagine the glare Kate had to be giving her boyfriend.

But then Kate dissolved into laughter, telling Lily all was well, and suddenly a deep pang hit Lily's heart. She wanted that. She wanted to tease and laugh with Allen. They'd done it so often before . . . but now?

"I've been relegated to the couch," Kate said as Lily slid to the ground and leaned her back against their fence.

"Probably smart of Kevin," Lily teased.

"Come on now. It's enough I get it from him. Et tu, Brute?" Kate asked dramatically.

"When it's the truth . . ."

"Ow, Sister. That hurt."

Lily imagined Kate clutching her chest. Kate had been the lead in two of Whisling High's plays back in high school, and she'd never lost her flair for the dramatic.

"So, enough about my sad cooking skills."

"And that you have a boyfriend to negate them," Lily added.

"It is kind of nice," Kate admitted. "But enough about me. How are you?"

Since it was the second time Kate had asked the question, Lily knew she wouldn't get away without answering it.

She drew in a breath before saying a word in order to give herself some time to think. How was she? On the outside, things were great. She and her family were home, together, and healthy. Lily's jobs were making ends meet, and technically, nothing was wrong.

So then why did this pit constantly reside in Lily's belly?

Did she want to tell her sister that last part? Or should she just concentrate on the positive?

"Things are good. Physical therapy is going really well for Allen. Amelia is driving me nuts one second and then the sweetest thing the next. Not much to report," Lily said, making the decision that she wasn't going to unload on Kate. Lily tugged the coat she'd slipped on as she'd escaped out the door a little tighter. The sun was out, but it was still a chilly November afternoon.

"Uh huh," Kate said in a way that made Lily pause.

"What do you mean *uh huh?*" Lily asked.

"Well, for starters, that pause before you said anything. You were sifting through your life, trying to decide what to tell me. You decided to give me the abbreviated version, right?" Kate said, causing Lily to purse her lips. Was she really that easy to read?

"What's really going on, Lil?" Kate asked.

"Allen's home. I should be thrilled," Lily said softly.

"But you aren't."

"I am. I really truly am."

"But . . ."

"But Belle." Lily tried to say the name of Allen's nurse without sounding vindictive, but she wasn't sure she accomplished it.

"Yeah," Kate said, telling Lily she didn't need to know any

more. Lily was sure her sister, heck any woman, could imagine how fun it would be to live with a woman who wasn't only beautiful but whose sole job was to take care of her husband.

"And if she weren't so . . . it drives me nuts that I can't quite put my finger on it. She doesn't overtly flirt. I mean, she whispers in his ear, which isn't exactly professional. But I've asked Allen what she says and its always totally mundane stuff. Like asking him if he really wants the blanket I gave him or if he wants Amelia out of the room."

"But you feel like she's undermining you?" Kate tried to understand.

"Yes . . . but no. I don't know. It's just . . . she's always there. Always. And she wakes up so put together and caters to Allen's every need. I tell myself it's her job, but then she'll give him a look when he isn't looking. I swear she wants him, Kate. And then I feel crazy because maybe it's all me. I'm so scared of losing him, everything is a threat."

"Does she do her job well?" Kate asked.

"According to Allen, yeah."

"According to you?"

"She doesn't work with me."

"Lily," Kate warned.

"I don't know. I feel like there were probably way more qualified candidates, but this one has the appearance of Allen's dream girl. It makes me wonder if that was the reason Gretchen hired her."

"One, *you* are Allen's dream girl. And two, if anyone would be so horrible, it would be your mother-in-law," Kate said.

Lily conceded, on both points. Even though it was harder to do on the former. Lily opened her mouth.

"I know you're going to say Belle looks like all the girls from Allen's past. But you are his present and future. I really don't think you have anything to worry about on that front."

Lily wished she could be so sure.

"But Belle isn't the whole of it," Kate said, and Lily wished for a second that her sister didn't know her quite so well.

"Eggshells. I'm just so sick of them," Lily said, knowing she didn't need to explain any more. She didn't have to tell Kate that she was scared to talk about anything real or even anything small with Allen.

"Still?" Kate asked.

"Mm hmm," Lily responded. "It's just—"

"Scary," Kate finished for her.

"The last time we tried to really communicate, it didn't exactly change anything," Lily said.

"You had that one conversation," Kate said, and Lily nodded even though her sister couldn't see her. Yes, they'd had one conversation almost a month ago that had dug slightly beneath the surface of their relationship. It had been good, but it hadn't been enough. They needed more. But Lily wasn't sure how to do it.

"Now Allen is home," Kate said.

He was. And that helped with everyday communication, but they needed to burrow to the roots of their problems. Could they get there?

"He's only home because you got off your butt and you fought."

That was true.

"When did you stop fighting?" Kate asked.

Lily stilled. *Oh*. Lily had stopped fighting. She hadn't even realized that was what she had done until Kate had said so. When *had* she stopped fighting? She knew her answer immediately.

"When it felt like if I fought, I would lose," Lily said. "It was easier when he was in Alabama because it felt like there was nothing to lose, but now . . . I have everything, Kate. Allen is living in our home. I can't lose that."

"So what do you feel like you'd like to talk about with Allen? If you could?" Kate asked.

That was easy. "I want to know if he's really happy here. Or if he wishes he stayed in Alabama. I want to ask him if *I'm* the reason why he hides out in his room. Even though he told me it wasn't me, it still feels like it is. And I want to ask him why he stopped kissing me." Lily said the last words so softly, she wasn't sure her sister had heard them. "I mean, I get Allen's physical limitations make our love life challenging," Lily said, disclosing as much as she was comfortable sharing. "But he could kiss me."

Kate was quiet for a minute, maybe more, giving Lily a lot of time with her thoughts. Lily hadn't realized just how much it hurt her that Allen kept a wall between them. He seemed to be keeping Lily at least an arm's length away when it came to any type of physical affection. There were certain husbandly roles that Allen could no longer fulfill, and Lily had known things were going to be different after the accident. But she'd assumed they'd find different ways to connect physically. Instead, Allen had completely pushed her away in that respect.

"You need to ask him those questions," Kate finally said.

Lily knew that she did. But when? When would she know that speaking from her heart wouldn't send Allen right back to Alabama with Belle and Gretchen? She sighed.

"What are you thinking, Lil?" Kate asked.

"I'm thinking I'm scared, but you're right." Lily shivered against the fence. She needed to go back inside soon.

"And you don't know when you should broach the subject?" Kate asked.

"Yeah." Lily sighed again and then closed her eyes. How wonderful would it be to just wish for things to be better and then have her wish come true? But wishes didn't work like that. Lots of hard work came before any wish came true.

"Whatever you decide, Lil, I'm here."

"I know," Lily said, feeling an overwhelming gratitude for her sister.

"But I would say something sooner rather than later."

Lily knew that her sister's advice was right on the money.

"When is Belle's next day off?" Kate asked.

"She gets a half day on Wednesdays," Lily replied.

"How about this? I'll come take over for you with the kids on Wednesday."

"I can't ask you to do that."

"You didn't. I'm offering."

Lily smiled. Her sister was a bit bossy. In the best kind of way.

"I'm sure Gen will be more than happy to give me the time off from the salon. I'll come watch the girls at Gen's, and you go home and make a dinner for you and your man. Then you talk. Because you have to, Lil. I can see this is slowly killing you."

The not knowing really was. But would Lily be ready to confront Allen by Wednesday?

"How about—?" Lily began, but Kate cut her off.

"I know next Sunday you wouldn't have all the girls, which might make it easier. But that just gives you more time to chicken out. This isn't the time to be fearful, Sister."

Lily knew Kate was right.

"Fine," Lily gave in as she stood and started for her backdoor. "And Kate?"

"Yeah?" Kate said, her smile easy to be heard, even over the phone.

"Thanks."

"What are sisters for?"

ALLEN HAD BEEN SURPRISED to hear Lily's car come up the driveway hours before she would typically be home.

"Where's Amelia?" Allen asked when Lily came in the house without their daughter but with bags of takeout from his favorite Thai restaurant.

"She's with Kate," Lily said, setting the bags down on the kitchen table. The only advice of Kate's she hadn't taken was the part where Lily made the meal. A special meal hadn't ended up very well for the two of them last time.

"Oh," Allen said, suddenly realizing why Lily was home early.

"I think we need to talk, Allen," Lily said as she patted the spot next to where she'd taken a seat at their table.

"I figured that. Is the food to butter me up?" he asked, his voice monotone and his facial expression unreadable.

"As long as it's working," Lily said with a smirk, hoping to start things off on the right foot with a little bit of fun.

"Do you have any Panang curry in there?" Allen asked as he dug into the bags.

Lily nodded.

"Then so far, so good." Allen cracked a smile, and Lily laughed, feeling hopeful about her relationship with her husband and having the confidence to move on in the conversation.

"I've got some questions I'd really like answered. I'm guessing you have a few for me too?" Lily felt that wasn't too much of a long shot. If she was holding back on asking Allen things that needed to be asked, Allen was probably doing the same, right?

"I'm not sure," Allen said quietly.

"Maybe you'll come up with a few while we're talking." Lily suggested.

Allen nodded.

"But first, food," Lily said with a grin as she got out two plates and began serving them.

Lily put Allen's plate in front of him, and Allen posed with his fork in the air. "Now I'm ready," he said, and Lily loved that Allen was adding to their light tone. He was in this. She could feel it.

"Okay," Lily began.

"Maybe start with an easy one?" Allen suggested. She could see the trepidation on his face.

"Yeah. Of course." Lily paused, meeting her husband's eyes. "Do you wish you'd stayed in Alabama?"

Allen's eyes bugged out as he tried to swallow his food.

Lily ran into the kitchen to grab a glass of water so that Allen could swallow down what he was choking on.

Allen gulped one more time, setting down his glass and his fork before turning to Lily. "That's an easy question?"

Lily shrugged. It was. At least compared to the others.

Allen sat back in his wheelchair and then leaned forward again.

"I'm glad I'm home and here with you, Lily," Allen finally answered.

Okay. So that was good. But why had it taken him so long to answer? Was he unsure? Lily felt her follow-up question might help to get a bit more insight.

"Then why do you stay in our room so much of the day?" Lily asked. "Well, at least whenever I'm around. I know you said you sometimes need a break, but I thought after our last talk you wouldn't be in there so often."

Lily had noticed that when she came home from work, Belle and Allen were often in the living room. But when Lily and

Amelia would go to join them, they'd leave to their respective rooms after just a few minutes of being together. It hurt her to think she was driving her husband away.

Lily blinked hard, willing the tears away. They would help nothing. She then forced a smile on her face as she looked at Allen.

"You have to be honest with me, Lily," Allen said softly as he watched her face.

"Honest?"

"If you want me to answer your questions honestly, you have to show your emotions honestly. I'm not afraid of your tears. I hate them, but I'm not afraid of them," Allen said.

Lily nodded. She could do honest. So she swallowed her fake smile, and Allen nodded.

"And now I'll be candid as well. I didn't mean to keep part of the truth back when we spoke last about me going into our room so much. I really thought it was because of my physical limitations and not wanting to scare the girls with my wheelchair. But since then, I've realized it's more than just that, and I wasn't sure how to tell you. So I just stayed away again."

Lily gave a small shake of her head.

"I know. I should've told you earlier."

"I should've asked. We've both been too scared," Lily admitted.

Allen nodded. "But not anymore?"

Lily felt her lips lift. "Not anymore."

Allen nodded again before he began to speak. "It's hard for me to be out here with you and Amelia." Allen crossed his arms over his chest.

"Hard?" Lily asked. She never imagined this would be his answer.

"Our life before . . . it was so good, Lily. Literally the life of my dreams. And then it was just gone one day. I knew I'd never have it back."

"But we could—"

"We can't, Lily. Not like it was. Notwithstanding my physical limitations, I'm not the same man."

"Do you still love us?" Lily asked.

"With all my heart," Allen responded in an instant. "Lily. I wish I were as good with words as you are. But . . ."

Lily waited as Allen searched for the right words. She could tell he would need time to articulate what he wanted to say.

"I don't blame the accident on you."

Lily's mouth dropped open, her face going slack with disbelief. What?

"It was my fault. I chose to speed. I always chose to speed. I chose to get you that gift that was out of our budget. I chose everything that put me in that hospital bed. And I had never been so angry at myself. I was so full of fury, I didn't know what to do. I couldn't let out the raging storm, but I couldn't keep it in. So I began to punish myself. And the very worst way of punishing myself was to hurt you. To push you so far away that you would never take me back. Because after what I did, I didn't deserve you."

Lily closed her mouth and turned her seat so that she was facing Allen's chair. She tugged on Allen's arm until he did the same. Lily scooted forward until her knees touched his. This was the most intimate position they'd been in in a long time, and it felt just right.

Allen began to speak again. "Telling you it was all your fault was the lowest of my lows. But at the time, it felt like the only thing I could do."

Lily nodded. She didn't exactly understand, but she was trying to imagine what had been going on in Allen's mind.

"Telling you that lie . . . it was the most terrible thing I could imagine saying to you. I knew I'd lost you."

"You never lost me," Lily said as she reached across both herself and Allen to take his hands in her own.

"I don't know why," Allen said as his eyes glistened with tears.

"Because I love you," Lily said softly.

"I know. But I don't know why you love me," Allen said.

"There are about a million reasons," Lily said, "but I'll start with I love you because of the way you look at Amelia. It began at the hospital, and you gave her that same sweet look this morning."

"Really?" Allen asked.

Lily nodded.

"I still do it?"

Lily nodded again. "I know that this has changed you. It has changed us. But the critical things, they're all the same, Allen."

He swallowed.

"You have to stop punishing yourself. Don't keep a wall up between us. Please." Lily didn't know when she'd fallen to her knees, but she had.

"I can't be the same man," Allen said softly as he held on to Lily's hands.

"I don't want the same man, Allen. Believe it or not, I've changed too."

Allen nodded. Lily knew he couldn't deny the changes in her.

"You're stronger than I ever imagined. Strong enough for both of us," Allen said.

"You've been strong enough for both of us plenty of times before. It was my turn."

"Lily," Allen said as he gripped her hands tightly.

"I know this won't change everything. I'm not asking for that.

But we have to talk. I needed to hear what you had to say," she responded.

"I should've said it before. But I was scared if I told you the truth . . . can you ever forgive me?"

Lily slid back up onto her seat. "There's nothing to forgive."

"Oh there's plenty to forgive."

"Not in my book. You went through a terrible trauma. You might wish you had navigated it differently, but you were, in your own way, still trying to do what was best for me."

"Always. But that doesn't change the fact that I hurt you."

"You did."

"So let me apologize, Lil."

Lily nodded. "Okay."

"Lily Andersen. I am so so sorry. Those words feel inadequate for the emotions I'm feeling, the sorrow that overwhelms me. I haven't been fair to you or our daughter. And each time I try to fix things, it just gets worse."

"It's okay," Lily whispered as she squeezed Allen's hand.

"It's not. But I hope one day it will be. I'll work harder," Allen promised.

"So will I," Lily responded quickly.

"We'll talk more."

Lily nodded. That would be necessary.

"And we'll get rid of your nurse?" Lily asked.

Allen barked out a laugh. "Really? Belle is your concern right now?"

"I kind of hate her, Allen. And I hate that I hate her, but I feel like she's another obstacle between us."

"Really? I thought she was taking on the work you didn't want," Allen said.

"What work would that be? Caring for my husband?" Lily said.

"Yeah. It's a lot of work, Lil. I don't want to be a burden."

Lily slid her chair even closer to Allen so that their legs were intertwined.

"*You* could not be a burden," she said, hoping her eyes that were gazing into Allen's were saying as much as her words. "But Belle is."

That same laughter shot out of Allen.

"Okay, she's gone," Allen said, allowing Lily's entire frame to sag in relief. "I should've realized."

Lily shook her head. "I should've said something sooner. And from now on, I will."

"Good," Allen said.

"You'll speak up too?" Lily asked.

Allen nodded.

"Okay," Lily said.

"We're good?" Allen asked, his face missing all of the strain it had been carrying for months. He literally looked years younger.

"Almost," Lily said as she climbed into her husband's lap and gave him the kiss she'd been longing to give.

Allen's body immediately responded, and as he wrapped his arms around her, Lily felt her entire body alight with an all-consuming fire. This was her husband.

CHAPTER TWELVE

"HELLO?" Alexis said into her phone, answering it after just the first ring. It was late, past ten pm, so she'd been hoping the call would be from Dalton. But when her phone screen read "No Caller ID," she knew it wasn't her boyfriend's cellphone. Still, she answered anyway with the small hope that maybe Dalton was calling from one of his restaurant's phones.

There was quiet on the other end, no answer after Alexis's *hello*. But it was obvious someone was on the line, and Alexis was just seconds away from hanging up. This would've been creepy in the light of day, but at ten pm and home alone, it was plain terrifying.

"Did you think this was him?" a female voice finally said.

"Excuse me?" Alexis responded, and then she shook her head at the absurdity of the call. "I think you have the wrong number."

"Is that what he tells you to say?" the woman asked.

What the heck is going on? Alexis began to pull her phone away from her ear. This was what she got for answering an unknown call. She felt like she'd entered the twilight zone and, honestly, she was done with it. She didn't want any part of this prank.

"Dalton's good at covering his tracks. I have to give him that," the woman said before Alexis could hang up.

Alexis froze. *What?*

"Do you know who I am?" the woman asked.

At this point Alexis was so confused, she wasn't even sure she knew who she was. But the woman knew Dalton's name and Alexis's number. Was this someone Alexis knew?

"I'll give you the benefit of the doubt that you didn't know what you were doing. But could you really be stupid enough not to know about me?" the woman asked.

Suddenly Alexis felt anger bubble up within her. Who was this woman? How did she know about Dalton? And where did she get off offending Alexis?

Suddenly it hit her with complete clarity. This was Dalton's ex-wife. He had warned Alexis that she was a bit unstable, but this phone call was proving she was more than just a *bit* off.

"Nina?" Alexis said the name of Dalton's ex to see if she'd get a reaction.

"So you do know about me."

Okay, so this was Dalton's ex. At least Alexis knew who she was dealing with. But how had Nina gotten her number?

Suddenly the line between them was filled with hysterical sobs. They were so loud and felt like they were all around Alexis, she wondered to herself if maybe she'd broken down. But Alexis got a grip and quickly realized she wasn't crying at all. She was still angry. The crying was coming from Nina.

"He said they'd stop. He just needed another project, and then they would stop."

What would stop? Alexis was curious, but she decided not to ask Nina any questions because it would be better to get her information from a person who was actually on their rocker.

"So we invested in another restaurant. But I should've known. The late nights. The calls in his office. It's all the same." Nina's sobs had suddenly disappeared, and she was back to spitting out her words.

This was insane. Alexis should just get off the call.

"How can you sleep at night? Knowing you're with a married man." Nina said.

Alexis felt her blood run cold. *What had she said?*

"Dalton divorced you," Alexis said, her first words in a long time.

Nina's laugh sounded maniacal. She had lost it. Officially.

"We are very much still married," Nina said, and then her voice was gone.

Alexis really thought about hanging up. Why was she entertaining a crazy woman? But the tiniest part of Alexis wondered if there was any truth to what Nina was saying. And that tiny part kept her on the line, waiting for Nina to return.

"Check your text messages," Nina said when she came back on the line.

Why not? She'd already stayed on the call. Might as well follow the unstable woman's instructions as well.

Alexis opened her phone and saw an unread message from a number she didn't recognize. She opened the message to see a photo. A beautiful blonde woman leaning back on a bed, her head right next to a nightstand. On the nightstand were a pair of reading glasses. Alexis immediately recognized them as the ones Dalton wore.

But any number of people could have those, right? Then Alexis saw the book next to them. The book Dalton had just told her the evening before that he'd been reading.

But that could be another coincidence, right? Dalton had never given her a reason not to trust him.

"You don't believe me," Nina said.

Of course Alexis didn't. Why should she?

"He's called you from this unavailable number before, right? This is our home phone. The phone he shares with me, his wife," Nina said.

Alexis felt nothing. She'd only ever gotten calls from Dalton's cell. Nina was wrong.

"Oh, he hasn't called you from here. He's gotten smarter," Nina said when Alexis kept quiet. "What about this one?"

Alexis heard her call waiting tone and saw that a call was coming in from Dalton. A FaceTime request.

Alexis suddenly felt a small squeeze on her heart. This could all just be coincidence too. Or maybe not. Nina was nuts. Who knew what she could be orchestrating? Alexis refused to believe Dalton was still married. That much she knew to be true. She trusted Dalton.

Because Alexis didn't want to continue playing Nina's games, she ignored the call.

"Answer the phone, Alexis. Don't you want to know how I know about you? He left his second phone at home, the one he uses to contact you. The idiot. It was easy enough for me to break in and find all of your texts. Did you know he was texting you while I slept right beside him?"

Nope. No. Dalton wouldn't have done that. Not her Dalton. Alexis pushed down the sick feeling that had entered her stomach. There were plenty of explanations for why Nina could have Dalton's phone. Not his second phone, but just his phone. Alexis had to separate the truth from the lies that Nina was trying to get Alexis to believe. Dalton might have needed to see his ex for divorce stuff or even restaurant stuff. He'd told Alexis the separation had been messy because they were still in business together. That was how Nina must've gotten his phone, and she was trying to scare Alexis off. Dalton loved *her*. That much Alexis knew.

"At least you didn't send him any nudes. That makes you a bit classier than the typical trash he goes for."

Alexis huffed. Of course she hadn't sent those kinds of pictures. But Nina misread Alexis's huff and used it as a reason to keep on speaking.

"Oh, did you think you were an original? The first affair?"

Nina's crazy laugh sounded again, and Alexis was done.

"You're his sixth," Nina said loudly.

Alexis physically shook her head. That had to be a lie. No woman would endure six affairs. Especially when Dalton and Nina had only been married for nine years.

"You wouldn't stay with a man who had cheated on you six times," Alexis responded, unsure of why she'd chosen to respond to that statement and not the many others. But Alexis just couldn't believe the lies she was being fed. Now she was only on the call to try to set Nina straight. To let the woman know she couldn't scare Alexis away.

"You would think that, wouldn't you?" Nina's voice went soft, and Alexis almost felt sorry for her. Maybe in her head she really did think that she and Dalton were still together? That thought prompted Alexis's next words.

"I get that you still love him. I would too. Dalton is the best man I've ever met. But you have to let him go." Alexis now hoped she could help Nina. Wow, had this call taken a lot of twists and turns. But Alexis hoped this was the last one.

"Have you met his parents?" Nina asked.

Okay, one more turn. But Alexis figured she should take it with Nina. Maybe they could go back to helping Nina let Dalton go.

But no, Alexis hadn't met Dalton's parents. However, she would soon. Dalton had promised he'd have time for them to all get together sometime during the holidays. The restaurant opening had just been so intensely busy.

"His brothers? Their wives? Their kids? His friends? His coworkers? Have you been to the restaurant?" Nina asked, reminding Alexis of a machine gun.

Alexis hadn't. Again, Dalton was busy. And the last one was Nina's fault. Dalton said Nina would get territorial if she heard that Alexis had been there. Dalton was going to tell Nina about them soon so that Alexis could go to the restaurant. Wait, was this what this was about? Had Dalton told Nina he was dating Alexis, and she'd come unhinged?

"Have you ever been to his home?" Nina asked.

Alexis swallowed.

She hadn't.

But that wasn't a big deal. She always worked late, and Dalton didn't want her riding the ferry alone at night. He always came to her.

"Sent you pictures of him at home?" Nina asked.

He hadn't. But that was because he spent the majority of his day at the restaurant. She'd been sent pictures from there.

"Does he have to get off your calls quickly? Even though it's one am?" Nina asked.

He did. But Dalton got hit with tiredness fast. He worked hard. It made sense.

"Have you ever heard a woman in the background of your calls?

That was the TV.

"Have you ever FaceTimed him while he was at home?" Nina asked.

"Yes," Alexis blurted out. "Yes I have!"

There. She had Nina. It wasn't often, but sometimes Alexis just wanted to see his face, say goodnight to a face instead of a voice. So Dalton would FaceTime her.

Alexis's call waiting beeped again.

Dalton. Again.

"Answer the call, Alexis."

"You say you have his phone. Why would I answer it?"

"Do you want to know the truth?" Nina asked softly.

For some reason, it was that quiet question that moved Alexis. She closed her eyes before pressing the button to take the FaceTime call.

Alexis's phone screen filled with the blonde woman sitting in an office chair. Dalton's chair.

"Does he call you from here?" Nina asked.

Nina moved the phone so that she no longer filled the screen and then scanned the room. The room Alexis knew well.

"If it was always so late when he was speaking with you, why was he never in his bed? Wasn't he always here?"

Alexis didn't know about every call, but for every FaceTime, he had been. But Alexis couldn't believe Nina. The woman was crazy . . . right? She was. Alexis had to believe in her boyfriend.

"Why are you in Dalton's house?" Alexis asked, suddenly feeling angry again. There had to be an explanation for why Nina was there. Dalton's life was still entwined with his ex. She could've arranged this to mess with Alexis's mind and Dalton's new relationship.

Nina turned the camera to film Dalton's desk, a sight she'd been shown often. But Alexis immediately noticed a difference.

"That picture," Alexis said quietly. She had never seen that picture before. The frame, all of it, had never been there.

"I'm guessing it isn't here when you FaceTime?" Nina asked as she zoomed in on a photo of Nina and Dalton kissing.

Alexis felt her stomach turn.

But Nina could've just put the picture on Dalton's desk. When she somehow broke into his house and somehow got ahold of his phone.

Nina stood up, taking the shaky FaceTime call with her out the door of the office to spaces Alexis had never seen.

The hall Nina entered was lined with photos. Pictures of men who looked a lot like Dalton, she was guessing his brothers, and other family filled the screen. Between each and every picture of relatives were photos of just Nina and Dalton.

Maybe Dalton hadn't had time to redecorate since his divorce? He was really busy.

Alexis tried to swallow past the lump in her throat. But was he really that busy?

Nina paused in front of an open doorway. "And this is our bedroom," Nina said as she let the phone zero in on the bed.

Alexis felt her stomach clench. She was going to be sick.

Nina finally moved on, going through a bathroom with skin and hair products on the counter that obviously belonged to both a male *and* a female. Then she stopped in the closet.

"Recognize this?" Nina asked as she held up a shirt Dalton often wore. Then she turned to the other side of the closet. It was full of women's clothes. Jam packed. Like it would've taken a full day of moving just to get all those clothes in.

"I'm going to text you the number of his real phone. The one he gives to his wife, his friends and family. The people he isn't hiding in his life. Call it. I'll teach you how to block your number. He'll assume the call is from me because the calls from the house are always blocked. See how he answers. See if it's the way he would answer his ex-wife's call."

Alexis felt her eyes swim with tears. This couldn't be real. This woman had to be lying.

And then the screen went black.

A text came through from Dalton's phone with a phone number and instructions.

Alexis's entire body sagged against her couch. This couldn't be true. It couldn't. Dalton loved her and only her. He'd have an explanation. Wouldn't he?

But did he really have another phone? Would he answer?

Even if he did, it wouldn't prove anything. It could always be the phone at one of his restaurants.

But the clothes and the pictures and . . .

Alexis had to call. She had to see if Dalton answered. Even if it was just so he could reassure her that this was all a hoax. Nina had done this all to break them up because she couldn't let Dalton go. Alexis had to call.

She followed Nina's directions and let the phone ring.

"Hey baby," Dalton's soothing voice answered, and Alexis almost responded. Until she remembered how she was calling. Her number was blocked. She was calling a number she'd never called before. Dalton couldn't know it was Alexis who had called him.

"I know I'm late and you're mad. But I'll be home soon, I promise. I just have this final paperwork to finish up, and then I'll make it up to you. A backrub? I love you, baby. Nina?"

Alexis dropped her phone.

"Nina?" Dalton said again, and Alexis had to turn off the call. She couldn't hear him say it again.

Her entire body went hot and then cold. Her muscles ached from how still she'd been holding herself.

Dalton. Her Dalton.

No. Nina's Dalton.

And with that revelation, Alexis ran to the bathroom and fell over the toilet.

———

ALEXIS HAD SOMEHOW AWOKEN that next morning and every morning after for four days. Life had moved on. Well, somewhat. Alexis had yet to speak to or text Dalton since that night. Four days and nights of no contact, and it was only the night before that Dalton had started leaving messages that he was worried about her. After four days. How had she thought he'd been attentive? Looking back on what they'd had with new, clearer vision, Alexis saw that Dalton had often neglected her during the days that he hadn't been able to come see her. But when he was with her, he'd be so invested that Alexis never doubted his true devotion to her. She could now see that all of the times he'd put her off, been too busy, or been unavailable, it had been because he was focusing on his wife and his real life.

And during all of his lies, Alexis had been busy making up excuse after excuse for him. That was one of the hardest parts to swallow. Dalton hadn't needed to cover up anything. Alexis, in her need to please, had done it all for him.

Her stomach churned again.

Her text tone went off once more, and she knew in her gut it was Dalton. Alexis fought the urge she still felt to run at his beck and call. Why?

Alexis finished getting ready for the day and then finally went to her phone. Sure enough, Dalton had texted thirty minutes before.

Alexis. Please get back to me. I'm worried about you. Please. If I don't hear from you by tonight, I'm coming out to Whisling.

That was enough to get Alexis's fingers moving across her phone's keyboard. The last thing she wanted was to encounter her soon-to-be ex.

I'm fine. Don't come to the island. I need space.

Is it something I've done? Please talk to me. I miss you.

Was it something he'd done? Um, yeah. But Alexis didn't have the time or patience to deal with lying, cheating Dalton. It would've been bad enough if he'd cheated on her. But Alexis had realized, while retching into the toilet that first night, that she was the other woman. He had made her the other woman.

I need time. Was the only text Alexis could manage.

I get it. I'm here for you. I love you.

Alexis wanted to scream and shout and rail at the man who had taken her love and trust and shattered it into itty bitty pieces. But that would take seeing him. And Alexis wasn't sure if she was ready to see him. Now or ever. Maybe she could just slip out of his life. Heaven knew he had enough in it without her.

The PI just got back to me. Check your email. Love you, baby.

Alexis stared at her phone and those last three words. How could he lie to her like that? How was it so easy for him to lead a double life?

Her thoughts began to spiral out of control, and Alexis knew they would drive her wild if she just sat there and reflected.

Alexis's actions during the last four days had felt jerky and out of place. She would move from one thing to the next quickly so that she didn't have to deal with her emotions and over-whelming concerns. Her motivation for moving was often just so she didn't think. This was another moment like that. She had to *do* something. So she checked her email. Typically, reading an email like the one awaiting her from the PI would've taken Alexis hours, if not days, to build up the courage to open. But Alexis no longer cared about much. Why not find out if yet another man in her life was a terrible person? The sooner Alexis got it over with, the better.

Alexis quickly scanned through the email from the PI. In past communication, he'd already given Alexis background info on her dad. Things she'd never known like his real name, birth date, and nationalities. He'd even sent her a picture of the dark haired enigma.

But this email was different. The PI had spoken to Alexis's dad.

Alexis's phone dropped to the couch after reading the contents of the email.

Her father wanted to meet her. In the PI's words, Alexis's father was thrilled to know his daughter had reached out and wanted to meet at her earliest available time.

Alexis felt a true smile light up her face. The first she'd felt since that awful night. Her dad wanted to meet her.

She quickly typed back a message to the PI, who answered immediately with Alexis's dad's phone number.

The PI had ended his latest email with the words, *He said to call or text as soon as possible. His exact words were, "I can't believe I get a chance with my child."*

Alexis worked on ridding herself of the darkness that had followed every part of her life for the last four days. Her father wanted to get to know her. Alexis. This was big news. Huge. Bigger than any cheating bastard.

Alexis swallowed as she looked at the number. A Seattle area code. The man who was half of her had been so close for so long. So why had he stayed away? Was that her mom's fault? Maybe. Who knew, since Margie wouldn't talk about the man. Suddenly Alexis remembered all of her own years living in the city. Had Alexis ever seen him in passing? Sure, Seattle was a big place, but she'd lived there for years.

Years. That was the time she'd missed with the man who was half of her. Had he just been waiting to meet her as well? She knew he'd known about her. Her mom had told her that much. But what else did he know? Why hadn't he reached out?

Alexis drew in a deep breath. There was only one way to get answers to her questions, and she held the key in her hand. His phone number. Should she call him? That was a quick nope. She would just stumble over her words. There was no way she could have a coherent conversation. So it had to be a text. Yes. A text she could compose and recompose until it was just right.

She hemmed and hawed over what to write. Nothing seemed adequate and yet everything seemed to be too much.

After twenty minutes of debating and rewriting, Alexis finally had a text composed.

Hi. This is Alexis.

Alexis pushed send before she could second guess herself yet again. It wasn't brilliant, but it would get the job done. It would get a conversation going.

Alexis? The response was immediately followed by, *I can't believe it's you.*

Ditto.

Yeah. I'm kind of feeling the same way.

I bet. I'm sure you have a lot of questions.

That was the understatement of a lifetime, but she didn't want to overwhelm the man.

Yeah. A few.

Was that a lie? No. Because she would start with just a few of her questions. Okay, it was kind of a lie. But what was she supposed to say? She guessed she could've just texted *Yeah.* That probably would've been better. But it was too late now. And Alexis wasn't going to take it back. Oh dear. She needed to stop fretting.

We should meet up and talk. I owe you this discussion in person.

That was good. And he did owe her. Probably more than just one discussion. But Alexis wasn't going to point that out. At least not yet.

She bit her lip as she nervously decided what she wanted out of all of this for herself. In recent days, she had imagined coming to this point with Dalton by her side. But that wasn't the case. And Alexis wasn't going to let Dalton ruin this moment for her. She was a grown, capable woman. She could do this.

I'm free whenever you are.

That was both a grown and capable message.

Lunch today?

Oh wow. That she had not been expecting. Probably not lunch today. Today. As in hours away.

But then Alexis began to wonder *why not*. She could get into Seattle in the next hour or so. She was already ready; she just needed to hop on a ferry. She might come back to Whisling a couple of hours after her shift at the food truck started, but Bess wouldn't mind covering for her. Not for this. So what was making Alexis hesitate?

She was scared. No, she was petrified. Because one nagging thought kept popping into her mind. Why had her mom kept this man from her for so long? Her mother loved her. Alexis knew that, even if they hadn't been seeing eye to eye recently. Her mother wouldn't have kept a good man away from Alexis. As soon as Alexis had seen Dalton's true colors, she had realized that was why her mom had had so many issues with him. Margie had seen what Alexis hadn't. So was it foolish for Alexis to jump into this new pot of boiling water now? Would she get burned just as badly this second time? This time by her father?

Alexis didn't know. But at this point, she felt like nothing could hurt her more than Dalton had. She was close to numb. If she was going to be hurt again, there was no better time. Alexis knew she could go to her mom and tell her all that had happened. Margie would cradle and love her, but Margie would also do what Margie did best. She would try to protect Alexis. And that would mean keeping her from this man who was the other half of her complexion. Alexis knew she would never have a dad in the traditional sense. The man had been out of her life for too long for that kind of relationship to begin. But maybe they could be friends or at least friendly? Maybe the teenage version of the guy hadn't been worth Margie's or Alexis's time, but he had to have changed in the last nearly forty years. So didn't Alexis owe it to herself to at least meet this man?

Her answer was a resounding yes. She quickly texted back before she could think better of it.

I can do lunch today. Where would you like to meet?

The coordinates to a cute cafe came through on Alexis's phone followed by, *Thank you for this chance, Alexis. I can't wait to meet you.*

Meet her. Okay, that was already more information than she'd ever had about her father. She'd always wondered if he'd been around for her birth before taking off. But he'd never met her. Why?

That was a question she'd get the answer to soon. But Alexis vowed to be smart. She'd given her heart to Dalton too easily. She wouldn't do that for any man, even her father, again. She'd take the ferry, drive to the café, and have a nice lunch with a man who had given her half of her DNA. But she'd do it all with a shield firmly in place.

Those first two steps of Alexis's plan flew by, and before Alexis knew it, she was parking in the lot of the cute café. Her hands began to shake as she put her car in park. She was about to meet her dad. *Oh my gosh.*

Thankfully, the severity of the moment hadn't hit her until that instant. Alexis wasn't sure she would've been able to drive otherwise.

But even as her heart ramped up in excitement, so much of this felt wrong. Alexis shouldn't be doing this alone. She was supposed to do this with Dalton. She shouldn't be hiding this meeting from her mother. Was she making a huge mistake?

Alexis gripped her hands together to calm the shaking and then breathed in and out the way her instructor, the one time she'd taken yoga, had told her to do. Maybe this was a huge mistake. But she was here. She'd made her decision, and it was a chance Alexis had to take.

She told herself all she had to do was move one foot at a

time. So she did. Out of her car. Across the parking lot. Into the café. She paused just outside of the front door. This was her last chance to back out. It had all happened so fast. Should she slow down? Leave and tell her father she needed a few more days, weeks, maybe months?

Alexis shook her head. Nope. She was here. She was going to do this. She had to do this.

She walked in and scanned the café and saw only one man sitting alone. A man who looked just like the picture she'd been sent.

The man looked up and met Alexis's eyes, and for the first time in her life, she stared into a pair of deep blue eyes that looked exactly like her own.

Okay. This was weird.

The man waved, so Alexis wound her way through the restaurant and sat across from him. Fortunately, her father made no move to physically touch her, and for that, Alexis was immensely grateful.

"Breathe, Alexis," her father said.

So Alexis did. She hadn't realized she'd been holding it for so long, and some of her lightheadedness disappeared when she did.

"Are you okay?" he asked.

Alexis nodded. Or at least she would be. Hopefully.

"I'm not sure what you know about me," the near stranger across from her said. Alexis had felt a connection when she'd seen his eyes, but then nothing. Shouldn't she be feeling more? Who knew?

Wait, he'd said something Alexis had wanted to respond to. Oh right. He wasn't sure what Alexis knew about him.

"Nothing," Alexis supplied through her jumble of thoughts.

"Okay. So I guess we start at the basics?" he asked.

Alexis nodded, even though the PI had given her a few of

them. Alexis wanted to hear it from this man. Her father. Was she really sitting across the table from her father?

"I'm Roger Banks. I grew up on Whisling with your mom, but my family moved during the middle of my senior year."

Alexis nodded. The math was right. Roger was a year older than Margie, and Alexis's mom had had her the summer between her junior and senior years.

"After that, I bounced around a lot. My family wasn't very well off, so I skipped the whole college step. I found jobs here and there and led a pretty vagabond lifestyle for most of my life."

Roger met her eyes, and Alexis felt a need to respond in some way. But she wasn't sure how to, so she just nodded again.

"But Seattle was always home base. I lived here for some of the eighties, most of the nineties, half of the two-thousands, and then I've been here ever since 2011."

Alexis nodded again. But if he lived in Seattle, why had he never come back to Whisling? Alexis decided to wait on that question and ask another that had come up during his explanation.

"Where's your family now?" Alexis asked.

"Here. In the city. Well, what's left of it. My mom passed about ten years ago, and my little brother died a few years after that."

"I'm sorry," Alexis said immediately.

Roger shrugged. "Life is hard."

Alexis swallowed as Roger went on. "My dad and I went into business together a few years back, so we work together and now we live together too."

Alexis wanted to ask if that was all the family he had, but it felt rude and almost like she was prying. Was she allowed to pry?

"No wife and kids. Is that what you were wanting to ask next?" Roger supplied.

Was it? Alexis guessed she would've gotten to that eventually. But did Roger have more kids like her? Without the wife or responsibility? She figured now wasn't the time to ask.

"Why did you leave Whisling?" Alexis asked. Although the question she really wanted to ask was, *Why did you leave me?* But Alexis was nowhere near ready for that.

"Your mom," Roger said, and Alexis's stomach dropped for her mother's sake. "My parents thought she was trying to rope me to her for life. They never really liked her. You have to remember, that was a really different time. Girls who got pregnant, it was their fault."

Alexis fought the urge to roll her eyes, and then she was hit with intense sadness. This wasn't just an anti-feminist moment she was hearing about. This was her mother's life. Margie had been blamed for getting pregnant. Even though Roger was very much just as involved.

"It wasn't right, but it was what happened. Mom and Dad told me we were going. Never coming back. And I was never very good at standing up to my parents."

"So you left," Alexis said, her heart aching for her mother. Poor Margie.

"In my defense, I was a kid. Barely seventeen, and my parents knew I couldn't handle being what Margie needed. Raising a kid."

"My mom was only sixteen," Alexis muttered, reminding Roger they had both been kids, but one of them had stepped up.

"I know." Roger shook his head. "If I could go back and change things . . ."

Roger didn't finish that sentence, and Alexis wished he would. How would he have changed things? Would he have stayed? Judging by the red that had creeped into his cheeks,

Alexis was doubting it. If Roger could change the past, he would've only ensured Margie never got pregnant. Made sure that Alexis didn't exist.

Margie had had a rough time of it, but she had never, not once, made Alexis feel like she would've changed the past to alter Alexis's existence. Even though she hated Roger with every part of her. On the contrary, Margie had only ever said that Alexis was the greatest blessing in her life. Yet Roger had implied he would've done the very thing Margie wouldn't have in less than ten minutes of conversation.

"I didn't mean . . ." Roger began.

Alexis put up her hand. Nothing he could say in that moment would make things better. It was best to just move on.

"Your mom didn't want me around anyway," Roger resumed, and Alexis let him continue. Even if she didn't like the responses, these were the questions she wanted to have answered. The ones she'd yearned to ask all her life but never had the chance.

"She knew I was bad news. I didn't hang with the 'in' crowd, if you know what I mean. I was into some," Roger looked at Alexis as if judging her age and then said, "not so legal activities."

Great. So her father wished she'd never been born and had been, maybe still was, a criminal. Alexis felt her heart rate ramping up. She was grateful she'd come into this with low expectations because even they'd been disappointed.

"So Mom asked you to stay away from me?" Alexis asked. The numbness from Dalton's betrayal was beginning to slip, and Alexis found herself hoping that she'd been right, at least in this.

"She yelled at me when I came to tell her we were moving. Told me she didn't want to see or hear from me again," Roger said with a nod.

"And that was it?" Alexis asked. Sure, Margie would've

railed at him. She was sixteen and pregnant and probably scared to death. Roger, as a grown man now, had taken the word of a sixteen-year-old girl and stayed away for thirty plus years?

"I'm glad we're meeting now. It's better this way anyway, right? Your mom raised you well, and now we can be . . ." Roger's voice trailed off.

Yeah, what could we be, oh wise father?

"You're saying you're glad that you missed all of my growing up years? The years where I wished and hoped that my father would appear and say that he, I don't know, cared about me?" Alexis said words she would've been too scared to utter had the rest of her world not just imploded. She was beyond caring about anything, especially what this selfish man thought.

"Um, no. I mean, I should've been there for you. But I couldn't. Your mom—"

"Was sixteen. *Sixteen,*" Alexis knew her voice was getting too loud for the café and noticed that eyes were looking in her direction. But she didn't give a flying goose.

"I was seventeen."

"Yeah, when she said those words. But what about when you were eighteen, twenty, twenty-five, thirty, forty? Did you ever think to check up on me then?"

Roger's face was blank, telling Alexis all she needed to know.

"I looked for you," Alexis said, the memories flooding back of a twelve-year-old girl desperately searching for her father in a world before social media. "I went to the library to try to access old newspapers on the island. I checked the yellow pages. I was twelve, and I did more to look for you than you ever did for me."

"I didn't know if you'd want to see me. I'm not rich or—"

"Do you think any little girl cares about that?" Alexis said, standing. She was done with this man. Her mother had been right. Yet again. And all Alexis wanted was to see the woman who she'd been so incredibly disrespectful to, who she knew would take her back with open arms. Because her mother loved her. The way a parent should. The way Roger would never be able to.

"Mom found out and made me promise to never try again. That I was better off not finding you. And I listened to her for over twenty years. I should've kept listening," Alexis said as she turned and walked out of the café.

Alexis wasn't sure what she expected to happen as she walked away. Maybe Roger running after her? Maybe the café-goers giving her a standing ovation? What she hadn't expected was the companionship of complete silence as she walked to the door and let herself out.

In four days, Alexis had lost two men who were never really hers to begin with. She tried to ignore the stabbing pain in her heart. She'd been rejected twice. Not loved enough . . . twice. And it was only when the world came crashing down around her that Alexis knew the one place she needed to be. With her mom.

CHAPTER THIRTEEN

"GO PEARLY!" Kathryn, Olivia's mother, yelled from where she sat on the metal bleachers next to Olivia.

Olivia watched as Pearl stuck her foot out for the ball and stole it away from the defensive player on the opposite team. She then got control of it before taking a shot on the goal.

Her shot went a bit wide, and by the drop of her shoulders, it was easy to see Pearl's disappointment.

"That's the way to be aggressive, Pearl!" Dean, Pearl's coach, called out. "You'll get it next time."

With those few words, Pearl beamed and ran down the field to help her teammates get possession of the ball that was going towards their goal again.

"He's a good coach," Kathryn said.

Olivia nodded. Dean was the literal best when it came to her girls. Not only did he know what to say as he was coaching Pearl, he knew what to say when they were tired after swimming or when Rachel was frustrated by her school work.

"Are you guys talking about Dean?" Elsa, the mom of one of Pearl's teammates, asked as she slid down from her bench behind them to sit right next to Olivia. Elsa began to shed off the jacket she wore over her bust-boosting tank top. Olivia wasn't sure how her ample breasts were able to say in the very little fabric supporting them, but they were. Thank goodness, since the nine-year-olds around them really didn't need that kind of eyeful.

Olivia also wasn't quite sure why Elsa was taking off said jacket. Although they were in the indoor soccer arena, it was still December and jackets were very much needed since it couldn't be more than sixty degrees.

"Aren't we so lucky he's following the girls?" Elsa asked, and Olivia nodded.

This was Dean's second year coaching Pearl through her community soccer league. Last year's team was so good that the girls and parents alike wanted the team to continue playing after the less competitive community season, so they'd created a club team. Dean had been gracious enough to continue coaching, even though the commitment meant that he would now be coaching nine-year-old girls' soccer nearly year-round.

"I can't help but think he has a bit of an ulterior motive," Elsa said.

Olivia looked at the other woman with raised eyebrows.

"Ulterior motive?" Kathryn asked the question Olivia had been thinking.

"Well, we do have quite a few attractive single moms on the team. All the eye candy any single man could want," Elsa said.

Olivia's eyebrows only went higher. Seriously? Did Elsa think that was why Dean was coaching? Then she didn't know Dean and his kind-hearted soul at all.

"But I'm thinking he's going to need a bit of a push to actually ask any of us out. He's gone out with so many of the other women on the island, but I think he's worried about hurting his relationships with the girls if he dates us moms. But we're all big girls, right? We would always put our girls over a man. Even one as beautiful as this one."

Elsa's eyes lit up with appreciation as she looked over at Dean, who was crouching so that he could talk to one of the girls who sat on the bench.

"I think I may have to give our Deany a push. Let him know that I'm up for any kind of fun he's up for," Elsa said with a grin.

Olivia swore she threw up in her mouth a bit.

"Oh, right," Kathryn said quietly, looking very sorry that she'd asked Elsa to elaborate. Olivia was sorry as well. She closed her eyes, willing the last moments of conversation to disappear from her memory.

"You got it, Pearly," Kathryn called out, pulling Olivia's attention back to the field. Pearl had the ball again, and she was racing with it down the field. Dean tried to give all the girls playing time in different positions, but he often allowed Pearl to end the game as a forward since she seemed to still have so much energy, even after nearly a whole game of running.

Olivia watched as Pearl appraised the goal and then took her shot. This time the ball hit the back of the net, and Pearl jumped with joy.

"Yes, Pearl!" Olivia cheered along with all the other fans in the stands.

"Just like a pro, Pearly girl!" Dean cheered.

Olivia noticed how Pearl's smile somehow grew wider with her Coach's praise.

Olivia had to admit the shot had looked quite pro-like. Especially for a nine-year-old.

The rest of the game went by quickly with no more goals scored. Except in Elsa's imagination, as she told Olivia just how she planned on snagging the attention of their daughters' coach. Olivia was more than glad to get up and walk away from the bleachers as soon as the game was over.

"That woman is quite the piece of work," Kathryn said as Olivia's dad joined the two of them. He and Rachel liked to watch the game standing up, so they would leave the women as soon as kick off happened and stand closer to the sidelines.

"What woman?" Rachel asked, catching her grandma's statement. Of course she had. Rachel never heard words that were spoken just to her, but if it was something Olivia hoped her older daughter would miss, it never happened.

"No one," Olivia said, shooting her mom a look that wasn't necessary because Kathryn already looked apologetic.

Even though they said nothing more, both Kathryn and Olivia watched as Elsa moved past the players and made her way to the coach. Elsa said something which Dean responded to, and then Elsa bent over in loud laughter, and Olivia became really worried for her top. But somehow everything stayed in place.

Elsa said something else, and Dean smiled but shook his head before turning to one of the girls who'd asked him a question. Elsa flipped her long hair and then called out to her daughter before leaving the field.

Oops. Looked like Elsa took her shot and missed the goal. Olivia tried not to be too happy about the turn of events, but that little jealous monster who reared its ugly head whenever Dean was around was pretty dang pleased.

However, her green-eyed companion shouldn't have celebrated too early as Olivia realized that Dean turning Elsa down meant Dean wasn't up for dating the moms of his players. Including Olivia.

A much needed reminder because ever since she'd come out of her melancholy over breaking up with Noah, her heart had quickened anytime Dean was around. She had tried to ignore it, the way she had for so long before Noah, but her emotions must've been unboxed while dating Noah because Olivia no longer felt able to compartmentalize all she felt for Dean. Her heart pattered, her stomach flipped, and she tended to say the most ridiculous things in front of the man whom she'd known for over half her life. She had basically become an enamored idiot, and she'd made it a point to avoid Dean now more than ever.

"I guess Elsa's conquest didn't go according to plan," Kathryn whispered when Rachel ran up to give Dean a high five after a game well-coached. Dean then fell into conversation with Olivia's dad as Rachel went on to give the girls on the team high fives as well. Olivia grinned at the awe-struck faces of the girls because a sixth-grader like Rachel had congratulated them. Olivia needed to be sure to tell her sweet Rachel how wonderful she thought her gesture had been.

"I guess not," Olivia whispered back. "Poor thing."

"Poor thing? More like poor Dean," Kathryn said.

Olivia figured her mother was right, but if anyone understood losing her mind when it came to Dean, it was Olivia. She really hoped she had the sense not to do what Elsa had done, but who knew what next week would bring. Olivia seemed bent on not keeping her dignity when it came to Dean.

"Yeah, I guess," Olivia said as the girls ran to Zia's mom who was giving out after-game treats.

"Did you hear Dean has been dating less?" Kathryn asked.

Olivia shook her head, but she'd assumed so. Even though she'd been avoiding Dean, she hadn't avoided looking out the window each night to see if his car was parked there by eight pm. And Olivia had noticed his car was home every night the whole week. And the week before.

"Do you know what life event of yours coincided with Dean dating less?" Kathryn asked.

Uh oh. Her mother was going to try to play matchmaker. As

if Olivia wasn't already in enough trouble, where Dean was concerned.

"Mother," Olivia warned.

"So you know."

"I can guess by the way you're acting. But I can assure you, Dean's dating or lack thereof has nothing to do with me," Olivia whispered.

But even as she spoke the brave words, Olivia's stomach took flight with butterflies. Could her mom be right?

Olivia hadn't checked for Dean's car right after her breakup. She couldn't. Her mind had been too consumed with Noah. Olivia had truly been heart broken. She hadn't acted heart broken for the sake of her girls, but it had taken time to lick her wounds over losing such a good man. Although, Olivia had to admit, even as she was depressed about Noah, seeing Dean always lifted her spirits. Did that make her a bad person?

"And no, it's not too early to date someone after Noah. You've been broken up for nearly two months."

"That's not what I was thinking," Olivia said, even though her thoughts were right along that line.

"Dean is the right guy for you, Olivia. He always has been. I know it, the girls know it, and I think you know it. You're just scared."

"I just broke up with Noah, Mom."

"Two months isn't just. And besides, you didn't love him."

"But I liked him a lot. And he deserves better than me moving on right away. That's *if* Dean is interested in me, which he's not."

"But you're interested in him," Kathryn said with a beaming grin.

Crap. Olivia had kind of implied that.

"Not right now," Olivia said in defense.

"Is Noah dating anyone new?" Kathryn asked.

Olivia shrugged. They hadn't exactly kept in touch after she broke up with him, and they definitely weren't sharing dating stories.

"So why should it matter to Noah if you're dating someone new?"

Oh. Olivia guessed that made sense, until she found a flaw in her mother's reasoning.

"But Dean is Noah's friend."

Kathryn nodded. "That's true. But if he's a good friend, he'll see you were meant for Dean. Not him."

Would Noah? Olivia doubted it.

"And you can't base your future decisions on a man from your past."

That was actually a good point. Without a single flaw. Why was her mother so right on the money? This conversation would be a whole lot easier if her mom was completely wrong about everything. However, even though Kathryn had made a good point, Olivia wasn't ready to admit that.

"But all of that is neither here nor there," Olivia said, ready to move on from their conversation. Because although two months had been long enough for her to not feel hurt about breaking up with Noah, that time hadn't changed the one big thing that was keeping Dean and Olivia apart.

"And why's that?" Kathryn asked.

"Because Dean isn't into me," Olivia said, and she walked away to round up her girls before her mother could respond. Kathryn stood frozen for a few seconds after Olivia left, then shook her head before joining Olivia's dad and Dean.

Olivia thanked Zia's mom for the snacks and then told her girls it was time to go. Pearl had already dug into her bag of treats and had been kind enough to give Rachel her fruit roll-up.

"I need to say bye to Grandma and Grandpa and Dean,"

Pearl said before running toward where that small group was still gathered.

"Me too," Rachel added, rushing after her sister.

Olivia realized she couldn't very well just stand there, mere feet away from her parents and Dean, without saying anything. That would just be weird. She guessed she'd have to say bye too. But could she get in and out of a conversation with Dean without making a fool of herself? She sure hoped so.

As Olivia slowly walked to her destination, her thoughts turned back to what her mom had said. Kathryn had been right on almost all counts. If Dean asked her out, Olivia would say yes. In a heartbeat. She had fallen in love with Dean soon after her divorce, and she might've always loved Dean, although that wasn't fair to Noah in the least. As much as Olivia felt badly about that, she could honestly say that she hadn't realized her feelings until now. And she'd certainly put her all into her relationship with Noah. That had ended for reasons other than Dean. Things they couldn't have worked around. In the end, she had to believe it was what was best for all of them.

But Kathryn had a specific, big blind spot when it came to her daughter. She believed any man did and should want to date her. But with Dean, Kathryn was wrong. Sure, he'd liked Olivia in high school. But he'd had his chance since. Many chances. And yet here they were. Still friends and neighbors. So Olivia would just have to learn to be content with the arrangement they had. And she was . . . for the most part.

Olivia joined her family and Dean just as Rachel was hugging her grandpa and Pearl her grandma. That left just Dean and Olivia in the circle.

"Thatta boy, Coach," Olivia said as she slugged Dean in the shoulder, making her immediately regret all of her life's decisions. *Thatta boy*? Slugging Dean in the arm? What the what was she doing?

"Thanks," Dean said as he turned his body so that he was facing Olivia. "But the win was all on the girls."

See, she said weird things and he somehow made their conversation coherent. If that didn't prove that she felt everything and he felt nothing, what would? But she could make this better, right? He'd gotten their conversation back on a normal track.

"I think the coach can take a bit of the credit," Olivia said, and then she winked. At Dean. Over a soccer game. Why was her body betraying her like this? She needed to get out of there.

Dean didn't respond verbally, but he suddenly opened his arms.

Olivia didn't know what to do. Oh . . . he was about to hug her. Okay. She could do this. It was a normal thing for friends to hug. Olivia walked into his arms and savored the feeling of being held against the strength of the chest she often dreamed about. She relished the spot for a bit too long but finally stepped away.

"Um, Mom?" Pearl said, and Olivia turned around to see her daughter just behind her, causing Olivia's face to flame. The situation was now obvious to her.

The hug had been for Pearl. Olivia had stolen her daughter's hug. Oh my goodness, Olivia had finally hit rock bottom.

Olivia stepped away, let Pearl get her hug, and then started for the exit. Her daughters would follow eventually.

Olivia heard her text tone go off, and she looked down to see a message from her mother.

Don't worry. Dean was enjoying the hug almost as much as you were.

Olivia just needed to die. Start over in a new body, in a new life. This one was over.

Only when she was outside of the indoor arena and heard the sound of small feet running behind her did Olivia turn around. She gave Pearl a congratulatory hug, and Rachel joined them soon after.

"Mom, why did you hug Dean when he was trying to hug Pearl?" Rachel asked innocently.

Yes, why had she done that? Olivia knew her face was on fire, but thankfully they had left the dome and were outside in the frigid air. Being away from the field meant Dean couldn't see her flaming face and the cold air could cool it down.

"Dean's a good friend. So I thought he wanted to hug me. I didn't see Pearl. Friends hug," Olivia said lamely.

Right. Friends hug. If anyone else questioned her, she'd use that line. It wasn't great, but it wasn't horrible.

"O-kay," Rachel said, still sounding confused as she and Pearl climbed into the back seat. Thankfully Pearl took over the conversation, giving them both a play-by-play of the game they'd just watched until they got home.

As Olivia drove past the house of her friend and neighbor, she decided she was done acting like a fool. She was a grown woman. She could put her feelings for Dean away and not be a complete mess every time she saw him. She could do it. She would do it.

Feeling resolved, Olivia got out of the car and followed her girls up to their front porch. Now, if only she could get rid of her feelings as easily as she could try to hide them. But Olivia had a hunch that these ever-growing feelings for Dean would never go away. And she would just have to live with that.

CHAPTER FOURTEEN

AFTER LUNCH WITH HER DAD, Alexis had had to go right into work. Thank heavens. Because she'd been left with no time for the self-pity party she'd desperately wanted to throw. Work had been her salvation, not only that day but every day after that. Work was the only thing waking her up every day. Literally. Alexis would wake up at noon, get to work by two, and then fall right back asleep after her shift. She knew she needed to talk to someone. Actually acknowledge her pain instead of hiding from it. The hours she slept away wasn't healthy, but it felt like all she could do.

She'd gotten home from work the night of meeting her dad wanting a clean break from all of the mess surrounding her. She started by officially breaking up with Dalton . . . over text. He seemed shocked by the breakup, even though Alexis had already asked him for some time apart. So Alexis assumed Nina hadn't told him about their little talk. A text might've been a wimpy way out of a six-month relationship, and if she'd broken up with anyone else in that same way, she might've felt guilty. But scumbag Dalton didn't even deserve that much consideration. After she told him they were done—she kept the text simple because she wanted no confusion as to what her text meant—Dalton texted back sweet nothings, trying to change her mind. Alexis tried hard to ignore his responses until it all became too much. She just wanted him gone, so she told Dalton why she was breaking up with him. Because the dirt bag was married. It was only then that he really began to freak out because Alexis told him that *Nina* had been the one to tell her the truth. Alexis realized then and there who Dalton cared about more. Not Alexis, the other woman, but his wife. And it was only then that her despair over Dalton gave way to anger.

Fortunately, anger was a whole lot more fun. So after the phone call, she went through her box of memories and rid it of anything to do with Dalton. That cute puppy? Gone. The bag of Hershey kisses she couldn't bear to eat because of their sentimental value? Digested. And the best part was burning each and every card the man had ever sent. Alexis was responsible and kept the small fire within her sink, close to a water source. But watching every piece of Dalton she still had literally burn? That was satisfaction.

In the weeks since Alexis's life had gone to hell, she'd kept everyone she knew and loved at arm's length. She had done a great job hiding her pain. No crying at work. That had been reserved for home. No running to her mom. She'd realized she didn't deserve that kind of comfort after all she'd done.

Alexis *had* been in contact with Rianne over text, so her friend knew the gist of things. She'd tried to get Alexis to come over and commiserate, but Alexis had told her she was fine. She just needed time. So Rianne had respected that. She'd given Alexis the space she craved. But then, even though it had been Alexis's choice, that left her completely alone. What a terrible catastrophe her life had become.

And to be entirely honest, Alexis didn't mind that much. Because she didn't want her dad. She definitely didn't want

Dalton. She didn't even want Rianne. She only wanted one person. A person whom she knew would take her back. But Alexis was having a hard time forgiving herself enough to visit that one person who could start to help her heal. Her mom.

So Alexis continued to work and sleep. Her job had helped her to avoid her pain since it was getting even busier with Stephen and Jana's wedding right around the corner. What used to be seven to eight hour days on the truck were turning into to nine to eleven hours. The longer she worked, the more she talked herself out of going to her mom. Alexis was still processing what had happened. She shouldn't bring her mom into things yet. But deep down, Alexis knew she needed her.

It was now a few nights before the wedding, and Alexis was working late with Bess once again, adding some final touches to the favors: kissing chocolate covered strawberries. Yes, Alexis had to create kissing strawberries while she was still incredibly furious with her ex. It wasn't a great combination.

"Um, Alexis?" Bess asked quietly from her stool. Bess had brought both women stools in the past few days when their hours had gotten longer. She'd said it wasn't good for them to be on their feet for so long each day, and Alexis knew that her own feet were grateful for the reprieve.

"Yes?" Alexis answered as she set down yet another strawberry couple that she had crushed.

"Is that your third destroyed couple of strawberries?" Bess asked.

Alexis nodded.

"Do you want to talk about it?" Bess asked, but Alexis shook her head immediately.

Bess had asked her the same question a few times in the past few weeks but had been as astute as Rianne, giving Alexis time and space to grieve in private. And Alexis still needed that time; she wasn't ready to talk to anyone about what had happened.

Sure, she'd texted Rianne, but she hadn't actually spoken the words out loud.

"Okay," Bess said quietly. Then she added, "Just know that I'm here. And if the wedding stuff gets to be too much, you can always opt out. You didn't sign on for this mess. I did."

Alexis shook her head again. She was grateful for the extra time at work. Heck, she was loving it. Sure, she hadn't known they'd be doing catering events when she'd first started working on the truck, but her light schedule before the wedding prep had begun had seemed too good to be true, especially when it came to the culinary world. Prior to taking the job with Bess, Alexis had assumed that long hours were the norm when working in a kitchen. Besides, Bess was paying her overtime for these extra hours. Basically her dream job had only gotten better right at the time when she needed to work more. So she didn't need Bess feeling guilty that she was overworking her chef when the food truck had been her one salvation.

"I love all of this wedding stuff," Alexis got out because it was at least half true. Alexis loved the cooking part, and that would be most of what they were going to do. The cutesy favors though? That she could leave.

Alexis took another set of chocolate dipped strawberries and began to fuse them together with some extra melted chocolate. Once she did that, she began to paint on the strawberry mouths with white chocolate they'd colored pink. Again, Alexis pressed too hard, and again, she crushed the strawberries. What was her problem?

"Um . . ." Bess said.

"Yeah." Alexis admitted defeat as she set down her piping bag and leaned away from the counter she'd been working on.

The anger Alexis felt whenever she thought about love, kissing, or especially Dalton had become her constant companion, but she hadn't realized she had so little control over it. She didn't want to be crushing these poor strawberries that Bess had paid really good money for. Maybe she should just go home.

Alexis was about to open her mouth to tell Bess just that when other words came tumbling out. "I broke up with Dalton."

"Oh," Bess whispered. Then louder she said, "I'm so sorry, Alexis."

"Don't be," Alexis said, shaking her head. The last thing she wanted was for Bess to feel sorry for her.

"Okay. I'm not sorry at all. Well, I am sorry for him. But definitely not for you," Bess said, causing Alexis to smile.

"Yeah. You should be sorry for him. *He's* the one who lost out," Alexis said, feeling surprised that she could joke about Dalton and the many pieces of her heart he'd left behind.

"Yes, he is," Bess reiterated. Then she left it at that. She didn't press for details. She didn't try to help Alexis let go of her pain and suffering. She just went back to work.

Alexis gave Bess another small smile as the older woman continued fusing strawberries. Somebody had to. The stack they were supposed to get done that night was enormous, and it was already after ten pm.

Alexis felt lighter after those few words, and because of that, she was ready to rein in her anger and help her poor boss. She took another two strawberries, fused them, and then got their mouths painted without a single berry being harmed. Thank goodness.

Alexis noticed that after her sigh of relief for not killing the strawberries, Bess tried to stifle a chuckle that was obviously directed at Alexis's apparent joy over making it through the process with a strawberry couple intact. Alexis accepted the muffled laughter without feeling any offense because it was extremely nice of Bess to just laugh about the strawberries' misfortunes. Especially because the poor woman was probably wondering if she'd have to go back to the dipping stage considering how many strawberries Alexis had ruined.

After that first strawberry couple was completed, Alexis was able to do another and then another until she was no longer worried she would crush the cutesy favors. And her thoughts began to wander again. As she and Bess worked in silence, Alexis wondered if she should tell Bess the whole situation. The only other person she'd even told about the breakup was Rianne, and Alexis had barely skimmed over the why of the breakup, even with her best friend. The why being that Alexis had come into the middle of a marriage. That she had been the other woman. The other woman. Was there a worse three-word combination in the English language? Alexis didn't think so. The turmoil of those three little words made her want to hurl as well as throw something hard. Preferably at Dalton's head.

She guessed at least there was a bright side to her breakup. Dalton and Nina had no connection to the island. If Alexis wanted to keep the reasons behind her breakup quiet, the residents of Whisling would be none the wiser. Because as much as Alexis admired and appreciated Bess, she didn't think she wanted to tell Bess the whole truth. Actually, maybe it was *because* Alexis admired Bess that she couldn't tell her the truth. Especially considering Bess's past. Her whole marriage had imploded when she'd been cheated on. Would Bess look at Alexis differently if she knew what Alexis had done? Alexis was sure of it.

She quickly made the decision that she would keep this tragic mistake to herself. No one needed to know the truth behind her breakup with Dalton.

But as she and Bess continued to work, the lack of conversation in the truck hit Alexis, and she knew she was missing a good opportunity to talk through her troubles with a woman she had grown to truly respect. Just saying those earlier few words of truth, that she'd broken up with Dalton, had helped so much. What would saying more do for her?

But since the reason for her breakup was off limits, Alexis moved on to the second cause of frustration and anguish in her life. The part of her distress that she did kind of feel ready to talk about.

Part of her distress. How sad was that? Alexis's life had become such a mess that she could divide her troubles and still have a whole conversation's worth to share with Bess. How was she here? How had she gotten to this place of so much hurt and rage?

By not listening to her mom. But Alexis pushed away thoughts of her mom because of how much they hurt. Her mom had been so right. And Alexis so wrong. Okay, her mind was not a fun place to be, and Alexis had to say something to Bess or she'd go insane.

"I met my dad," Alexis said quickly.

"What?" Bess asked. This time *she* dropped her strawberries.

"Shoot," she muttered as she bent over to clean up the mess and then turned up to Alexis. "I'm sorry for my interruption. Go on."

Alexis pursed her lips. "He was nothing like I hoped he'd be. He had no excuse for not being in my life other than the angry words of a sixteen-year-old version of my mother. He knew about me, but I got the impression he was never really curious about who I was or what I'd become."

"Oh, Alexis."

"I think he would've been fine having a relationship. He seemed eager over text, but . . ."

"The man was nothing like you hoped he would be?"

Alexis nodded. "He's selfish. He was a selfish teenager, and now he's a selfish adult. There's no way I could count on him. I could easily see him dropping a relationship with me if he couldn't get anything out of it. He also may not be on the right side of the law."

"Oh," Bess breathed.

"Yeah. I can totally see the reasons why my mom kept him away," Alexis said finally, and that was when tears pricked her eyes. Why had she done this all on her own? Why had she pushed her mother away? The one person who'd always loved her, and Alexis had treated her like dung.

"Oh, Alexis," Bess said as she pulled Alexis into a hug.

Alexis cried against Bess's shoulder for nearly a minute and then realized how unprofessional her behavior was. She was on the clock, for goodness' sake.

She sat back up, straightened her shoulders, and then went back to her strawberry job.

"It's okay to be sad. And mad." Bess looked over at the crushed strawberries. "And anything else you want to feel. That was a lot to get hit with separately. But at once? You are a tough woman."

Alexis shook her head as she fused together another set of strawberries. She didn't feel tough. She felt guilty and angry. She felt betrayed and sad. She felt a whole lot of things, but none of them was tough.

"You are," Bess reiterated. Then she asked, "Was your mom upset?"

"About me meeting my Dad?" Alexis asked, and Bess nodded. It was common knowledge among anyone who knew Margie that she had no love for her ex.

"Probably," Alexis replied.

Bess's eyes narrowed. "You've talked to your mother about this, right?"

Alexis paused as she finished drawing a set of lips.

"Alexis," Bess said, her voice going up in disbelief.

"We haven't been on the best of terms and . . ."

"You need her," Bess said.

Alexis nodded. She couldn't lie.

"And she'd want to be here for you," Bess added.

Alexis wasn't sure about that. Her face must've shown her indecision because Bess said, "She would."

Alexis finally nodded. Margie would. But Alexis was sure she wasn't deserving of her mother's unconditional love. Because even after everything that had happened between them, Alexis knew what would occur. Her mother would hug and love her and somehow make everything right.

And that was why Alexis needed to stay away. After all she'd done, she didn't deserve for her mother to make things right. Even Bess didn't know the worst of Alexis's sins. She'd dated a married man.

Ugh. Her heart clenched with disgust.

"Call her," Bess said, taking the strawberries and the piping bag out of Alexis's hands.

"I can't," Alexis said.

"Right now. I know this is one hundred percent overstepping my bounds as a coworker, but you need this, Alexis. As a friend, I have to push," Bess said as she walked over to Alexis's purse and took out her phone. "I'll leave to give you privacy," Bess said after she handed Alexis her phone and then started for the door of the truck.

"Wait, no, I'll leave," Alexis said while standing up, unwilling to let Bess take more time away from the job she had to get done tonight. She wouldn't make Bess just stand outside of the truck when she could be working hard right where Alexis sat.

As Alexis crossed paths with a returning Bess, she figured this meant she was calling her mom. And although part of her was still hesitant, most of her was grateful for the push Bess was giving her.

"Fine, but leave, leave. Go home. I'll finish these berries."

"I can't leave you."

"I'm telling you you have to leave," Bess said with a smile. "You have no choice."

Alexis really did have the best job in the world, and her boss had a good deal to do with why her job was so incredible.

"Fine. But I'm staying extra late tomorrow," Alexis promised, retrieving her purse from under the back counter.

"We'll see," Bess called over her shoulder as Alexis walked off the truck and into the cold night air. The food truck's space heater couldn't reach her out here, so she hurried to the warmth of her car. At least it would be warm after she turned it on.

Alexis held her phone in front of her as she waited for her car heater to kick in. Although the ocean wind couldn't hit her in her car the way it had during her jog to the secure space, Alexis still shivered.

As she continued to eye her phone, Alexis wondered just how upset Bess would be if she came in tomorrow not having called her mom. She decided she didn't want to find out.

She scrolled down her recent calls, speeding past the numbers associated with Dalton, Nina, and her father. She really should erase her call log. All the way at the bottom was Margie. She was typically first or second on this list. But Alexis had chosen a man over her mother. She'd written off her mom's actions as wrong and crazy. She hadn't even stopped to question if her mother might actually be right. And now Alexis was paying for that.

She pressed the number before she could back out, and the phone only rang once before it was answered.

"Alexis?" Margie's familiar voice calmed Alexis immediately. This was home.

"Mom," Alexis said, willing the overwhelming urge to cry to stay at bay. At least until she got a few words out.

Alexis connected her phone to her car speaker so that she could talk to her mother as she drove and decided to make her way home.

"Is everything okay?" Margie asked.

The tears wouldn't stay away. After all this time. After all Alexis had done. Her mother had one simple question: was she okay. How could she have ignored that kind of love?

"I'm sorry for the scene I caused at your house. That was out of line," Margie continued when Alexis didn't speak.

"Our house, Mom. I can't imagine you're even half as sorry as I am. I feel horribly for the way I've treated you. That I put Dalton before you. That I put finding my father before you. You were only trying to protect me."

Margie was quiet for a few seconds before saying, "I was. But I went about it the wrong way. I was still using the same tactics I used when you were a child. But you're a grown woman now. I should have trusted you more."

"But you were scared," Alexis said for her mother. She knew that had to have been what had made Margie keep the secret the way she had.

"And ashamed. I chose the worst option on the island to be the father of my child. You deserved so much more than that," Margie said.

Alexis felt as if she were finally beginning to understand. "But you were sixteen. And you didn't know you'd get pregnant. You've made up for it every day of your life since. You have nothing to be ashamed of, Mom," Alexis insisted.

"That's sweet of you to say, Hun. I'm not just filled with shame when it comes to choosing your father but also with the way I dealt with the entire situation. I think I thought that if I could just keep him far enough away from your consciousness, we'd be safe. You wouldn't hurt, and neither would I. I was wrong."

"So was I. So wrong, Mom," Alexis said softly, feeling her eyes brim with tears. "I broke up with Dalton."

"Oh?" was all her mother said, but Alexis knew she wanted to cheer for joy.

"You can scream and shout for joy if you want," Alexis said.

"Oh no, sweet girl. I know you're hurting, and you being hurt is the last thing that makes me want to scream and shout for joy. I'd be happy to scream and shout at Dalton if it would help anything," Margie said.

Alexis laughed. She actually laughed. A full hearty sound she hadn't heard in over a week.

"I miss you, Mom," Alexis said. The words felt so wonderful to say aloud.

"Oh, I miss you," Margie replied.

"I have to tell you something else, Mom," Alexis said, hating this part the most. But she had to be completely honest when it came to her mom. She wouldn't feel good about their relationship unless she was. But man was it going to suck. Talking about her mistakes when she'd decided to pursue finding her father was one thing, but this . . .

"He was married, Mom," Alexis said softy, and then she waited for the shocked exclamation.

"I'm sorry, Alexis," Margie replied just as softly.

"Why are *you* sorry? I'm the one who was the other woman," Alexis spat.

"Love can make us do crazy things," Margie said, and Alexis realized what her mother was assuming.

"I didn't know, Mom," Alexis said. There was no way she would've dated Dalton had she known. "His wife called me, and I didn't talk to him again."

"Then why all the guilt, Alexis Rae?" Margie exclaimed. "*You* did nothing wrong."

"I dated a married man. Pretty sure that's one of the cardinal sins, right?"

"*You. Didn't. Know.*" Margie said each word slowly. "You did nothing wrong," her mother reiterated.

"Then why do I feel like I did? I feel so dirty, Mom." Alexis let all that she'd bottled up spill out. "I thought it was love. True love. I was planning a wedding and babies. How was I so stupid?"

"Because he was a charming man who made it his mission to get you to fall in love with him."

"Did he know I would be an easy mark? Is that why he dated me?"

"Alexis, no. We are not going down this road. There is nothing wrong with you, my dear girl. That man," Margie spat out the last word, "that vile man took advantage of you and your sweetness and kindness. He saw a beautiful woman who was unmarred from the cruelty of the world, and I truly believe he loved you. In his own selfish way."

"Am I bound to only have selfish men in my life?" Alexis asked, remembering that had been the very word she'd used to describe her father.

"Heaven knows I'm not the greatest example when it comes to choosing men," Margie said, "But I sure as heck hope not. You're too good to be stuck with men like Roger and Dalton."

"Am I?" Alexis asked the question she was scared by most of all.

"You are," Margie said forcefully. "You are the best person I know."

"Even after I kicked my mom out of my house?"

"Your mother was being a bit unreasonable," Margie said, causing Alexis to smile. Man, she missed her mom. What she wouldn't do for just one hug.

"I should've listened."

"I should've been more supportive," Margie said as Alexis pulled into her driveway and saw that a car she recognized was already parked in it.

"Mom?" Alexis said into the phone as she got out of her car and ran to her mother, who had just gotten out of hers.

Alexis slid her phone into her pocket just as her mother embraced her. She was finally getting her wish.

"I'm so sorry, Mom," Alexis said into her mom's shoulder.

"Shush now," Margie said as she held on to Alexis as tightly as she possibly could. "We've already gone over all of that. Now it's time for healing."

Alexis relaxed into her mom's arms. Healing. Now that sounded like the perfect next step. And she knew that with her mother by her side, she might actually succeed.

CHAPTER FIFTEEN

BESS GROANED as she rolled over in bed and realized it was already eight am. She and Alexis had stayed at the truck until after midnight finishing all of the food for the wedding that could be cooked a couple of days in advance. And today the food truck would be closed for regular business as Bess and her crew finished food preparations for the wedding of her son and daughter-in-law tomorrow.

Tomorrow. Her son was going to be a married man tomorrow. Where had the time gone?

But there was no time for Bess to reminisce. She'd blocked out time for that and all her mother-of-the-groom responsibilities later that day during the rehearsal and subsequent dinner, and then of course the next day at the wedding.

However, this morning and early afternoon had to be all about cooking and getting the last things ready so that tomorrow, Alexis would just have to heat things up and set things out while Bess enjoyed the wedding day with her family. But none of that would happen unless Bess got to work. Pronto.

She found a baggy t-shirt and a pair of leggings that she

deemed a worthy outfit for the first part of today since she'd be seeing very few people and would be working her booty off. She quickly got dressed, since she'd showered the night before, and pulled her shoulder length hair back into a no-nonsense pony-tail. Well, she guessed there was a bit of nonsense since some of her shorter hairs fell out of it, but most of her hair was being pretty obedient.

After a quick brush of her teeth, some lotion, and a swipe of deodorant, Bess was ready for the day. There was no need to take time for breakfast since she'd be sampling plenty of the food she would be preparing.

She and Alexis had decided to divide up most of the day's cooking. Bess and Olivia would cook here in Bess's kitchen at home and Alexis and Cassie would get their work done on the truck. The amount of food they needed to make for the wedding was too much for one space or the other. Fortunately, the recep-tion hall that Jana's family had rented out for the big day had a beautiful kitchen area, along with a couple of industrial-sized refrigerators that could house all the food Bess's kitchen and the food truck couldn't. Bess realized that was something she would have to think about before deciding if she could do this type of catering gig again. Fridge space. Right now she didn't possess enough on her own. Maybe she could purchase a few more and keep them in her garage? But today wasn't the time to worry about that. One event at a time.

The menu planning had been a bit of a rough road. Jana and Steven had gone over every possible type of cuisine and had finally landed on a buffet with steak, chicken, and seafood. They had told Bess they didn't care about the other side dishes and salads—she could decide those for them—but they figured those meats were what a wedding meal should be.

But then Jana had come to Bess crying, about two weeks

before, telling her the menu was all wrong. It didn't feel like her and Steven at all. She loved Tex-Mex, and Steven loved Italian food. They were serving neither at the biggest day in both their lives. Bess had gotten out of Jana that she'd felt pressured to have a typical wedding meal, but what she really wanted were fajitas and chicken parmesan. Bess had laughed and told her of course she should have exactly what she wanted. Plus, who didn't love a good fajita? So although the last minute change in menu had been a bit of a pain in Bess's behind, it was worth it to see her future daughter-in-law happy.

Serendipitously, Jana had come just moments before Bess had had to finalize the food order with her vendors, and in all actuality, most of the order had remained the same. Who knew both meals would use so many of the same ingredients?

So with the new game plan, she and Alexis had prepped the non-green salads, both pasta and potato, the day before, and green would happen today. Yesterday, they'd also prepared the pans of chicken parm. They would sit well for a few days until Alexis could cook them at the reception hall. Today was fajita and sides day since many of the ingredients that were piled on fajitas would taste better fresh. And thankfully, dessert was being outsourced to a bakery on the island.

Jana had told her family that she not only wanted to get married on Whisling but she also wanted to use as many local businesses as she could. She'd fallen in love with the island almost as fully as with Steven. At least that's what Steven liked to tease her about.

Bess heard a knock at the door and hurried over to open it. As she left the kitchen, she noticed the time on the clock ready eight-forty-five. Olivia wasn't supposed to be there until ten.

"You're early," Bess said, opening the door.

"I know," Dax responded with a gigantic grin. "But I didn't think you'd mind."

"Dax!" Bess exclaimed as she jumped into his arms, kissing him quite thoroughly. He was supposed to arrive a little after noon in order to escort Bess to all of the wedding festivities.

"I caught an earlier flight. I figured you might need me?" he said.

Bess nodded immediately. She wasn't about to turn down any help.

"Then put me to work, Boss," he said, his grin never wavering, and Bess couldn't help but kiss him one more time.

"If you keep this up, we might not get the food done until tomorrow," Dax teased before stealing another kiss, and Bess realized they really did need to get to work.

"How about you get started on seasoning the steak? I'll work on the shrimp," Bess said.

Dax nodded, pulling the ingredients out of the fridge that Bess would need. "What have you been eating?" he asked, his head still inside the fridge. "This thing is full of wedding ingredients."

"I may have been a patron at our local restaurants a bit more than usual these past few days," Bess admitted.

Dax laughed. "Jana and Steven owe you."

"I'm having fun," Bess said. And for the most part she was, especially now that Dax was here.

"We're in charge of the meat and pepper mixture," Bess said. "The girls at the truck are making the pico and crema mixture. They'll move on to green salad and any other details we may have missed, and we'll move on to homemade tortillas."

Dax's eyes went wide at the word *homemade*.

"I've been perfecting a recipe. They are really, really good. I've got the dough ready, so it won't be too difficult. I have it all under control. Although I do have to make about two hundred of them. Jana thought two tortillas per guest would work out well."

"Two hundred? In five hours?" Dax's eyes somehow grew in size.

Bess chuckled. She could understand his hesitation. But she was sure the task sounded a whole lot worse than it really was. Especially because she'd invested in a couple of tortilla presses and a griddle that could cook eight of them at a time. "More like three hours, after all this other prep. That's why we'd better get to work."

"Yes, Ma'am," Dax said with a bit of sass, earning him a swat on the backside from his girlfriend.

The two worked side-by-side for an hour before Olivia joined them. She began to prep the peppers and onions, and soon Bess was sautéing up two huge pans of fajita fillings. Then she sent Olivia to the venue with multiple pans to put into the fridges there.

"Now we move on to the tortillas," Bess said with a grin. She was stressed and her feet were already killing her, but she was loving every minute of cooking with Dax. He could make even the worst of days happy, and this had already been a happy day . . . but he'd still managed to make it better.

"This is what we'll need?" Dax asked as he eyed the pile of ingredients that Bess had placed strategically together on her kitchen table, and Bess nodded. She was about to get to work when Dax took ahold of her hand.

"Do you think I could talk to you about something before we do that?" Dax asked, pulling out a chair for Bess to sit in. "I promise it won't take long."

This seemed serious. Bess nodded as she sat where Dax had offered, and then Dax sat in the adjacent chair, all while never letting go of her.

"I'm moving," Dax said.

Bess felt her heart drop. LA was already far enough in her book, but was Dax going back to Nashville? She had always known this would be a possibility, but Dax moving felt like a step in the wrong direction. They would now be in different time zones and . . . Bess couldn't freak out. If he was doing this, it was because it was what was best for him. She knew he wouldn't make the decision lightly, and she had to respect it. Even if she didn't like it.

"Oh," Bess said.

"My LA office is running smoothly, even though we've recently acquired some big name clients along with some up and coming actors. But I've hired five new agents, and they are all exceeding my expectations. One agent is just for Julia, of course."

"Of course." Bess smiled at his joke. He appreciated his biggest client, but she'd always been a handful—much more needy than any of his other clients.

"That really is wonderful, Dax," Bess said, truly amazed by her boyfriend. He was so good at what he did. But even as she swelled with pleasure, a small, jealous part of her that she wasn't proud of wished Dax was a little less great at his job. Then maybe he wouldn't be moving further away from her. But the smart part of her knew that wishing for anything but the best for him was just plain self-centered. So she pushed the jealous part away and grinned at her incredible boyfriend. "So LA no longer needs you?" Bess asked, hoping she sounded as proud of him as she felt.

Dax nodded. "What can I say? I'm good at my job."

Bess's smile widened. He was. And she really was so proud of him.

"So Nashville?" Bess asked.

Dax shook his head.

Not Nashville? Then where? Would Dax open another office? Oh no. New York?

"Nashville has been running smoothly without me since my

move out to LA. My clients love their agents, and although I'm needed every once in a while, the day-to-day can be done without me."

"That's great, Dax," Bess said honestly because, even if he was going further away, she was thrilled for his success.

But what did that mean for them?

Then it hit Bess. Dax was coming to tell her goodbye. All of this—helping her cook, being her wedding date—was his farewell tour. She blinked back the moisture that threatened her eyes.

"So I think I'm going to come home," Dax said, and Bess felt her entire body go slack.

"What?" she asked, her eyes wide with disbelief.

"I'm coming home, Bess. For good."

This time tears not only threatened, they overflowed. But they were the good kind. The really good kind.

"You are?" Bess asked as she stood.

Dax pulled her down into his lap. "I am."

"But your job. I can't ask you to leave LA."

"You didn't. You wouldn't. I know you wouldn't. But I want to, Bess. I'm not exactly retiring, but I've put over two decades into my job and nearly all of that time into this business. It is thriving. I'll still be CEO and will have to check in on the offices every month or so, but they don't need me, and I don't need them."

Bess leaned her head against Dax's.

"But do you know what I need or, better phrased, who I need?" he asked.

Bess shook her head just because she wanted to hear him say the words aloud.

"You, Bess. I hate being so far away. I hate that our dates are so few and far between. I hate that we can't move forward because I'm always leaving."

"I should fight you harder on this. Tell you I don't need you to come home," Bess said.

"I would just fight right back. I've made up my mind, Bess. And even though I love you with all that I am, I'm not doing this for you. I'm doing it for us."

Bess felt a smile take over her face. If she thought she was happy before, she wasn't sure what the right word was to express how elated she felt now.

"So I guess that's that?" she asked.

"That's that."

"You're moving home?"

Dax nodded.

"For good," Bess added, loving the way those words sounded.

"For good."

Dax was moving home. To her. Bess figured there was only one thing to do.

She pressed her lips against the lips of the man she loved and wound her arms around his shoulders. He gripped her waist and pulled her closer to him as he returned her kiss just as fervently.

Bess relished his touch, the feel of his skin, the touch of his lips. It was only the sound of a car alarm going off somewhere down her street that reminded her of all she still had to do that day.

Bess reluctantly pulled away from Dax's kiss.

"How do you feel about making about two hundred tortillas to celebrate?" she teased.

"As long as I'm with you, every day is a celebration."

"Oh, you are smooth, Dax Penn," Bess said, giving him one last kiss and then stepping away from him. She hated to do it, but it had to be done.

She grinned back at Dax as he followed her to the counter. He was moving home. Suddenly, visions of Dax being with her every day filled her head, and Bess felt a deep satisfaction she'd been missing for a long time. Dax was coming home. More than that, Dax was becoming her home.

CHAPTER SIXTEEN

OLIVIA HAD FELT BADLY LEAVING Bess's before the tortillas got started, but Bess had assured her it wouldn't take too long to cook them, and someone did need to get the fajita fixin's to the venue. Plus, Bess had Dax there to help her.

Still, Olivia was only willing to leave when Bess had gone over the timetable and it looked like Bess would be ready in plenty of time for the rehearsal and dinner that would be starting in a little over four hours.

Speaking of Dax and Bess, Olivia loved that they'd found one another. She also loved that her brother was home more because of his relationship. But Olivia could do without the constant hand holding and kissing. How they did that while they cooked—Olivia only knew because she'd seen it, and she really wished she could wipe the picture from her mind—was beyond her.

It was one thing to know her boss and her brother were in the honeymoon stage of their relationship. It was another to see it. Not that she was jealous or anything. Okay, Olivia was completely jealous. She had a feeling she wouldn't care in the least that her brother and Bess were so lovey-dovey if she had someone of her own to love.

And with that sad thought, Olivia pulled into her driveway and then walked a few houses down to her mom's.

"I'm back," Olivia called as she walked into her mom's house.

Her girls sat at two of the stools in her mom's kitchen, feasting on probably too many chocolate chip cookies, if the streaks around their mouths told the truth.

"Hi, Mom!" her girls said around mouthfuls off cookies.

"How much sugar did you feed them, Mom?" Olivia asked, eyeing a half full jar as Kathryn joined them in the kitchen. Had her mother really fed them half a jar of cookies in only a couple of hours?

"Just enough," Kathryn said as she kissed her daughter's cheek in greeting and then sent her a smirk.

"I should leave them here with you for a sleepover," Olivia threatened.

"But you won't," Kathryn said, her smirk just as annoying as ever.

Olivia shook her head and had to laugh at her mom. Even though her mother loved to push her buttons, Olivia knew she would be lost without Kathryn's help and guidance, especially over the past few years. For that, and so much more, Olivia loved her.

"How were the lovebirds?" Kathryn asked immediately, wanting the scoop on Dax and Bess.

Olivia was pretty sure the only person more excited about Dax and Bess than Dax and Bess was her mother. Kathryn was thrilled that her oldest had finally settled down, and the fact that it was with a woman from the island was the cherry on top.

Olivia had worried that Kathryn would think Bess was a bit too old for her son because of their eight-year age difference and because Kathryn and Bess had been neighbors and friends for years, but she hadn't minded at all. She loved Bess and she loved Dax. She'd realized from what she knew of them that they would work well together, the same way Olivia had.

"Lovey," Olivia said, feeling a mixture of disgust and jealousy.

"I'm taking it he told Bess the news?" Kathryn asked, her smirk long gone. Now she was beaming. Kathryn had cried for over ten minutes when she'd heard her oldest was moving home, and it had only served to help Kathryn love the idea of Dax dating Bess even more.

"He was going to tell her after I left, but I'm sure she'll be thrilled. Well, maybe not quite as happy as you are," Olivia teased.

"Hey!" Kathryn swatted her daughter with a dish towel. "When your daughters grow up and move off the island, you'll understand."

"Impossible," Olivia said as she turned to her girls. "You two will never move away, right?"

"Never, Mama," Pearl said seriously.

"Well, maybe for college," Rachel said.

Olivia shook her head. "Never, Rachel Birmingham."

"Fine, never, Mom," Rachel said, placating her mother.

"Good," Olivia said before turning back to her mom. "See, I don't have to worry about it."

"Yeah, yeah. Well you go on and take your smug self and your girls home," Kathryn said before kissing each of her grand-daughters on the sides of their heads and then ushering them to their mom.

"Thanks, Mom," Olivia called out as she made her way toward the door with her daughters. "Love you!"

"Yeah, yeah," Kathryn remarked sassily. Then she added, "Love you three!"

Olivia laughed as she left her mom's, and the girls ran ahead to their own home. They were screeching about something as Olivia started down her driveway, so she hurried her steps because she couldn't tell what emotion was behind the screeching.

As she got to the back of Dean's house and into their shared yard, she saw that, fortunately, they'd been screeches of pleasure —if there was such a thing—and Buster was to blame.

"We've missed you!" Pearl exclaimed, even though they'd seen the dog merely days before. Although the girls did typically see Buster more often than every four to five days. But between Olivia's work schedule and the girls' practices, performances, and all that culminated at this holiday time of year, their little family had been busier than normal.

Olivia knew she'd missed seeing Buster's owner, who she hadn't seen for even longer than that. Somehow she'd managed to avoid Dean not only at home but at soccer, as well. Pearl's team had had a bye that week, so there'd been no game nor need for practices.

But it had been better for them not to see one another. Well, better for her. She'd needed to get her bearings after her last embarrassing run-in with Dean.

As the girls nuzzled and played with Buster, Olivia looked around to see if Dean was anywhere nearby. He wasn't in the backyard, so Olivia assumed he must've let the dog out and was still in his house. That wasn't typical for him. Especially if he heard the girls playing with Buster. But maybe he'd noticed how incredibly awkward Olivia had been at the game and was avoiding her for the time being too? Maybe he'd figured out that Olivia needed time to deal with her feelings for him?

Her face flamed at just the thought. If Dean ever knew all that she felt for him . . . a lump grew in her throat and somehow, even in near-freezing temperatures, her face got blazing hot.

She drew in a couple of deep breaths, helping herself to

relax and her face color to return to normal. Dean didn't know. He couldn't know, right? Well, whether that was true or not, it was what Olivia decided she had to believe.

Resolved, she pushed her embarrassment away and watched Rachel throw Buster's ball as far as she could, hitting the fencing of Dean's yard and causing the girls to erupt with giggles when Buster had to skid to a stop just before hitting the fence. The sight of the dog putting on his breaks *was* rather entertaining.

She looked down at her watch and realized she needed to get inside and get dinner started. Work the next day would be pretty hectic as well, and then she would be attending Jana and Stephen's wedding as a guest. They'd been kind enough to invite all of Bess's employees, along with her neighbors who resided in their little cove.

This big, beautiful wedding was the kind of event Olivia typically would've tried to avoid since her divorce—for some reason the gossips loved to bring up failed marriages at the start of new ones—but knowing it was Bess and people she loved hosting, Olivia was actually kind of looking forward to the next evening. She just had to get through the busyness of her day and make it there.

"I'm going to go in and start dinner," Olivia called out, and the girls just waved their hands to show they'd heard her. They didn't care where their mother went as long as they were able to stay out there with the dog.

"I work, cook, clean, and this is the thanks I get," Olivia muttered as she started toward her home. Just as she walked away, she noticed the back door to Dean's house open. The object of too many of her recent dreams came out onto his back porch and then jogged down the stairs to join the girls and Buster.

As much as Olivia longed to stay and watch as Dean joined the party, she knew it was probably for the best that she was removing herself from the situation. She just couldn't be normal around Dean right now, and it wasn't fair to him. He deserved his friend, but instead he was getting another woman who got all flustered and giggly when she spoke to the most eligible bachelor on the island. She was being ridiculous, and she needed to get her act together before she could be allowed to spend time with the man.

Olivia waved at Dean before unlocking her door and stepping into her home. That was good. She'd had a normal, neighborly interaction. She could do this.

Olivia put her purse and coat away and then changed into a pair of joggers and a sweatshirt. As one of Bess's employees, Olivia didn't have to dress up each work day as much as she would've had to for an office job, but she did have to at least wear a decent pair of pants and a shirt that couldn't also be worn to sleep. And although her work getup was comfy enough outside of her home, there was no way Olivia was going to wear those clothes for longer than necessary.

She'd been reacquainted with her fondness for joggers, leggings, and sweats ever since divorcing Bart. The man hadn't liked her to dress so casually, and even though all three bottoms had been her favorites before marrying her ex, Olivia had happily given them up. Man, Bart had literally controlled every aspect of Olivia's life. Who knew that class reunion would be the start of the best period of her life?

Olivia stuck the chicken she'd been marinating all day into the oven to bake and then put a pot of rice onto the stove to cook. She opened her fridge and debated between sauteing up some green beans or roasting a pan of broccoli. She decided on the latter since she already had her oven going. She filled a baking sheet with a bunch of broccoli from a bag and then massaged it with a good amount of olive oil, salt, and pepper.

Roasting veggies was a trick Bess had taught her. Olivia's

mom was a wonderful cook, but she hadn't been a big roaster. Bess was. She'd shown Olivia the kind of flavor that could be derived from just a simple cooking method, and Olivia and her girls had fallen in love with it. Her girls never turned down a chance to eat roasted broccoli.

Her front door opened as Olivia was bent over the oven, putting the broccoli in and checking on the chicken.

"Wash your hands," Olivia dictated to whichever of her daughters had come inside.

"Yes, Ma'am," a deep voice that very obviously didn't belong to either of her daughters responded.

Olivia jumped, knocking her head on the stove hood, and then stood to face Dean, trying not to grimace too hard at how clumsy she'd just been and how much her head hurt.

"Woah, that was quite the hit," Dean said, rounding the counter so he could join Olivia in her kitchen. He moved Olivia's hand that was holding the back of her head and gently parted her hair so that he could see where she'd smacked it.

"I think it's fine," Olivia said, trying not to sound as out of breath as she felt. But Dean was standing so close. His chest was against her arm, his fingers entwined in her hair, and his gentle breath on her neck.

"I think so too. Even if it wasn't, I don't know what I was expecting to do, checking up on the wound. I'm a lawyer, not a doctor," Dean said, causing Olivia to laugh.

And of course it wasn't a dainty, sweet laugh. It was a loud, upsetting guffaw that was way too much for the cute little joke Dean had said. Olivia worked on reining in her laugh and also her wayward emotions.

"The girls told me to just come in, but I still should've knocked," Dean said as he took a step back.

Olivia immediately missed the feel of his chest against her.

Man, he had a nice chest . . . and face and arms and legs and smile, the list went on and on.

"It's fine. I just expected a girlier voice," Olivia said.

"I would hope so," Dean replied with a grin that Olivia returned.

It was only after smiling up at Dean for too long that Olivia realized she'd been staring. She needed to pull herself together. Olivia now wished she'd sautéed green beans instead of roasting broccoli just so she'd have something to do. The pot of rice was self-sufficient, so she decided to clean instead. She found her kitchen cloth and began to wipe down all of her counters.

"I just had a talk with the girls," Dean said, causing Olivia to pause.

"Is everything okay? Is it soccer?" Olivia asked as she froze mid-swipe, a look of concern on her face.

"Everything is fine. Maybe even grand. Depending on how this conversation goes."

"Grand. That's quite the expectation," Olivia said, grateful to be talking about her daughters. Somehow her girls entering the conversation made her act a whole lot more normal. Olivia went back to her cleaning.

"It is." Dean put a hand on Olivia's arm, causing her to stop yet again. He took the kitchen cloth from her hand and set it next to her sink. Then he held both of her hands in each of his own.

What was Dean doing? This would not help her resolve to treat the man like a friend and friend only. He was holding her hands. He was—

"Olivia," Dean said.

Olivia could only manage a nod. Her mouth seemed to have lost all ability to work.

"Will you do me the honor of being my date tomorrow evening?" Dean asked.

Oh. Olivia let out the breath she'd been holding. All of that anticipation for this? He had already talked to the girls, so that had to mean this was a big group thing. Her girls, Olivia, and Dean. It was a friendly date that made sense because they'd both been invited to the wedding. They would take the girls, maybe ride with her parents. It would be a neighborly affair.

"Sure," Olivia answered, trying to keep her voice steady. But Dean had begun to run his thumb against the inside of Olivia's wrist. What was he doing now? Did he know what that simple touch did to her? She needed to get him out of there before she did something she couldn't take back. Like jump into his arms and kiss him.

"Do you want to drive? Or I can drive?" Olivia offered nonchalantly.

"Um, no. I think you might've misunderstood me. I'm usually much better at this, but I guess this is what happens when you finally ask out the girl you've been in love with for over half your life," Dean said.

Olivia froze. What did he say?

"Yeah, didn't mean to say that and freak you out," Dean said with a self-deprecating laugh.

"I'm not freaked out," Olivia squeaked.

"You should see your face, Liv. You're definitely freaked."

"No, I'm . . ." Should Olivia tell Dean what she felt for him? He'd kind of already laid his cards on the table.

"I guess I might be freaked out," Olivia amended, "but not for the reason you think. It's the kind of freak out a woman has when a man she really, really likes asks her out."

Dean smirked. Oh dear. She'd just fueled his ego.

"*Really, really*, huh?" Dean asked.

"'That's nothing compared to *in love with for half your life*," Olivia pointed out.

"Yeah, but it's still much better than I'd hoped for," Dean said.

Olivia allowed him a little smugness because that had been pretty cute.

"So this is a date date?" Olivia asked, feeling foolish as she said the juvenile-sounding words. But she had to be sure.

"For how much more of this conversation will you be doubling up on your words?" Dean teased, and Olivia swatted at his chest. His hard, muscled chest.

"But yes. This is as datey of a date as I've ever had," Dean said, his voice becoming much more serious.

Olivia pursed her lips, feeling giddy and nervous all at once.

"A penny for your thoughts?" Dean asked.

"What does *as datey of a date* mean?" Olivia asked.

"It means I've already talked to your girls and asked their permission for me to date their mom. It means I'm planning on this date being the first of many. It means I want to skip the whole getting to know you phase of dating because I already know you, inside and out. It means I already love you, Liv. I probably always have."

Olivia gasped softly at Dean's powerful declaration. But as shocked as she was, she had to let him know he wasn't alone in his feelings.

"I think I like *as datey of a date*," Olivia said as she took a bold step closer to Dean.

"I think I like *as datey of a date* too," Dean replied, wrapping his arms around Olivia and pressing his lips softly to hers. Her chest filled with flurries and her stomach heated as Dean tugged her closer and she wove her arms around his neck. Years of long-ing, passion, and friendship exploded between them, and Olivia was sure that without Dean, she would've fallen into a heap on the ground. Dean deepened the kiss, and Olivia threaded her hands through his gorgeous hair—something she'd done many times in her dreams. But dang if reality wasn't a million times better.

"Mom?" Pearl's voice penetrated her consciousness.

Had the girls come in? Olivia and Dean both jumped away from the other, their faces burning as if they'd been seventeen and caught by their parents.

"They were kissing. I think they're going to do a lot of that now," Rachel said with a knowing smile.

A smile? Olivia liked that.

"Does that mean Dean is your boyfriend, Mom?" Pearl asked.

Did it?

Olivia opened her mouth, but before she could even look at Dean, he said, "It does. Are you two okay with that?"

"Yes," Pearl gushed as she ran into the kitchen to hug her mom and then Dean.

"Yeah, me too," Rachel said a lot more calmly than her sister. "It means when you get married, Buster becomes our step brother," Rachel added with a mischievous smirk.

Olivia's cheeks went red for the third time in less than an hour as her daughter said the *m word*. What would Dean think?

"It does," Dean said as he took a step closer to Olivia and wrapped an arm around her waist.

He wasn't freaking out. In the least. Okay. She nuzzled into Dean's hold. She could get used to this.

"You girls wash your hands and then set the table for dinner," Olivia said, even though she wanted to enjoy the moment for even a few seconds more. Dean liked her, no, he loved her. Oh my goodness. And she was going out with him, and he was her boyfriend. Olivia's mind was still whirling. The last fifteen minutes had been some of the best of Olivia's entire life.

"Is Dean staying for dinner?" Pearl asked as she opened the utensil drawer after washing her hands.

Olivia looked up at Dean for his answer.

"I'd love to," Dean said, and then he dropped a kiss on Olivia's forehead, causing her heart to flip flop and then flip again.

"Yes!" Pearl cheered.

Pearl set forks and knives on the table as Rachel went to fill water glasses and Dean helped to fold napkins. Olivia was about to take their dinner out of the oven when she paused, taking another glance at her family. They were working together, they were joyful, and never in Olivia's life had things felt so right. A peace filled her heart, telling her she was finally on the right road. The road that would lead to happiness.

A smile filled her face as she finally turned to get the chicken and broccoli. Her life's twists and turns had been hard, but they'd brought her here. For that, she had to be grateful.

CHAPTER SEVENTEEN

LILY LAUGHED as Amelia squealed from her new favorite position in all the world. She loved to sit on Allen's lap as he wheeled himself anywhere. She'd learned to hold on well so Allen could typically use both of his hands to wheel himself with Amelia settled in his lap. Lily felt it was the perfect arrangement.

Their little family traveled with the large crowd of wedding guests from the outdoor venue where the ceremony had been held to a tent where they would have drinks and appetizers. Then after the bride and groom had taken enough pictures for posterity and beyond, the entire group would move to *the* tent where the reception would begin.

"Lily, Lily!" Maddie called out as she ran from where she'd been holding her dad's hand to join Lily, Allen, and Amelia, as well as Kate and Kevin, who'd just joined them.

"Hey, Maddie Moo," Lily said as she spun Maddie in her arms, causing the big skirt on Maddie's flower girl dress to poof out.

"Spin again," Maddie shrieked, but Lily shook her head. She knew Maddie all too well. This would be the first of many more *agains* if Lily gave in. Maddie nodded mournfully. But then she realized she was the focus of not only Lily's attention but also Kate's, Allen's, and Kevin's, so she grinned. She was always delighted to be the center of the show. It was a big reason why she'd been such an excellent flower girl. The flower petals may have all been in big clumps along the aisle, but Maddie's smile and the determined way she'd taken on said aisle had made up for her lack of throwing prowess.

"Hello, Maddie, Amelia and gang," Deb said as she passed their group on her way into the tent. From the way the woman was huddled into her husband, Luke's, arms, and hurrying into the warmth of the heated tent, Lily was grateful to get any kind of greeting at all.

Although there had been numerous heat lamps to warm up the outdoor wedding, Lily was sure many people had still been a bit colder than they would've liked. But Jana had wanted a wedding next to the stunning shoreline, and since the rain had held off, there'd been no reason to keep her dream from coming true.

Even though the ceremony had been a bit chilly, the entire wedding scene of Jana's visions had come to life. From the gorgeous leafless trees that had been spun with twinkle lights to the trellises that had been built around the guest seating area in order to be covered with gorgeous December greenery. Just behind the couple was the rocky beach that gave way to rolling waves. The venue couldn't have been more spectacular, and the words and vows exchanged had brought a tear or two to the eyes of those in attendance.

Lily smiled as Deb finally got all the way inside the tent and slowed her steps, a look of satisfaction relaxing her face. Lily imagined Deb wasn't just satisfied with where she stood right then but also with her life in general. From what Lily had heard, Deb's new gallery was thriving. She'd even hired her sister to come and take over some of the day-to-day operations because it had become too much work for just her. And from the way Deb was snuggled close to her husband, Lily assumed all was more than well on that front.

"I'm starving," Maddie declared as their group walked into the tent that had been decorated as a winter wonderland. Soft jazz played in the background, snowflakes and starlights lit up the ceiling, and evergreens created paths toward the tall tables where people could enjoy their food and drinks.

"Me too," Lily admitted, and she looked around to find waiters serving canapes. This and dessert were the parts of the menu Bess hadn't prepared.

A waiter paused in front of them, offering bacon-wrapped asparagus. Lily took one for herself and then gave one to Maddie. The little girl beamed as she took the offering and then slid down Lily's side to the ground.

"I need to find my mom," Maddie said, and since Lily saw Gen just a table away, she allowed Maddie to go find her mom on her own. But Lily kept an eye on her until she was back in her mother's care.

After making sure Maddie was alright, Lily scanned the room. Her gaze paused on Alexis as she came into the tent to hand something to the group manning the bar, and then she exited as quickly as she'd come.

Lily could imagine a wedding was the last place Alexis would want to be. It was only because Lily had overheard a quiet conversation earlier that day between Bess and Margie that she knew Alexis had broken up with her boyfriend and had had a horrific experience meeting her dad. Lily hadn't meant to eavesdrop for so long, but she'd been waiting to ask Bess a question about the wedding lineup that Gen had asked Lily to pass on. Even as Lily tried to give the women their space, she also wanted to be close enough that as soon as Bess was free, she could ask Gen's urgent question.

Bess had asked if Alexis was okay, especially considering where their work had taken them that day, and Margie had assured Bess that Alexis was. Or at least she would be soon. She'd taken huge strides in the past few days, and Bess chalked that up to Alexis and Margie's mended relationship.

"Hello all," Gen greeted as she joined Lily and her group at their table.

"Hey, Gen," Lily responded with a grin as Gen juggled Cami in one arm and Maddie in the other. The woman was officially a pro at being a mother of two. Lily had made the mistake of asking Gen if baby number three would be coming any day soon, and Gen may have bitten her head off. It was safe to say Gen was content with her life just the way it was.

Lily held out her arms for Cami, who Gen gratefully bestowed on her friend.

"The flower girl did a super job," Allen said to Maddie, causing her to grin widely. Allen had made major progress on not only his relationship with his daughter, but with Maddie and Cami as well. All three girls were such a big part of Lily's life, so Allen was making sure they were a part of his as well. He was trying to make Lily and all she loved a priority. Especially Amelia. In the few weeks since their last discussion, Allen had not only won Amelia over, he was now officially the favorite parent again. And Lily wouldn't have it any other way. They still had a ways to go when it came to their relationship, but they were trying, and they were on a much better road than before. Allen finally understood that giving up on them was not an option.

"Yes, I did," Maddie said confidently, causing the group to laugh.

"Yes you did what?" a resplendent looking Bess asked as she

joined their small party. Lily could not imagine a more beautiful mother-of-the-groom. Bess wore a pale green dress that perfectly showcased her curves and brought out the greens and golds in her hazel eyes.

"I did flower girl," Maddie said.

Bess nodded. "You did such a good job," she replied.

"Yup," Maddie said, and Lily chuckled again. Man, she loved that girl.

"The wedding was beautiful," Kate said wistfully, and it might've been Lily's imagination, but Kevin appeared a bit nervous.

"It was, wasn't it," Bess said. "All of the beauty was due to Jana and her family."

"The beauty that is being very well documented," Gen teased as she eyed the three photographers dotting the room. "Speaking of which, you were able to tear yourself away from pictures?" Gen asked, nudging her sister's shoulders.

"The mother-of-the-groom gets the best jobs. I made the food, and now after just a handful of pics, they've let us go," Bess said with a smile.

"And now she gets to spend the evening with her date?" Dax asked as he joined the group and put a tender arm around Bess.

"That's the hope," Bess said, grinning up at her boyfriend.

Gen had been unable to keep the fact that Dax was officially moving back to the island a secret from Lily and Kate. She was just too thrilled for her sister, and it looked like Bess felt even more ecstatic about the situation, if the look she gave Dax was any indication.

Bess, with her lovely updo and gorgeous dress, looked stunning, and Dax was dashing in his black tuxedo. The two made quite the pair, and thankfully they would now be a complete set on Whisling.

"Oh shoot. I forgot I needed to tell Jon something," Bess said as she left the group, taking Dax with her. "I can introduce you to Jon's date," she said to her boyfriend before they were out of earshot.

"Looks like all is well there?" Lily asked Gen.

"Jon and Bess have finally figured out a good relationship for the two of them. They co-parent well, and now, apparently, they meet the others' significant others. I think it helps that they both found people who are just perfect for them," Gen said as she watched her sister speak with Jon and Jon's date.

"She's pretty," Lily said about Jon's date.

"And young and malleable and completely adores Jon. I think she's what he needs," Gen said.

Lily nodded. From the little she'd heard of Jon and Bess's last breakup, Jon did seem to need someone who was able to put his needs before her own most of the time.

Another waiter stopped by, and this time Lily took two shrimp puffs just for herself. She really was starving. She'd noticed Allen and Amelia had broken into the snacks Lily kept in her purse for a rainy day. She didn't blame them.

"Oh, and there is the couple of the hour," Gen said joyfully, causing Lily to look up. She fully expected to see Steven and Jana, but instead it was Olivia and Dean, entering the tent hand-in-hand.

Lily laughed at Gen's joke. The natives of Whisling at the wedding had had a heyday when they saw that the couple who should've been together months ago had finally found their way to one another. All were pleased for them except for the few single women attending. Not that Lily could blame them; Dean was quite the catch.

Dean led Olivia around the room and seemed to stop in a somewhat awkward spot. They weren't near a table and they weren't exactly in a walkway. Dean pointed up, and Lily laughed when she and Olivia noticed at the same time that they were standing under the mistletoe. Dean took full advantage of that mistletoe and kissed his girlfriend so intensely that Lily had to look away. It felt too much like invading their privacy to watch such an intimate kiss.

Lily felt a warm hand take ahold of her own, and she looked down to see Allen's fingers entwining with hers. He grinned at her as he pulled her hand to his mouth and kissed her wrist, promising that they'd have a kiss just as intimate as Olivia and Dean's very soon.

Lily felt her heart bloom with love for her husband. He was here. Holding her hand. And he'd told her just earlier that day there was nowhere he'd rather be. Lily had taken those words to heart. She was still adjusting to being Allen's full-time care-taker, and she knew physical therapy continued to be challenging for Allen, especially because he'd hoped that with enough hard work, he could beat his paralysis. Right now that didn't seem likely, but Lily took courage that Allen was trying so hard, not only in his therapy but with her and Amelia. Life was good.

"Let us welcome the reason we're all here, Mr. and Mrs. Steven Wilder!" a voice said over the microphone, interrupting the music.

The crowd began to clap and cheer as Steven and Jana danced their way into the room. They were followed by their bridal party and then Jana's parents along with Bess and Dax and Jon and his date. The entire group looked elated not only to be there but to be together.

"And if you know Jana, you know how much this girl loves to dance," the emcee declared, garnering a laugh from the crowd. "So we'll start off the evening as well as end the night with dancing."

Wow, that was different. But Lily liked it.

The dance floor cleared, and Steven took Jana into his arms

before sweeping her around the dance floor in a way that had to have been practiced. It was just too perfect.

Lily watched Bess wipe a tear from under her eye as she gazed at her son and new daughter-in-law. She shared a grin with Jon and then stood on her tiptoes to give Dax a kiss. Lily was glad they were figuring out how to work this whole blended family thing.

Soon the bridal party and parents with their significant others joined in on the last part of the song. Then all in attendance were asked to move to the dining tent that sat just adjacent to where they were.

Lily quickly found her groups' assigned seats and motioned for her family to follow her. They were in the middle of the room with Olivia, Dean and Olivia's family on one side of them, and Deb, Luke and their kids on the other. Gen and her family sat closer to the front of the room and the bridal party.

As groups were called table by table to fill their plates at the buffet, Lily studied those around her and the smiles on each of their faces. Lily knew Bess and her family had endured a lot to be there on that day, standing together as a group knit in love. Bess had endured and prevailed the same way Lily and many of her friends had. Lily had watched as Bess toiled and labored to make her relationships work, and in the end, the one that had stuck was the one she was meant to be in. Lily truly believed that. Just like she truly believed she was supposed to be right where she was, as well.

Wasn't that the way life went? Hard work, divine intervention, and a bit of luck combined to give you your hand. One could either embrace it or fight against it.

The rest of the reception flew by, and after hours of food, dancing, and fun, it was time to call it a night. In fact, Amelia had fallen asleep in Allen's lap nearly two hours before.

"Hey, before we head out, let's take a quick walk along the beach," Allen said.

Lily looked at him with wide eyes. "Allen, it's midnight and nearly freezing out there," she said as she eyed their baby in his lap.

"We'll leave Amelia with Kate. And I know it's cold, but please, Lil?"

Lily couldn't say no to that. Besides, a walk along the midnight shores with her handsome husband did sound enticing.

So with Amelia in Kate's arms, Lily took her husband's hand and followed him as he led her out of the tent and down the path that took them to the rocks and sand. Lily wasn't sure what Allen's plan for his wheelchair on the uneven ground was, but she would let him figure it out.

Allen stopped just before the packed dirt became small rocks and loose sand and took Lily's other hand, moving her so that she was standing right in front of him.

"Lily Anderson, you amaze me."

Lily grinned.

"I know it's freezing, so I'll make this quick," Allen said as Lily shuddered. "But I feel like we need a restart."

Lily nodded. That was what they were doing.

"And so I want to say to you, before God and no witnesses," Allen continued, and Lily laughed. "That I promise to love you and only you from this day forward. I promise that when times get hard again, and they will, that I will stay with you. I won't run. And I won't let you run."

Lily pressed her lips together as she tried to contain her emotions. She wanted to see Allen clearly. She didn't want a wall of tears marring her view of the man she loved.

Allen continued. "We are in this together. For better and for worse. Forever and ever."

Lily nodded.

"I love you, Lil. Thank you for not giving up on me. For not letting me give up on me."

Lily dropped into her husband's lap and kissed him with everything that she had. "I could never," Lily said.

"I know. And that's just one reason why I love you so," Allen said, causing Lily to grin.

As much as Lily wanted to stay there cradled in Allen's arms forever, she knew they had to move or they might freeze to death.

Love was a funny thing. It could be the strongest force on earth, and yet it could be shattered in a moment. When it was on your side, it was the best thing in the world. But when it was only one-sided, it was as horrible as any doomed fate.

She walked back into the tent with Allen at her side and noticed that Gen, Bess, and Deb, the very best of friends, were dancing crazily together and thoroughly enjoying every minute of it while Alexis stood on the side of the dance floor with a ghost of a smile on her face and her mother's arm linked through hers. Olivia was also on the dance floor in Dean's embrace, the place she'd been all evening.

Love had worked for Lily and Allen. She hoped it would also work for all of her friends, but she knew if and when it didn't, there were other kinds of love to make things better. Because if one kind of love broke, there was always another to heal it.

And in the beginning, the middle, and especially the end, love would always be there.

Made in the USA
Las Vegas, NV
18 February 2022

44157258R00134